THE HOLLOW MAN

THE HOLLOW MAN

Paul Hollis

Eagle Spring Publishing

Let me be no nearer
In death's dream kingdom
Let me also wear
Such deliberate disguises
Rat's coat, crowskin, crossed staves
In a field
Behaving as the wind behaves

— "The Hollow Men" by T.S. Eliot

CHAPTER 1

It was a dream. I am fairly certain of that now. A shadowy sixteenth-century cathedral emerged from the mist, and I found myself waiting for a funeral procession to begin. Except for a large rat that brushed past my leg, I was alone in the darkness, although it felt like someone was watching me. The tower bell tolled sharply, and each numbing stroke sucked a little more confidence from my bones, right through the muscle, and it settled like sweat on my skin. I wanted to push the melting courage back inside to strengthen my spine, but I couldn't move. I was getting weaker by the second, and my body would no longer support the weight of my own thoughts.

The heavy timber doors of the church swung wide, and in the winter moonlight, I saw a robed priest appear at the doorway. With his head bowed over scriptures for the dead, he mumbled soothing passages as he baby-stepped down three stone stairs to the ground. Six pallbearers followed him, carrying their burden, solemnly gliding along the gravel path to the waiting coach and restless horses. Their footsteps made no sound on the hard surface, even though they passed so close that I could smell death on the air around them. Gaunt, hollow eyes reflected heavy hearts, but the men persevered to the coach where they lowered the plain casket to the earth.

The coffin was a small mahogany enclosure made for a half-grown child. The top was covered with a pale red lace that stood out against the anemic landscape. A sudden stale breeze caught

1

the cloth and blew it into the night. A thin, pallid girl of perhaps twelve sat up in the box and began clapping in time to the tolling bell. She slowly turned, pointing in my direction, and I saw blood running down the side of her face from a bullet wound near the scalp. The child beckoned me toward her.

"I can help you," she said, not quite looking at me with colorless, blind eyes.

"I've already told you that you can't. No one can help me now," I said.

"Yes," she emphasized.

"How?"

"Come closer." She absently wiped at the blood, but it only smeared her ashen face.

"Can you stop the bell from ringing?" The sound scraped across my raw nerves.

"You're a strange policeman," she smiled. "Why do you still search for him?"

"You know why. He slaughtered half the British Embassy, including you and I need to find him."

"Be careful of Chaban," she said. "He is a creature of evil and he's brought you here to witness his power over you."

She stared past me into the dark night. I turned in the direction she was looking to see if someone was standing beside me, but there was no one in the blackness that swallowed us.

"Where is he?" I asked.

She suddenly frowned.

"He's been watching the watcher for a long time now. Look behind you, not in front."

With vacant eyes still fixed on the dead unknown, her watery figure faded to a thin wisp and blew through me, leaving cold fear in its wake. My soul parted like the Red Sea and when it closed again, there was another scar. It was always the same. I needed more, but she was gone.

The sound of the bell shook the emptiness twice more before the gray-black dissolved into total oblivion and I started to wake. The telephone was ringing; it hadn't been a church bell at all. My head was heavy, and my body was barely functioning. Unsteadily, I reached for the pillow that covered the handset.

"Si?"

"Status?" the voice asked in English.

"Unchanged."

"Suspend surveillance on Chaban. I need you to go to morning Mass."

"It's Wednesday," I said.

"It's Madrid. People go to church every day in Spain."

"Who's the mark?"

"Luis Carrero Blanco."

"The prime minister?" I stumbled over the words.

"I'm short-handed, kid," the voice admitted. "You're right there. You'll do."

I had followed dozens over the past year but none so high ranking.

"Mass is at nine o'clock," he said. "A dossier is in the news box next to Museo del Prado."

A thread of moonlight filtered through the window and reflected on the clock's face. Still two hours until dawn. I rubbed crust from tired eyes with both hands. It had been a long time since I'd had a full night's sleep. Every time I closed my eyes, the little girl was there waiting for me. I desperately needed to hibernate for the rest of the winter, but for now, I'd have to settle for a strong cup of coffee. December had already been a long month, and it wasn't over yet.

Generalissimo Francisco Franco himself had hand-picked a close confidant as his successor and for the last six months Luis

Carrero Blanco has served as prime minister of Spain. He had fought with the Nationalist forces in the Spanish Civil War and had quickly become one of the leader's closest collaborators. After the Nationalist victory and installation of Franco as Supreme Commander of Spain, Blanco's power had grown with El Caudillo's favor. Last June, when he had been appointed prime minister, Blanco had also been named top deputy to Franco. Now that the dictator's health was failing, it was only a matter of time before Blanco assumed control of the country.

At 8:50 a.m. on December 19, 1973, I was standing across the street from San Francisco de Borja Church on Calle de Serrano, waiting for the traffic signal to change. With its large buildings and attached park, the grounds covered a city block in the heart of Madrid. The church was at its center, standing majestically in a nondescript, middle-class neighborhood. Separated by a wide passage on the right, the monastery and office complex occupied a five-story, U-shaped structure with an inner balcony overlooking a courtyard. To the left lay an unattended tract of land with a dozen barren trees irregularly clumped amid several rough patches that I believe someone once called a lawn but it was now decayed and brown from neglect. The park had become a casualty of the dry Spanish winter and big-city pollution.

The inside of the church was not unlike a thousand other Catholic churches across Europe. The altar boasted an elaborate backdrop ornately fashioned from gold and other precious metals brought back from the New World. The nave floors and pews were made of beautiful padouk wood from Southeast Africa. But the dossier noted San Francisco de Borja's most prized possessions were its collection of sacred relics. In the treasury lay the full body of a mummified saint in holy dress and an assortment of fingers and tongues from martyrs who had stuck out an appendage a bit too far in mixed company.

Somewhere there also had to be the proverbial strip of wood salvaged from the table at the Last Supper. Every church had one, a chunk of blackened cedar or cypress nailed to a wall where every tourist might stand in awe of its place in history. If all the pieces could have been somehow reassembled, the dinner table would have been massive. I imagined Christ yelling down a hundred-meter table to Peter or John, "I said pass the potatoes, not the tomatoes! Oh, never mind!"

I was brought back to reality and no doubt from the brink of eternal damnation for my thoughts by the short, ball-shaped figure of Luis Carrero Blanco walking along the prayer alcoves lining the side of the main hall. He wore an expensive cream-colored business suit and had a flamboyant stride, but what impressed me most were his bushy eyebrows which preceded him by two paces. Accompanied by his full-time bodyguard, Police Inspector Juan Fernandez, Blanco genuflected and crossed himself before settling into the second row.

Seeing a single bodyguard with a top-ranking official was not all that uncommon these days in Europe, but this pair seemed more like old friends. They sat shoulder to shoulder and spoke quietly, exchanging soft smiles. The two men had been together for many years, and perhaps a little complacency had set in. After all, the last head of state assassinated in Western Europe was back in 1934. Those were wild times. Today, the world was much more civilized, and Franco was certainly in control of his own country. With harsh restrictions on personal liberties, any disruption under existing martial law would have been unthinkable.

I turned toward a hand on my shoulder.

"Sir, I see you are English," said an unshaven man standing over me. His speech was heavily accented but understandable.

The man wore a light brown wool overcoat that would have flopped open had he not held it together with fists in his pockets. Heavy boots and a pair of loose-fitting broadcloth pants made me think he may have been a farm worker. The hair around his cap was shiny black, though flecks of gray dotted his beard stubble, and I guessed his age was close to fifty. He was uncomfortable, apologetic, standing next to the pew.

"No sir, you're mistaken," I said.

"Ah, yes, American. My first thought," he confirmed to himself.

I wondered why Americans were so easily identified wherever we went. I prided myself in disappearing within the thin cultural fabric of a country no matter where I found myself, but obviously, I was still being schooled on exactly how to blend into the surroundings. These lessons were important for a humble government tourist like me. Be invisible or be dead. There was no in-between when one was finding people who did not want to be found, watching people who did not want to be watched, and learning from those who did not want to teach.

"Mass is beginning." I tapped a finger to my lips.

Pushing me down the pew with his body, the Spaniard slid in beside me and crossed himself. We sat in silence, pretending to listen to the liturgy. I heard a heavy rattle in his breath above the priest's Latin. He was a man who needed a cigarette. For some reason, that bothered me but his five-day stubble really irritated me, mostly because it took me forever to grow facial hair. Even then, my cheek would still be as barren as the top of an old pirate's head and feel as smooth as a French prostitute's thigh.

"I'm a poor student. I don't have any money," I whispered.

"I know what you are." My eyes snapped in his direction, but the Spaniard was intent on the sermon as the priest professed something in the name of our Lord, Jesus Christ. Finally, he said,

"Tell America that España will soon be free again."

"What are you talking about?"

"You know as well as me, young one. Do not make us send you home in a box." He smiled. "We are no threat unless we're threatened." He crossed himself and rose to leave.

"Do you mean because Franco's ill and he'll die soon?"

"I thought you were smarter," he sighed. The man stared down at me for a long time before turning away.

It wasn't far from the truth when I said I had no idea what he was saying. Since arriving in Spain the week before, my entire focus was on tracking the man who recently held an embassy for ransom, and I was so close I could smell his aftershave. But early this morning I was jerked off course and ended up in church, sitting next to a misinformed lunatic. I needed time to figure out why I was now babysitting a prime minister.

Mass ended before I could feel sorry for myself or my circumstances. Blanco leisurely but deliberately moved back down the aisle toward the front of the church. Like those around me, I made the sign of the cross as I rose, pretending I knew what I was doing. But to get it right, I relied on a phrase I had been taught in the schoolyard as a kid, "spectacles, testicles, wallet, and watch."

By the time I reached the door, the two men were climbing into the back of a Spanish-made Dodge Dart 3700 GT. To many, a compact automobile would have been an absurd choice for an armored car on the streets of New York or Chicago, but in Europe with its narrow lanes and tight corners designed for horse-drawn carriages and pedestrian traffic, this small car was the perfect choice. While shielding its occupants against imaginable harm with more than 3,000 additional kilos of steel plating and reinforced glass, the Dodge offered both agility and speed to navigate the congested inner city.

The car pulled away from the curb and rolled down Calle de Serrano, past the one-way Calle de Maldonado that dumped out traffic in front of me. I followed lazily on foot, not really thinking about what I would do now. As the car reached the next intersection at Calle de Juan Bravo, it turned left. I thought the driver might use the maze of one-way streets to circle back to the government offices along Av. de Burgos. On a whim, I cut over on Maldonado and ran nearly to the next block before stopping to catch my breath at Calle de Claudio Coello. I was bent over and exhaling heavily as the Dodge cruised by. Luis Carrero Blanco met my eyes for one slow-motion second, and then the vehicle was gone.

CHAPTER 2

Thursday started out overcast and much chillier than the day before, having dipped to 1° centigrade overnight. I was regretting not bringing my gloves and scarf, as a cold gust cut through my long coat. The bitter weather reminded me of winters growing up in Chicago. No matter which way I turned, the swirling wind was still in my face. The frigid air seeped through my clothes and froze muscle as hard as bone.

I was glad to see the inside of San Francisco de Borja, not that it was much warmer, but at least the sharp bite was gone. Blowing on my cold, dead fingers did little to soothe them. I felt like one of the relics near the altar and thought about lighting a few prayer candles to heat my frozen hands, but a large man was kneeling in the alcove having a serious conversation with his faith. The oversized cross on the wall above his head reminded me it was probably not a great idea to disturb him in the off chance his appeal was actually a dialogue. I pulled open my coat and stuffed numb fists into the thin warmth of my jeans pockets.

I was late for Mass and Blanco was already in his usual second-row pew with Fernandez. An early morning meeting with an informant within Franco's inner circle had thrown off my schedule, but it had been worth it. The man had told me that because King Alfonso XIII had gone into exile without abdicating when civil war erupted, Franco has technically been ruling as regent to the King since his victory.

Without royalty on the throne, he was only able to govern by the grace of a sovereign coalition, which continued to support the Nationalists. However, the group had most recently been growing restless. It was now time to bring a Spanish king home, and Blanco's directive was to restore the monarchy to its former glory. But the new prime minister didn't seem the least bit interested in giving up his recently gained power and so far he had resisted the mounting pressures. This information added to what I'd already learned.

The hours had slipped away the prior day while I had examined the prime minister's life. The dossier had been good, but nowhere near complete. I had buried myself in library microfiche reading everything I could find concerning Blanco. In putting together the puzzle pieces, I had seen where his thoughts lived and I had discovered what scared him. I had been introduced to his few friends and his many enemies. As a man, he was overbearing, arrogant and dogmatic, with a taste for control when it came to other human beings.

Apart from his own actions, spreading political and economic discord had further damaged Blanco's popularity. The Madrid news agency Sabado had been printing a number of leftist bylines criticizing the lagging economy and El Mundo had just broken the story that he received threatening letters over the past week because of an upcoming trial for ten minor political dissidents. A mole had identified the men within their ranks as a group to be monitored. It wasn't known how they had jumped so quickly from Spain's watch list to accusations of civil crimes against the government but with their arraignment only two weeks away, the impending trial had attracted more than a little grassroots attention and it had all been negative.

While the priest offered communion, I moved to the aisle on the far side out of direct sight of the nave and walked closer to the altar. Blanco and Fernandez were the last to accept the sacrament and strolled to their seats as I reached the front. I sat in a pew opposite them and listened as the priest ended the concluding rite with a few announcements regarding the upcoming Christmas holiday and asked us to remember the poor and downtrodden during this time of year.

As soon as the priest was gone, I moved quickly into the center aisle to beat the crowd outside. I wanted to see how the common masses related to Blanco and how he responded to them. But when I looked up, the Spaniard from yesterday was standing at the back of the nave, watching me. His gaze was so piercing it stopped me dead in the aisle.

An icy dread wrapped around me, sending shivers down my spine as he slowly crossed himself. A long sigh parted his thick lips. Disappointment lined his face. What are you trying to tell me, old man? What?

A heavyset woman walked into me from behind and pushed me aside, muttering to herself. She was dressed in black and walked bent over a wooden cane. Her gait and rounded back vaguely reminded me of a beetle waddling home.

I looked back for the Spaniard, but he was already going through the front of the church. As the thick door slammed behind him, a cold burst of air filled the hall with a foreboding of the weather outside. Not waiting for the prime minister, I buttoned my coat, braced against the chill and pushed through the main doors.

The armored Dodge was idling at the curb and the driver waited on the sidewalk beside the rear fender. I turned left, then left again on Calle de Maldonado following the Spaniard. The space between us grew; he moved fast for an old man. I thought of yesterday's conversation as I strained to catch up. Something had troubled me about the exchange, but I couldn't decide what it was.

I was coming up on mid-block when I heard the rattle of the Dodge's powerful engine pass through the intersection behind me and suddenly I knew what it was. I walked faster as the Spaniard disappeared on Calle de Claudio Coello.

The prime minister's car crossed in front of me no more than twenty meters away, moving casually around a double-parked taxi near the intersection. I ran as a deafening explosion catapulted me backward over a row of parked cars.

CHAPTER 3

I lay on the pavement, listening to the ringing in my head coming from deep down near the brain stem. It felt like I was still running. I tried to roll to the side, but I couldn't find the ground. There was no way to steady myself, and I fell back twice before the motion around me finally stopped. I struggled to a sitting position. My body was numb and my lungs were empty, like I had been jolted awake from a bad dream. If the cement-faced buildings around the corner hadn't absorbed the full impact of the blast, I wouldn't have been waking at all.

I checked my ears and nose for blood and flexed my muscles as I stood the rest of the way. My legs wobbled but I eventually found my way between the parked cars to the building and leaned a hand weakly against the wall. My body wouldn't straighten and my breath came in spurts. From somewhere, I felt the spray of water on the wind.

A teenage girl faltered along the sidewalk. She was saying something, but the words were muffled. I placed unsteady hands over my ears and popped them to clear the cotton from my brain. The girl mumbled, barely above a whisper, "Es loco ... todos están muertos ... huir rápidamente." I still couldn't catch it all. I knew she was only making noise to prove she was still alive.

I edged my way to the end of the building. I had expected massive destruction and total chaos, but the street was far worse than any cataclysm my imagination could create. The sight was a surreal, colorless collection of nothing. Everything was gone.

There was no sound except for the ringing in my head and no motion other than the thick dust and smoke hanging in the air. There was no length, width, or breadth to calibrate what I was seeing. I couldn't touch it or make it more real.

Eventually, my brain began to measure some depth, collect loose pigment into colors and reconnect images into movement. There was a gaping hole in Calle de Claudio Coello from sidewalk to sidewalk, ten meters across, and it was rapidly filling with water and sewage. Building faces had several layers of skin cut away, exposing raw bones of rebar. Cement chunks and crumbled asphalt created uneven footing, and drifting dust cast a ghostly shimmer across the unsettled air.

A sharp, high-pitched moan came from the ground at my feet. It sounded like a crying cat. I stepped back involuntarily when I saw a woman lying face up near the wall. Blood had streaked the film of white dust on her face, and one leg was twisted at an odd angle. Vertigo caught me, and it looked like her body was hovering above the sidewalk. Kneeling, I couldn't hide the tremble in my voice.

"Señora, ¿estás bien?"

She made no reply. Her breathing was shallow, but her eyes were open wide, fixed on the imaginary distance. Pulling the injured woman up by the underarms, I rested her head and shoulders against the block wall, afraid she might bleed out before I could stem the blood flow. I stripped off my shoes and used my socks as gloves to wipe her face, feeling for the source of her wounds.

"¿Qué le duele?" She stared, unable to tell me where she hurt. I found a laceration on the top of her head and pressed a sock on it to stall the bleeding. "¿Se puede sostener esto? Hold the sock. Can you do that?" I lifted her limp arm. She wasn't responding. "Come on, lady, get with me."

14

I placed her hand in mine and squeezed gently. She didn't have the strength to fold her fingers around mine. I bent close to her face.

"Me mira. ¿Puede ver mi cara? Look at me. Um. ¿Puede usted mirar aquí?" I asked in a soft voice.

She blinked and saw me for the first time. Through wincing lips, the woman mouthed questions, but her voice wouldn't come. She lay back, exhausted.

Her chest quit moving and her eyes suddenly rolled up. Was she still breathing? Dammit, I didn't need this right now. I pinched her nose and forced a hard breath into her lungs. Air caught roughly in her chest and she began hyperventilating. My face reddened; she had only fainted.

"Calm down. You're all right. That's better," I said. "Escúchame. Ayuda está en camino. ¿Entiendes? Help is coming. Señora, do you understand?"

She tried to swallow on a dry throat, causing a long, deep coughing attack. Until it subsided, I could only hold her head and hope she didn't reopen the wound. I had no water to give her.

"Por favor, mantenga el vendaje en el lugar. Press on the top of your head here."

The woman finally moved a hand to mine.

"¿Cuál es su nombre?" I asked.

"Ana Dominga Santiago Pena," she struggled to tell me her name.

"Okay, Ana Dominga. Ayuda está en camino. Do you understand me?"

She nodded. I did not know if help was on the way or not. I hadn't heard sirens or approaching vehicles of any kind. The wind whistled in my ears obscuring all sound but the dammed ringing. Where was everyone?

"I need to go. Mantenga la calma y trate de no moverse. You

15

have to stay here. Okay?"

Slipping my shoes on bare feet, I tried to get up, but she grabbed my forearm. Her eyes darted to the scene in front of her, then back to me as she finally understood what happened. Apprehension creased her face and she started to cry. Tears rolled off her cheeks, caking in the dust.

"No...." That single word was at once filled with fear, pleading and loneliness.

The woman had a surprisingly powerful grip on my arm, and it took some time to gently free myself. Her breathing was stabilizing, and she was moving more now. I rose, afraid she might try to follow me, but she remained on the sidewalk. Feeling the woman's eyes bore into my back, I looked down at her and held up a hand to let her know she should stay where she was.

I looked around. What am I doing here? I was just supposed to watch and learn. I felt the buildings closing in on me and the compressed air tightened around my chest. A full minute went by before the twinge of panic passed. I took a shaky breath.

The crater was almost filled with black, thick water. I didn't want to know what was floating in it. Dust had cleared below eye level but continued to roll across the ground like marsh gas. I peered up and down the street. The prime minister's car was gone.

Debris lay thirty meters in either direction, but there was not a single tire track leading away from the hole. I knew it was probable the motorcade had been in front of the explosion and potentially missed the full impact, but it was doubtful the vehicle had escaped without some damage. Had it held together long enough for the driver to gun the occupants to safety?

The blast wasn't the result of a gas main accidentally igniting. There was no question it was man made, but the stench of sewage masked other odors, making it impossible to catch the residual aroma of explosives like dynamite or C4. The smell of gooey tar or sulfuric acid fumes could have let me know what happened.

From the deep depression, I knew the detonation point was underground rather than at street level. The energy was channeled upward. Concrete and stone were evenly sheared from the building fronts on both sides of the blast, all the way to the roof lines. If the explosion was at or above the pavement, such as a thrown or propelled weapon, the hole would be more of a divot in comparison and the main force would have caused a blast dome. Every direction would have been a path of least resistance, causing a fireball that would have destroyed outward from its center.

So, if a charge was buried, how did it get there? Yesterday, there had been no fresh asphalt or cement or any other indication of digging in the area. The sewer was a possibility, but usually not dry enough to ensure that dampness-sensitive dynamite would ignite when needed. Besides, the sewer pipes ran beneath the sidewalks so an explosion centered there would have caused more damage to one side of the street than the other.

I moved around the flooded cavity, examining the buildings across from the church. Off on an angle, a thick safety door had been blown off its hinges and lay in splinters several meters inside the hallway. Water was streaming from the opening.

I stepped through what remained of the entrance. On my right was a staircase leading to walk-up lodgings above the storefronts. In the stairwell was the door down to a basement flat. Water was sluicing from under the gap. I pulled out two picks from an inner pocket and went to work on the keyhole. Almost immediately, I heard the tumblers click. God, I loved Europe. Not entirely because most doors have hundred-year-old locks that were easily defeated, but that added to the charm.

The door opened onto a descending set of stairs, flooded up to where I stood. Frustrated, I came back out to the street and disappeared through the next entryway. The hall was dark and my knee crashed into a black pipe jutting from the wall. Grimacing, I used six of my favorite adjectives to curse my luck before lashing out with a side kick that drove the conduit back into place. I didn't see that the basement door behind me had been pulled off a hinge and hung by a prayer. I almost tumbled backward down the stairs.

The smell of sewage caused me to breathe through my mouth. Black water was knee deep and rising swiftly as I descended into a tiny, sterile apartment. A short hall led to a kitchen where the cabinets were standing open. I waded closer. It was hard to say if the floating trash came from the floor or was washed in with the street litter. I was just hoping I didn't kick a body while making my way through the sludge.

Something caught my eye on the counter. It was a small box of stick matches soaked through from the spray. I scooped it up and shook off the excess water. The printing had blurred on the wet paper but I could still make out the scripted name Café Iruña on the cover. I shoved the box in my pocket.

A loud snapping noise startled me. Shotguns! I spun, expecting the worst.

Instead of men chambering rounds, I saw a metal door trying to hold back a mountain of water from ruptured underground pipes. The seal around the outside had been jarred loose and a shooting stream was playing with a dangling strip of molding. I added another liter of liquid to the street waste I was standing in.

Sloshing through the deepening water toward the bedroom, I tried not to get any wetter than I already was. The room was heaped with debris. Someone had removed a huge amount of dirt from beneath Claudio Coello and piled it against the far wall.

Judging from the volume of mud and rock, the cavity beneath the subsurface had to be big enough to hold a hundred kilos or more of munitions.

I heard the whisper of the first sirens approaching.

A crowd of a dozen had formed on Calle de Claudio Coello. Some of the onlookers were standing alone, staring at the hole, wondering what happened, while others were talking quietly among themselves, certain that they knew. A tourist was snapping pictures like he was on a high school field trip. This would be one exciting story to tell when he returned home.

The first patrol car arrived with lights and siren blaring. Before the car came to a full stop, the passenger jumped free and forced his way between the water and the growing crowd. He pushed spectators back to a perimeter of five meters. Several wanted to argue, but the policeman was insistent, and in the end he moved everyone away from the sinkhole.

A second and third patrol car skidded up behind the first and an ambulance wasn't far behind. Someone called for help with an injured woman holding a sock to her head. She was trying to walk. Two men were explaining it would be better to remain for treatment, but one was punched and the other kicked for their kindness. The woman was going home.

The medical team got her seated on the curb, but she continued struggling against one attendant while the other recorded her vital signs. It looked like she'd live unless the medics dragged her to the water's edge and drown her. I would have.

I melted into a group of bystanders, listening to eyewitnesses who claimed to have seen the event. It wasn't likely I was going to learn anything useful since the Spanish were not known for retelling great stories, at least on purpose. I wanted to be sure I wasn't mentioned while the last twenty minutes were retold. I hadn't seen anyone except a hysterical youth and the injured woman, but it wasn't definite whether someone had seen me.

"¿Qué pasó aquí?" An officer waited with a pencil and notebook poised.

An eyewitness thought hard about the question. He looked at the policeman, then at the ground and back again at the policeman. The man's face reflected little of the confidence he tried to muster. Several in the crowd moved close around, ready to help him with the story.

"No sé," the man finally said, admitting he didn't know what happened.

"Hubo una gran explosión," suggested another.

I wondered what his first clue had been. Everyone was talking at once now, offering wild theories and other speculations of the obvious. Some said it had to be the Russians. Others thought it might have been the Americans. I almost threw the French into the mix for fun.

The police officer asked if suspicious people had been hanging around.

"Esa mujer se lesion," said a man at the back of the crowd. He thought that old woman over there might be faking her injuries.

Did you see anyone before the explosion?

"Yo vi a un sacerdote, el cual estaba en la ventana de la casa parroquial," offered another man. Jesus, he'd seen a suspicious priest in the rectory window. The policeman glanced up and held the man's gaze for several seconds, then went back to taking notes.

CHAPTER 4

Clouds had obliterated the rest of the sky, bringing a fast-approaching rainstorm on a sharpening wind. The sky was dark gray. The weather was noticeably colder, and the chill had soaked through to my bones. I was wearing a threadbare great coat made to be cool rather than warm. My scarf and gloves were back at the hotel, my socks were wrapped around some old lady's head, and of course, my feet and legs were wet to above the knees. Did I mention the explosion that had almost killed me? So far, this had not turned out to be a morning of wise decisions.

I made my way north along Calle de Claudio Coello in the direction the prime minister's motorcade had been traveling. The rubble under my feet reminded me of a war movie I had seen as a kid where the bad guys had hidden in bombed out windows and doorways, waiting patiently to shoot at the good guys.

The enemy in that movie had been definable. They had worn uniforms of another color, had carried different weapons and represented national goals in opposition to our own. They had mobilized to take away our land, our resources and our freedom. I don't believe a war would ever be fought like that again. Now, the evil lived among us and I had no idea who they were, how they looked or what they wanted. The little training I received from my handler had not covered unknown forces like this and I was scared to death.

"Cortar el agua!" Someone was shouting to turn off the water.

At the end of the five-story church annex, there was a wide corridor separating it from San Francisco de Borja. Walking traffic was welcome to cut through the grounds for a soulful stroll between Calle de Claudio Coello and Calle de Serrano. It was a place where one might talk to God.

Heading back toward the front of the church, my priority was to get back to the hotel for a change of clothes and a warmer coat before putting any effort into finding Blanco. However, partway down the lane, I noticed seven or eight people standing in a secular garden staring up at the windows. Curious, I walked around behind the group.

On a balcony overlooking the lawn lay an automobile precariously perched on its right side. My brain slipped a notch. I didn't know what I was seeing. The undercarriage was sealed like a child's toy. I couldn't make out the engine, wheel struts, or exhaust pipes. No matter how I turned my head, the scene still looked like some trick of light and mirrors in a circus sideshow. Was it a prank? How did the car get here?

Moving a few meters to the side, I recognized the rear trunk lid of a Dodge Dart 3700 GT. It was the prime minister's armored car. No one was going to believe this. I didn't believe it and I was standing here looking at it.

If the car had been positioned a fraction before or after the exact point of impact, it would have carried the vehicle on an angle away from the explosion, landing somewhere along Calle de Claudio Coello. But, unbelievably, Blanco's car was here, wedged on the catwalk just meters above my head. A freak of time and tide put the motorcade squarely on top of the dynamite and launched it twenty-five meters upward and over the church building. If not for the reinforced steel chassis, the armored car would have vaporized during the explosion.

There was no need to check for survivors. They were all

dead; the driver, the bodyguard, and the prime minister. If the explosion hadn't smeared the ceiling of the car with blood and bones, then certainly the impromptu flight and mid-air collision with the balcony would have left no one alive. The churchyard was deathly quiet.

I asked a man if he saw what happened.

"No, yo oyó," he replied. He hadn't seen what happened, but he had heard it. He had been startled by the sudden explosion and ran out of the rectory across the way as the car fell in a big whoosh on the ledge. He wanted to help but didn't know how that was possible now.

The man was barely breathing as he glanced at me. He crossed himself, and I saw then that he was a priest. Dressed in only a short-sleeved cotton clerical shirt with nothing on his bare arms, he didn't seem to mind the cold except for an occasional shiver. The collar at his throat was tight against a bulging neck and he was rubbing the back of one hand with the other. The priest continued to stare.

"Padre, por favor recen por ellos."

"Los conductores en el coche han ido a Dios." I supposed he was right. A prayer now would not reach them in time. They were already with God.

Had he been to see the explosion yet?

"Sinceramente, me temo." The priest's voice was breaking.

"Padre, que está bien, pero alguien puede necesitar su ayuda."

I doubted if anyone needed his services now, I was just making conversation. There was the one injured woman but I hoped by now she had been taken to the hospital. If there were others nearer the impact, someone in heaven was already sorting out the pieces. I placed a hand on the priest's shoulder. He took a deep breath and gave me a timid smile before turning toward the walkway. I meant the gesture to comfort him, but he took it as a prompting to help on Coello.

I considered the prime minister's resting place a final time. I was stunned, amazed and baffled all at once. Like most early acts of terror, this target was specific, personal, and damage was focused on a distinct, definable enemy. It was fast, clean, and effective. Three were dead to my count, with only one innocent wounded. So why was there such overkill with those in the car? There was no doubt a fraction of the dynamite would have produced the same result, minus the missile launch. The extreme force did, however, tell me something about those who carried out the assault.

The old Spaniard had not been working alone. He had people, money, and experience at his disposal. They had hit the car hard at the right time and place to enable the most force with the least fallout. They wanted Blanco dead at all cost. As bad as the consequences were going to be, government reprisal for a failed attempt was far worse for the group. Punishment because of success was considerably more bearable than punishment because of failure.

And government reprisal was coming. Within an hour, the Nationalist Army would be here. As a result of today's incident, it was inevitable that martial law would be tightened in the major cities by evening. There would be an immediate show of military might, complete with an early curfew and a ban on crowd gatherings. Movie theaters would close, parks would be patrolled and groups of more than ten would be disbursed. For the next few weeks, not much more than eating and breathing would be allowed.

For the army, it was a waiting game as much as anything else. They had to know the murder was too irresistible to go unclaimed for long. Someone would eventually want the regime to know who was responsible and why. Consequently, I had that much of a head start to learn what I could before Franco found them. And he would find them.

Back at the entrance to Calle de Claudio Coello, I was stopped by a policeman waving me off.

"Alto!" He demanded. "La calle está cerrada." I knew someone would eventually stop me.

"¿Qué pasó aquí?" I asked.

"Un asunto de la Policía."

"Tengo que ir por este camino." I told the policeman that I needed to go there, pointing to the left away from the blast site.

"¿Cuál es su negocio allí?" He looked at me sternly.

"Mi hotel," I answered.

The officer waved the back of his hand several times toward the end of the street, telling me at once that I could go, that I was a nuisance, and that he was an important and busy man. His stare warned me not to dawdle. I wandered down the way without looking back until there was no rubble beneath my feet.

The police were busy keeping spectators from the immediate area. I watched an officer intercept a woman as she approached the depression and a shoving match ensued. Another man was yelling about needing his car. It had been buried under a chunk of concrete.

The crime was spread out in front of me, no more than forty meters away. The buildings were battered and bruised, the rupture in the street was still bleeding, and thick dust had buried the dead. It was quiet. I scanned the windows and paced the road. Talk to me, I thought. Tell me a secret. Show me what Blanco hadn't seen.

I was betting against a pressure plate on the pavement. Getting the right car would have been nearly impossible on a busy street. Chances were better that a spotter had had a direct line of sight to the target from just outside the fallout zone. Somewhere like here. It would have been foolhardy to remain in the blast zone and risk being hit by shrapnel as the world exploded. Intentional suicide hadn't yet become a part of the terrorist playbook.

The church side offered a slightly better sightline of Claudio Coello, though anyone standing there would have been exposed. I examined the pavement along the curb, walking up and down several times. The gutter was remarkably clean, like it had been recently swept. A spotter wielding a broom could have been an excellent cover while he killed time waiting for Blanco's car. Stepping on the narrow sidewalk, I saw something near the building.

I picked up three cigarette butts. The tobacco was a popular brand of French unfiltered smokes that smelled awful when lit. Chaban was addicted to these. So was half of France, though their popularity didn't stretch much beyond the border. Great, so far I'd eliminated exactly zero of the Spanish population as suspects, and now the French probably couldn't be ruled out either.

Was this what the little girl meant? Had the Blanco assassination brought Chaban to Spain? Was I too late to stop him again? I had to find some answers before the death toll went nuclear. Think!

If the spotter stood here, where was the triggerman? I focused on the other side of the street. It was congested with parked cars, an outdoor fruit stand, a pharmacy, postcard racks, public trash cans and telephone lines. Nothing was out of the ordinary.

Crossing over, I noticed a tangle of wires hanging from a communications pole. As I moved an open trash receptacle for a better look, something inside caught my eye. My hand swept through the morning garbage, revealing a small black box. Could it be the detonator? I slipped it inside a coat pocket and turned back to the pole.

The thin, insulated wires hanging at my knees were not telephone or heavy impact electrical coils or any other type that belonged with utility bundles. I crouched. The triggerman had strung the detonation wires on the utility poles and now they were lost among the cluster of cables that brought power to Claudio Coello.

"What's happened down there?" A tall, sandy-haired man asked in English. I glanced at him and stood up. He wasn't looking at me, but rather he gazed down the way.

"No idea," I replied.

"Looks like an old fashioned mess."

"I guess so," I said.

"What'd you find there?" The man asked, pointing toward the wires.

"Nothing, I was tying my shoe."

The man eyed my feet.

"You might catch your death in wet boots," he said.

"It's been raining." I said.

The man nodded once.

"You're in the way," he finally said. "Tell your boss to get you off the streets before you get hurt. Leave this to the pros or you will be sorry." He stared at me. Finally, he said, "You need a haircut."

"Do you know any good barbers outside of Langley?"

"I hear there're still a few good ones left in Vietnam."

He grinned and walked with his hands in his pockets toward the activity at the end of Calle de Claudio Coello. He never glanced back, so I guessed he didn't feel the two words I carved into his rear with my eyes. By not looking around, he was also telling me he had a partner. Another agent had his back and my head in his crosshairs.

CIA involvement was bad news. They seemed to mix up the black and white of every situation, so answers continually came out in shades of dark gray. Because of their well-known techniques, CIA activities were generally at odds with those employed by the DEA, ATF, FBI, NSA and sometimes the Constitution of the United States.

So was the nature of CIA intelligence. It was often a random give and take with illegal entities, occasionally prospering in exchange for information and other forms of enlightenment. During the early years of Vietnam, the company was notorious for its operations with drug traffickers and gun runners. Like the old saying about cops having the best drugs, however, the CIA had the best information, but they didn't like to share.

That's one of the reasons the NSA scattered people like me on the ground. My job was to verify intercepted communications and learn firsthand if this information was a precursor to danger arriving on American soil. These assignments were, however, in direct violation of NSA's charter, so my orders were clear; get it done as quickly and quietly as possible, without causing any blowback on the agency.

I took a deep breath and scrutinized the wires once more, then turned in the direction of my hotel. It would have been nice to have stumbled across a signed confession or a stone tablet identifying the responsible group, but nothing that obvious caught my attention.

The morning's adrenaline was fading. My eyes were burning, my throat was dry and I had to think this through. I knew the what, the when, the where and the how. I needed to identify the who and the why. Where I would find one, I would find the other huddling with it.

Just before reaching the end of the block at Diego de Leon,

THE HOLLOW MAN

the clouds opened up and it began to pour.

CHAPTER 5

"Avez-vous apprécié le feu d'artifice?"

"Speak English so we can both be clear here."

The sandy-haired man stared into a pair of stone gray eyes. Finally, the Frenchman bowed his head in mock deference.

"Certainly, I asked if you enjoyed the fireworks."

"I know what you said. What the hell did you think you were doing? This isn't what we paid for."

"You wanted a roadblock eliminated. I don't remember the method coming up."

"My people didn't intend this to go international. Dying quietly in his sleep was what we had in mind. I thought you could manage something simple."

"That's your style, not mine." A car passed by the alley entrance. "You had a problem that required a quick solution. I had a need to test a focused blast. We both learned something, didn't we?"

"This is the first I've heard of that."

"Well, then we know what you learned."

"I don't give a rat's ass. Fix it and fix it now."

"Relax. It's handled. Look past the end of your nose. A plan's in motion."

"I guess you won't mind if we give you a little help this time."

"Actually, I do. People in my way tend to die."

"If this comes back to me, then you're the dead man."

The knife blade sliced through the carotid artery before the sandy-haired man could react. The stunned agent fell back against the wall, clutching his throat. He tried to run, but stumbled and fell on his face. The Frenchman curiously watched the body as it shook uncontrollably on the pavement. The legs kicked out, looking for a foothold, but the struggle soon faded to a slow twitching and finally nothing. He bent and wiped the knife blade on the man's shirt.

"Don't threaten me. I already have one idiot following me around Europe. I don't need another."

CHAPTER 6

Exhausted, I shed my wet clothes in a pile at the door and fell on the bed. I shut my eyes, but instead of resting, I wrestled with another fretful sleep. It was a fabrication to call it sleep, really. It was more like wandering through the strung-out mind of a speedball junkie coming down from the mountain. There were many things to see and hear and smell and taste, but nothing made sense except the longing for past euphoria. Horrible sights and sounds clashed with rotting odors and distasteful flavors. I wanted to throw up everything, my stomach, my brain and my heart, just to call an end to it all.

Somewhere between twilight and no light, she came again. I woke instantly, but fatigue forced my lids shut again. The air was stale. The smell of decaying matter wafted around me. I couldn't see her but I knew she was there. I pulled myself up against the headboard before I could keep my eyes open. Sitting in the coffin with her hands on top of the side walls, she was smiling at nothing in particular.

"I can't do this anymore." She pretended not to hear me. I sighed. "I'm breaking all the rules. He tells me to find people and learn from them. Don't get too close, he says. But how in hell do I learn by watching television? So, I move in and I get a scrap here, a scrap there. Then he says, 'I gotta have more.' Why don't I just walk into their kitchen then and ask 'em to give me their recipe for disaster?"

"You are stronger than you think," she said, just above a

whisper.

"Tell that to the thousand bugs crawling around my head. Some of them, most of them, are as old as me and that's not what they're saying."

"That's your father talking to you," she said.

"It doesn't matter," I shrugged. "He told me the same things. His demons are my demons now. So what? Tell me, how do I learn from all of this?"

"Learning is one thing, understanding is another."

"Then, how do I understand what happened today? Who killed Blanco, and why?" I asked.

"How do I know who killed your prime minister? I've been dead for a year."

"Nine months and seventeen days."

"Has it only been so long? Well, I can't calculate that sort of time here. It already seems like forever." She sighed and looked down at her lap as the air left the room. The silence was unbearable.

I'll tell you what forever is, I thought. It's going to be forever before I can settle this mess and get my hands on Chaban.

"Dammit! I'll never find Chaban now," I said in frustration.

"You'll find him or you won't. I cannot say but the blame isn't yours to bear. I enjoy your company, which is the only reason I come."

"I will find him just the same, as soon as I get this Blanco thing tied up." I reaffirmed.

"Why?"

"To give you justice."

"Justice is for the living, not the dead. It makes no difference to me now." She wiped at the blood. "You are a curious man. Why do you spend your time with the dead?"

"I get claustrophobic around people."

"You have no friends? Just me?"

"Plenty," I said.

She replied with a wan smile. We both knew she was right. There was no denying it. I was alone and preferred it that way when my back was solidly against the wall. I didn't need people getting in the way.

I threw my legs over the side of the bed before I really wanted to get up. I was exhausted. My lungs were on fire. My head felt like a block of wood. My mouth was so dry the gums had receded from the teeth. My eyes throbbed and no amount of rubbing would ease the pain.

I walked across to the bathroom for a glass of water. The lights were off and that was fine with me because I didn't want to face the mirror. I knew what I'd find; an emaciated, empty child barely hanging on to the last thread of sanity.

The little girl was the only person to ever see through to my unsound soul. Though I covered it with armor, used magic to vex the groupies and donned disguises to mislead the casual observer, she still seemed to know everything. I didn't have the heart to tell her my sleep had been more peaceful before her ghost began to discuss my shortcomings with me. Those were long and unsettled nights and when she didn't come, I lay awake waiting for her.

I suddenly remembered the detonator. Tugging on dry clothes, I found my coat on the floor next to the door and pulled the box free. I sat heavily at the small desk across from the bed. In the night light coming through the window, the palm-sized device resembled a Lionel train transformer. A black metal box no more than a ten centimeter square, there were two wing-nut electrodes on one side ready to stream an electrical current when the switch on top made a connection.

With an all-purpose tool, I extracted four screws from the bottom and the cover dropped away. Six nine-volt batteries fell out, bundled together with plastic tape and connected with soldered nichrome wiring to the undercarriage of the electrodes. There was nothing else, but it was enough to create a spark large enough for a hundred kilos of dynamite.

The mechanism was simple but effective. There was no obvious signature, and I wasn't positive I even had the right device. Any high school kid with a basic knowledge of electricity could have built this in 30 minutes.

Banging on the door interrupted my thoughts. I checked the clock. It was 11:40 p.m. That wouldn't be room service.

"Policia Municipal. Abra la puerta! Open the door, Señor!"

It sounded like half a police division stood between me and the stairwell down the hall. If I went that way, I'd be in handcuffs within ten seconds. I glanced at the fire escape. Expecting to find me sleeping, the police may not be guarding the emergency exit. And this did qualify as an emergency.

"Policia Municipal! Tenemos una orden para su arresto!" What the hell had I done this time?

I threw open the window and cold air flooded in. If I thought the jail cell waiting for me would have been any warmer, I might have invited the police in for donuts and remained for the consequences. Instead, I grabbed my coat and disappeared through the window.

There was commotion behind me. Someone was on the fire escape at the landing above. I took the stairs two at a time and when I jumped the last few meters to the ground, a policeman's hard head caught me under the chin and we both went down.

I pushed off the policeman. As he fell away, he managed to snare the bottom of my coat and I was dragged down again. Struggling up, I grabbed his wrist and kicked his underarm. He loosened his grip immediately and the numb limb dropped to the ground. I just added resisting arrest to whatever charge was in the warrant.

"Alto! Alto ahi!" I heard the metal fire escape rattling under the weight of heavy boots. As I rounded the corner onto Calle de Goya, I glimpsed two new policemen on the ground in the alley behind me. One was examining his injured colleague, and the other was in pursuit. The long burst of a whistle screeched above the shouts. Its shrill sound cut through the darkness like a mortar shell seconds before hitting the ground.

When I first arrived last week, I had plotted an exit route, hoping I might never need it, and here I was wishing the plan had been better. There was no choice now. Already breathing hard, I had to get out of sight before the man chasing me caught up or a radio car cut me off. I had to make it to the wall.

I turned off Calle de Goya at the next alley, ran to the far end and turned right into a neighborhood that changed from business to upscale residential the farther I moved from the main street. My only chance was in the walled estates of Madrid's most wealthy. With my adrenalin running thin, I spotted the three-meter wall I thought I could climb if I hit it at a dead run.

My shoe buried itself in the brown winter vines about halfway up and the foothold was enough to catapult me to the top. Broken shards of glass cemented in place along the crest bit into my leather gloves and coat sleeves as I went over the top. Landing in the soft mud between the wall and a row of hedges, I stood motionless, expecting an interior light to flood the yard and a pack of crazy-mad mongrels to catch my scent.

I heard footsteps jogging past. Men were shouting directions, asking questions. As soon as the police were out of earshot, I ran along the wall until it curved around toward the estate. It was a short hop to the back of the servants' quarters from there. I sat between two garbage cans to wait. It was unlikely the police would search house to house in this neighborhood and they certainly wouldn't imagine such an endeavor at this hour.

Tomorrow was another story. Now that my game piece had been exposed on the board, I needed a new way to travel undetected. I needed a disguise.

CHAPTER 7

An old man hobbled down the front steps of an unassuming stone co-op in a modest neighborhood a block off Calle de Silva in the Gran Via district of Madrid. He wore a shabby coat too large for his thin, frail body. A cap was pulled down tight on short-cropped, graying hair and an unkempt beard hung to his Adam's apple. The lines of a hard life were etched across a sagging face. He leaned heavily on a cane as he walked the two blocks to the Santo Domingo underground stop where he boarded a subway bound for the main railway station.

Sitting in a rear-facing seat, he paid no attention to others in the coach, preferring to concentrate on the tunnel beyond the moving train. Madrid's rush hour had ended a few hours before, so the car was empty except for six mid-morning travelers hoping to catch an early lunch or find a bargain in one of the upscale boutiques currently springing up in the downtown area. Two soldiers passed through the car without seeing the old man. He huddled down further in the seat and shoved his hands in his coat pockets.

Atocha Station offered train service to outlying Spanish provinces and most of the rest of Europe by way of the French frontier. The station was housed in South Central Madrid between a pair of beautiful old buildings framed in burned orange brick with white stone trim. Its interior lobby was illuminated with daylight from broad windows and an endless skylight draping the curved roof more than twenty-five meters above the pedestrian traffic. In the center stood an enormous fountain, drained and converted into an elaborate jungle-styled terrarium. Two sister gardens stood on either side of the concourse leading to the departure area.

The station was in chaos this morning. People were queued everywhere and most of them were in the wrong line. There were no information counters to direct traffic and without proper signage, there wasn't a way to identify the purpose of any window. Frustrations were boiling. Adding to the nervous energy, national guardsmen roughly patrolled the ticket area. Looking for someone.

The old man wandered into a telephone kiosk, pulled a numbered ticket from habit and patiently waited his turn for an open booth. There were nine people in front of him, but it was still the fastest way to get a local Madrid operator. He browsed through the turntable of telephone directories to kill time. Finding the Madrid business listings, his fingers ran through the pages scanning for the name he needed. There was no listing in Madrid. He moved through directories for neighboring locales with the same result, no such company.

"Hey, viejo. ¿Es tu turno? Me deja ver su billete," said an impatient man. Was it my turn already? thought the old man.

"Aprovechar mi turno si no puedes esperar," he said. Take my turn if you can't wait, he thought.

"Me deja ver su billete." The impatient man continued to bully the old man.

"Aquí, tómar!" You want to see the ticket. Here, take the damned thing.

"Es su turno!" The complaining man shouted to the growing audience.

"Yo no necesito el teléfono. Me dejen en paz!" I don't need the god damned telephone now.

"Pero tiene un billete, viejo estúpido!" The irritable customer walked away, still miffed that the crazy old man had taken a ticket he never intended to use.

Twenty minutes later, the old man had worked his way around the turnstile to the northern provinces without finding the listing he needed. His irritation was showing as he slammed a directory back into its slot. It had to be somewhere in Spain! The name wasn't French. Dammit! It had to be here.

Suddenly there it was two books from the end. I should have started at the back, he thought. Café Iruña was in the famous bull fighting city of Pamplona in the middle of Basque Country, and there was only one restaurant with that name. Now he had something—I had something—and I finally knew where I was going.

It was well known that Franco didn't have many friends among the Basque. They had mounted the strongest resistance to el Caudillo's nationalist army during the Civil War and, therefore, had suffered the most during its long aftermath. I heard open animosity between the two had been buried to some extent, albeit under a thin film of dust. With the assassination of Blanco though, the hatred may have just risen from the dead.

The ticket seller told me there was only one express train each day to Pamplona, and it had already left this morning. However, there were still a number of good local commuters this afternoon. In fact, one was leaving in half an hour. I bought a second-class ticket for 450 pesetas and went looking for a quiet place to wait.

With my cane leading the way, I approached a marble bench near the corridor leading to the platforms. A young couple and a lone man were already sitting there, but I thought I could still squeeze in. The three suddenly stood and moved away in different directions as if they all remembered they had somewhere else to be. Respect for old people was not yet dead here in Spain, I thought. As I turned to sit, two armed soldiers were standing in front of me. I sank with my head bowed. My disguise was about to be seriously tested.

"¿Señor, ha visto a este hombre?" One of the guardsmen held up a photograph.

I was staring at my own face.

It was a grainy black-and-white image of me standing in a shattered doorway on Calle de Claudio Coello. CIA. Anyone else and I wouldn't have lasted ten seconds before being arrested or shot. They were watching the entire time. I wondered if Franco had thought to ask how they had gotten the photo and why I wasn't already in custody. That was probably supposed to have happened when the police knocked on my door last night. Whose side were these bastards on?

I read the short description under my portrait. I was wanted for questioning about recent subversive activities in Madrid. Bomb-making materials had been discovered during a search of my hotel room and I had been seen plotting with other known enemies of the state. As a suspect in the prime minister's brutal slaying, I was to be considered armed and dangerous. I disappeared last night during a running gun battle through central Madrid.

"¿Este hombre? No. ¿Qué ha hecho?"

I didn't look up.

"Queremos hacerle algunas preguntas."

The soldier was saying one thing but what he really meant was I had won an all-expenses paid vacation to Zamora Prison with all the fetid air, rotten food and 60-watt sunshine I wanted. On festival Sundays, inmates were usually entertained with demonstrations of inhumane torture and beheadings in the prison yard. Audience participation was always welcome.

"No es una muy buena fotografía," I said, commenting on the poor quality of the picture.

Rising with the help of the cane, I ambled toward track 17 on a near side platform. As congested as the narrow strip between trains was, everyone avoided my meandering path as I approached. The second-class cars marked for Pamplona were at the rear of the train, so the walk was shorter than expected.

As I stood in front of the coach door wondering how to tackle the climb, a hand violently grabbed my bicep. I stiffened and looked around. The police had recognized me. There was nowhere to run. A large soldier forced me up the steps as I tried feebly to resist. The young officer shoved me aside at the top and pushed around me. Three other passengers passed in quick succession before I could move.

I found an empty compartment near the entrance and settled into a seat at the window. Leaning back against the leather cushion, my eyes involuntarily closed. I heard a group shuffle past the door, deciding on other accommodations after hesitating a moment. Sharing a berth for eight hours with a sick old man must not have been an inviting thought. I drifted but was startled upright when an annoying black-haired child rapped hard on the window and laughed.

Two more militiamen mounted the second-class car and moved down the corridor, knocking on compartments. The taller man opened my sliding door and stood looking down at me. Struggling to stand on my cane, I began coughing, lost my balance and fell back against the bench. It was not the most graceful I'd ever been, but I had to admit, it was a nice piece of acting all the same. The soldier squinted at me and closed the door without saying a word.

Almost imperceptibly, the train rolled out of the Atocha station toward its destination 400 kilometers to the northeast. I watched the concrete runway outside my window. The platform abruptly ended, and I was alone again on another steel highway, taking me nowhere near home. We moved through neighborhood winterscapes of grays, blacks and muddy browns until the depressing city eventually fell away, changing to flat country, then briefly to orange groves and finally to fields of winter corn that ran up to the tracks on both sides.

Not far into one of these corn forests, the train slowed and hissed to a stop. There wasn't a station or platform in sight. In fact, there was no sign of civilization above or beyond the high stalks, not even a path cut through the rows. Yet a woman was standing at the track with a small suitcase at her feet.

She adjusted the low bun in her hair and pulled herself up the coach stairs. Her black dress was calf-length and the hem almost hung up on a heel as she navigated the first step. She caught herself quickly. When she passed my compartment window, her weathered face revealed a much older woman than I had first thought. She made her way up the corridor as the engine began to pull again.

We were back to full speed by the time the train exited the dense cornfield. The engine clipped along at 80 km/h on the top end but stopped so often that the maximum speed was rarely achieved for very long. Madrid to Pamplona was a busy route and the train was very accommodating to travelers. We waited long periods at station platforms, and passengers were picked up and dropped off at the oddest times and places along the way.

The terrain had long since changed to barren field after barren field when the sun finally dropped behind acres of uninspiring and fruitless grape vines. I fell into a fleeting sleep with my head braced against the intersection of the couch and the window. Vaguely remembering the train climbing into unbroken foothills and winding through soft, low mountains, I was jolted awake by the breaking of the diesel engine as it descended into the rounded valley known as Cuenca de Pamplona.

Famous for the running of the bulls during the San Fermin Festival each July and forever immortalized by Ernest Hemingway, Pamplona was nestled on a green plateau surrounded by mountains in a region officially called the Chartered Community of Navarre. The city spread out on both sides of the Alba River and was home to 140,000 people and another 20,000 tourists during the summer months.

The train rolled to a gradual stop in front of a poorly lit, but bustling depot. I precariously descended the coach steps with my cane tapping the way. Straightening myself, I tentatively wandered through the throng of passengers who crowded the platform and station house. Finally, standing outside on the road, I smiled, buttoned my coat and faded into the night.

CHAPTER 8

The next morning, a bright sun rose into a clear sky. The clouds had scattered overnight, and by the time Pamplona awakened, the air was crisp but not overly bitter for the high altitude. Shopkeepers in the old city were out early, washing down sidewalks and readying open-air stands for the day's patrons. Cut flowers smelling of jasmine, gardenia and lilac sat in displays next to fruits and vegetables that decorated colorful bins and table tops. Fresh beef, lamb and chicken were displayed in shop windows and on a narrow lane off to the right, fishmongers presented the daily catch of North Atlantic cod, hake and haddock stretched out on beds of ice.

Like many European cities, the oldest development of Pamplona at the city's center was ringed by ancient battlements. Built and rebuilt through almost two and a half millennia to serve a number of masters, the borough's current wall system dated from the late sixteenth century. Though the city was much larger now, having grown far beyond the original enclosure during subsequent economic booms, inside the remaining historic fortifications was still known as the old city.

Appropriately named the "City Café," Café Iruña opened onto Plaza del Castillo in the heart of the old city. This area was the original site of a castle built by Navarrese King Louis I in the fourteenth century to guard the southern flank of Pamplona from invading armies. Since then, it had witnessed bullfights, battles, military parades, political demonstrations and good old-fashioned markets. I strolled through the tree-lined, uneven quadrangle toward Café Iruña at the far end before settling at a bench on the west side, about halfway down the open-air plaza.

I pulled out a newspaper and flapped it open just below eye level. I had already read the front-page story, vaguely outlining an undetermined explosion in Madrid that killed Luis Carrero Blanco and another about the nationwide search for an unidentified American college student wanted for questioning in an unrelated matter of some importance. The prime minister would continue to be big news for weeks to come, but my story was thankfully buried, without a picture, twelve pages back. Both stories were official government communiques released to the press by the national news arm of Franco's cabinet.

I peered at the immense, 14,000-square meter courtyard. Automobile traffic was not allowed in the square and pedestrian access was restricted to pathways on the northeast and southeast corners. A narrow alley on the west separated the mass of buildings looming behind me. The rest of the plaza formed a tight, walled enclosure lined with a myriad of upscale boutiques, cantinas and family-run bodegas stretching along the ground-floor locations below, converted five-story office complexes. The tall buildings made it impossible to know what might be coming at me, and there was no place to run when it did. It was the proverbial logistical nightmare, but this café was the only lead I had.

The plaza was busy this morning. People strolled arm in arm, and singles traveled in their own worlds. No one was in a hurry. A pair of young lovers paused at the gazebo in the center of the concrete square. During a long kiss, their arms explored each other's bodies with the desperate hand signals of tortured love. A lone man walked his dog while trying to read his own newspaper. The large animal stopped to relieve himself several times without the owner's notice. Three teenage girls sauntered along, entangled in smiles and whispers.

There was nothing unusual except for the distinct lack of a military presence. Pamplona was not exactly a million miles from the martial law that had seized the rest of the country, but I hadn't seen a single soldier since my arrival. As the center of Basque activity against Franco, Pamplona should have ordinarily housed more combat-ready troops on a regular basis than in all the rest of Spain combined. Where were they?

I left the plaza without looking back.

An hour later, a man with a blocked shoe and a turned-out foot limped into Café Iruña and sat heavily at an outdoor table to the far left of the main entrance. He adjusted his glasses to read the short mid-morning menu displayed on the table. The bright sun was quickly warming the day; nevertheless, he ordered coffee, traditional ojen and fried pastry. He sipped the hot liquid halfway down, then lifted the ojen in shaky hands and emptied it into the cup. That was the only way he could drink anisette, but the 40 percent alcohol kick was worth it.

The plaza crowd had grown since the morning as the early wanderers gave way to devotees of the chic and the haute couture. Before lunch and dinner were the best times for the Spanish to see and be seen. Both men and women modeled their latest fashions as if they were on the Madrid or Paris runways. Of course, attitude and bearing were as important as what one wore. Settling back, the man watched the promenade in the plaza.

But not all in Pamplona were fascinated with this custom. A pair of young men sat two tables away, unaware of the show beyond the restaurant's railing. Hunching over their coffees and speaking in quiet tones, they were concerned with little else. And likewise, they were invisible to the spectacle around them.

The old Spaniard from Madrid entered the plaza, walking

rapidly toward the restaurant. Glancing over his shoulder several times before flicking his cigarette to the ground, he found his way to the young men. Landing lightly on the plastic chair, he broke into their conversation. His voice was low and urgent, and the others nervously listened.

Something was wrong. I couldn't make out what. Their words were lost in the noise of the plaza. I struggled to hear. Suddenly, the old man focused on me. He recognized me. Crap! I can't run in this disguise. I was dead before I could stand up. Was a crippled guy the best I could do?

I decided to deliberately exaggerate my handicaps. I pushed my thick glasses up on my nose and absently lifted a deformed foot into the aisle. He stared at me. I raised the coffee and ojen with trembling hands. He still wasn't sure but, making some internal decision, the old Spaniard nodded and turned back to his friends.

I finished the coffee and signaled for a check. The waiter examined the empty dishes, wrote a number on the ticket and set it near my hand. I pulled 40 pesetas from my coat. He counted the amount in his palm and disappeared through the main restaurant entrance, returning with the small change. I waved him off, but he placed the saucer with 7 pesetas, 50 centimos on the corner of the table and turned the edge of the tablecloth over it.

I stood awkwardly and limped to the table where the three men sat.

"May I sit?" I asked.

The man from church abruptly stopped talking and peered up at me as I removed my thick glasses.

"You are the American from San Francisco de Borja," he said. "Have you come to kill us?"

"No."

The question surprised me. I slowly removed my hands from

my pockets and held the lapels open to show I wasn't armed. The old Spaniard motioned for me to sit, and I fell into the remaining open chair, using my hands on the table for support. The blocked shoe felt like I was continually walking up stairs and my calves ached.

"It's not safe to be seen with you," he said.

"I was going to say the same to you."

I turned to the other two men. Closer now, I saw they were just boys trying to look older in a world where longevity somehow translated to wisdom. They were younger by three decades than their companion, perhaps my age, but probably younger. One sat up defiantly under the scrutiny, steeling himself to leap across the table at me.

"Do you speak English?" I quietly asked them.

"They barely speak Espanish," the old Spaniard answered for them. "We are safe with English. They are Basque patriots who have refused to learn anything other than their beloved ancestral language."

"I only want information. I'm here to understand, that's all. I won't cause you any trouble," I said.

His eyes darted ceaselessly from person to person.

"I'm alone, sir."

"Then you aren't CIA," the man said flatly, and nodded. "Posta elektronikos da," he said to the two patriots, explaining that I was a friend.

"Are they involved with you?" I asked.

"They're ETA and therefore claim involvement in all actions against Franco's tyranny. It's the nature of young fools who need a cause to focus their energy and anger."

Euskadi Ta Askatasuna, or ETA, roughly translated in English to Basque Homeland and Freedom. The organization had been founded about fifteen years before and rapidly evolved from a group promoting traditional Basque culture to a paramilitary force bent on independence from Spain at any cost. In the past five years, they had claimed or were blamed for a few dozen killings and kidnappings, though these were of little consequence to the world in general and probably to Spain as well. But the assassination of Luis Carrero Blanco was a major leap forward in their terrorist capabilities if they were indeed responsible. ETA would gain the fear and respect they sought.

"Did you kill Blanco?" I asked.

"Me?"

"You tried to draw me into the explosion."

"I warned you to stay away. I was there to stop it but I was too late. Now, I have come to stop ETA from doing something stupid."

"Then who is responsible?" I asked.

"Rumor says no one wants responsibility, so ETA plans to take advantage of that. They have as great a need to be recognized for the killing as the Generalissimo has to place the blame on them. Besides, it coincides with a plan they were preparing called Operación Ogre. Good foresight or poor judgment, I do not know which."

"What's Operación Ogre?"

"It's nothing more than paper," he said. "Yet it's the thing that put all of us in motion."

"Who? What are you saying?"

"Let me ask you, boy, how did you find your way to Pamplona?"

"This restaurant brought me to you. I found a box of matches from Café Iruña in the basement where the charge was concealed."

He shook his head sadly.

"You were led here. ETA did not drop matches there or any

other place in Madrid. They haven't left the highlands. However, I did see DGSE, KGB and your CIA in Madrid weeks ago. I'm surprised MI6 wasn't there too. Why?"

"If you're asking me, I don't know."

"Many are interested in the Blanco crime. Did one of them execute it? Take some advantage from it? Watch and await the outcome? Who knows? But I can tell you all of them have talked to ETA during these last months offering support for Operación Ogre."

He looked at me sadly.

"My organization is forbidden from intervening in political matters, only the crime, so I do not know more than this," he said.

Interpol is involved, too? Christ, everyone has a part in this except Warren Beatty and Faye Dunaway, I thought.

"My job is to keep a tense peace here in Spain," he continued. "I have done that for many months. Now it's literally exploded in my face and I'm back to the beginning." He glanced at the pair across from us. "ETA may be the only group not involved but in the course of time, all roads are made to lead here. ETA will be condemned for the murder, like it or not."

"Why are you here then?" I asked.

"Here is where the loose ends are tied. It seems we were all brought to Pamplona. You came with your matches. ETA received a note from an informer in Madrid. If they wanted to capitalize on the assassination and leverage it for future operations, ETA was to meet him here. So they sent these patriots. I have come to help two young fools live a little longer. Now, three." The old Spaniard glared at me. He coughed and collected his cigarette pack from the table as he prepared to leave. "Go home, boy."

"Wait, is ETA a danger to America?"

"They are a danger only to themselves."

51

"Who is behind this?"

"If you don't know, then watch your back. Your friends are not your friends. It's dangerous here. We all must go. Goazen," he said to the others in Basque.

As he stood to his full height, a hole appeared below his right cheekbone. Blood and brains sprayed flecks of glitter across confused patrons behind him. He dropped hard to the paving stones. Dazed customers stared. A woman finally found her voice and screamed. I fell to the ground and crawled to the dead man.

One of the Basque patriots was looming over me with a pistol pointed at my head. I held up a useless hand to stop him. A second sniper bullet shattered his spine. The other man turned and caught a round that ripped his throat away.

I pulled the old man's pockets inside out, coming up empty. There was no identification, no money, and no keys. How the hell had he expected to pay for lunch? I looked at the other two. People were running all around now. There was no way I could get to the boys, so I covered my head and curled into a fetal position, hoping the stampede wouldn't kill me.

Arms pulled me to my feet and a waiter dragged me inside the restaurant.

"¿Señor, Estas herido?" He asked after we were safe.

"No, bien. Gracias!" I was out of breath and my chest was pounding.

The low whine of sirens spiked in the distance.

"¿Hay una puerta trasera?" Was there a back door or another way out?

"Pasar por la cocina."

The heavy steel door off the kitchen opened onto a perpendicular, residential street that led away from Plaza del Castillo toward the river. The buildings on each side rose straight to the sky, siphoning away light and oxygen from my path.

Feeling claustrophobic, I limped away from the back of the restaurant, trying not to attract attention as the first of the sirens reached the plaza and droned to a stop.

People absorbed in conversations and each other hurried in the opposite direction, barely noticing the handicapped man lamely walking away from the plaza. I hobbled through the jovial crowd, politely standing aside when necessary to allow the right of way for passing groups. Anticipating someone following, I looked back as I stood in a doorway. No one was coming, and the rooftops were clear.

CHAPTER 9

"I need you," I said.

"No 'hello'? No 'I miss your lovely voice'? No 'I'm sorry for leaving you in Cannes'?" I could actually hear her grinning as she paused. "What can I do for you, my love?"

I didn't know what to say or where to begin. The restless noise on the telephone line buzzed in my ear, reminding me of Calle de Claudio Coello.

"Doc, are you in trouble again, or do you really miss me?" She asked.

"Would it help if I said both?" I asked, in a cavalier manner I didn't feel.

"Please don't tell me you're involved with the general?"

"Why do you ask that?"

"Because I know you weren't in Rome last week with the Pan Am hijackers."

"How do you know that?"

"Because I didn't see you there. So, are you in trouble?"

"Right up to my eyeballs," I admitted.

"Brilliant. Are you always this unlucky or do you wander around with a death wish hanging at the end of a spear?"

"It's complicated."

"It always is, isn't it?"

"Are you free?" I asked timidly.

"Darling, I'm never free. But for you, I'll make the exception. Meet me on Sainte-Marguerite at ten o'clock tomorrow. Can you manage that?"

With pleasure, I thought. I was over my head and needed help desperately. As a field analyst who technically didn't exist, I had no other place to turn. The CIA would have killed me themselves if they knew for sure the NSA still had me on the ground. They didn't like the competition. Zita was British Secret Service and as close a friend as anyone could ever have. And to set the record straight, she left me in Cannes.

I took the afternoon train to Barcelona's Franca Station and hopped on to an overnight sleeper to Marseilles using a West German passport and a pair of coke-bottle glasses to get through customs. I slept without worrying, without thinking, without dreaming. There was something about a rocking train that worked like a narcotic massage on my muscles. Five minutes after leaning back, I was comatose for the duration.

I woke with a slight dehydration headache but otherwise felt good for a change. Arriving in Marseilles at 6:30 a.m., I checked the schedule board in the main station lobby for the next train east. A commuter left in an hour for the short hop of 130 kilometers to Cannes.

There was time for a continental breakfast. My stomach growled to remind me I hadn't eaten in twenty-four hours except for a bag of crisps and an orange Fanta from the vending machines in Barcelona. I devoured three breakfast baguettes with butter and jam at a stand-up kiosk before thinking about the café au lait cooling in front of me. French coffee was tastier than the mud served in Spain, but I still needed plenty of milk and sugar before I could drink it.

The commuter finished final boarding by the time I reached Track 3 and the engine had already shuttered to life. I caught the shadow of a towering man at the far end of the platform as I jumped onto the rolling coach. He took a particular interest in the train's departure and stepped into a telephone booth as the last car rolled past.

Leaving the city behind, we carved a tenuous path through the rocky foothills before finding the coast again at Toulon. A tourist's first glimpse of the Mediterranean Sea was always memorable. With the water as blue as the air above it, the line between them was difficult to determine. The morning light danced on the wispy waves, playing with the occasional yacht like a school of curious dolphins.

We traversed the cliffs above Le Lavandou, eventually settling on the middle ground between the rising slopes of the Alps on one side and the coastal cities of the French Riviera on the other. Technically, Le Lavandou was the beginning of the famous Côte d'Azur, though the beauty continued to build and reached its full stride at Saint-Tropez, running for another 100 kilometers to the Italian border at Ventimiglia. This was when most people decided if they had to die somewhere, it would be here.

To escort the beauty and wonder of the senses, the whims of the rich and famous were met with style, class, and service along the coast. Hotels owned lush beachfront properties where nearly naked bodies could bask in luxury. Everything else was only a waltz away, including the top-end boutiques and open-front cafés that lined the promenades. It was not uncommon to bump into a movie star or real estate mogul or even a princess while shopping or dining along the strand. After all, when they chose to return to Earth, the world's aristocrats ran with the rest of us along the Riviera.

I stepped off the train in Cannes, half expecting her to be waiting for me, but then I knew she wouldn't be there. The station was as I remembered. A delicious outdoor paradise welcomed tourists from up and down the coast. Palm trees and colorful vegetation decorated the platform. A life-sized mural of an impressionistic vision of Cannes covered the station wall with pastels of unimaginable brilliance. And, of course, the pirate pigeons still hopped about on the tracks, scavenging for morsels of food. They reminded me of pirates because most of the older birds sported talons with missing digits and some had only a peg leg remaining after making the poor choice of landing on the track's hot third rail.

I walked to the commercial docks off Bd. d'Alsace to the west. In winter, there was a reduced schedule leaving for Île Sainte-Marguerite every hour on the quarter hour. It was a little after nine o'clock, so I purchased a ticket that included access to the old prison grounds and waited aboard the ferry for the departure call.

A light breeze was coming off the salt water, making the heat dance as it rose from the sandy beach. I unbuttoned my coat to let in the balmy air, closed my eyes and turned my face toward the sun. I missed the warmth. The average high temperature this time of year in Cannes was 14°C, and it was already well past that.

The ferry engines jumped to life and vibrated the deck under my feet. As we pulled away from the dock, the moored sailboats pitched on the small waves coming off our launch. Their hulls bounced against tire bumpers tied along the pontoon slips jutting out into the small harbor. The bulky boat slowly moved out past the breakwater, revealing a regatta of yachts and sailboats against the backdrop of the open sea.

I turned nonchalantly toward the few passengers at the rail around me. A tour group of elderly couples on holiday stood cuddled in twos and fours, admiring the view. There were also a few college students who were possibly on winter break. Only one woman had that American look. We locked eyes for a moment, looking away only when the ship's whistle sounded and surprised a large furry dog lying off by himself near the stern. He ran into the pilot's cabin with his head down.

Île Sainte-Marguerite was a fairly low-profile, heavily wooded island originally home to a monastery. When it was demolished and the monks were spread to the four corners of the seventeenth century, the holy buildings were replaced with fortifications to protect Cannes and the mainland of France. But within a hundred years, the fort was converted to a barrack and finally a federal prison where a number of notorious criminals were incarcerated, including the Man in the Iron Mask.

To the left of the small marina where the ferry docked stood the tiny village of Sainte-Marguerite. A rather undistinguished refreshment kiosk now closed for the season greeted us at the wharf as passengers exited the gangway. I walked along the narrow road where seven or eight cottages huddled unevenly among a grove of sorrowfully anemic trees. The path up the hill to the prison was at the end of the cobblestones near the most prominent structure in town, a converted six-room bed-and-breakfast that stood on a point overlooking the coast.

It had been close to three months since Zita and I had last stayed here. This was one of her favorite places. She once told me all the world's woes melted away on Île Sainte-Marguerite. There was no sorrow, no despair, and no disappointment. The island was a place to recharge and a time to settle priorities. She could relax here, letting the warm wind blow the cares from her dark auburn hair and take them out to sea. It had been too bad we couldn't have stayed longer, but a little less than a week was all we had. Zita had reluctantly boarded a plane to Rome, and I had been called to Paris where I picked up surveillance on Chaban.

As I turned out of the woods at the top of the incline, the deserted prison came fully into view approximately 150 meters farther on. Open on two sides now, the courtyard was covered with dirt, patches of wild grass, and fist-sized rocks. To the left of the harsh, colorless prison was the old church where she would be waiting.

I checked the time. It was a little before ten o'clock, so I decided to stop in the prison to clear my head. For me, reality faded to a fine mist inside those walls and I was alone to bargain with the voices in my head. I had long since given up trying to reason with them. I only wanted to quiet them for a while. Stop the screaming. Stop the criticism, for a few precious weeks. Maybe I could convince one or two to take a vacation here until I was done with this mess. I would promise to fetch them by the end of January.

The cell of the Man in the Iron Mask was easy to find; it was the only room with heavy wooden, double doors along the hard-packed clay corridor. I stepped inside and the ambient world fell stone silent. Reason and belief no longer existed as I looked around.

The room was less than three meters long and three meters across. The floor was dirt but had been worn as hard and shiny as rock by the relentless pacing of feet over the centuries. The pressure of the thick air forced me back against the wall and I reluctantly sank in a corner.

The voices came all at once, sniping at my skin like a swarm of mosquitoes. I tried to swipe them away, slapping and scratching at my arms and legs. A low, taunting hum started in my head, rising to murmurs of incrimination and loathing. I came here for conversation, but the demons were all screaming and I couldn't defend myself. I had hoped I might have more time before it came to this.

"What are you doing here? You couldn't do anything right if your life depended on it!"

"Don't tell him that. He might think he has a change."

"For hell's sake, he knows he's crap and he's going downhill fast. Look at him, whimpering like a half dead dog."

And it continued until my head was bursting. There would be no bargaining with the monsters today. I shook off the feeling of creep and struggled up, using my back against the wall for support. My legs were numb and it was difficult to stand. I was light-headed and couldn't immediately focus. And they kept talking.

Expecting to find the doors locked, I was a little surprised they were standing open, one swung in and the other swung out. I clamored into the corridor, paying no attention to the cries and whispers calling me back. Hurrying into the sunlight, I began to breathe again.

The nave of the old church was rectangular, perhaps 7 x 12 meters, with a low altar at the far end. The room stood empty, and it was in serious need of repairs. The paint on the walls had peeled like old skin and the crumbling plaster had separated from the core of the structure. The roof had deteriorated and seagulls had moved into the rafters. Only two windows remained intact, and they were covered with centuries of grime.

To the right of where I stood was a narrow wooden companionway leading to the choir loft above the back of the nave. I mounted the staircase expecting to see her. Instead, a lone man was leaning over the railing, gazing down into the church. He didn't move for a long time. When I finally turned to go, he spoke.

"It's about time you arrived. I was growing tired of waiting," he said, with his back still to me.

His English was heavily accented with a sing-song, flowing cadence. I said nothing as he turned to face me. The Frenchman was in his thirties, wearing summer tourist clothing, but otherwise he was unremarkable. Not particularly tall or particularly short, he reminded me of someone who could fade into a crowd with little trouble.

"Que voulez-vous?" I asked.

"Oh, in English please. I need the practice," he answered.

"What do you want?"

"The question is more, what do you want, is it not? The one you seek from Paris. That man no longer exists. He sent me to tell you this." The Frenchman spoke matter-of-factly.

"Really?"

"He has been with God for the last few weeks, talking things over regarding his future."

"And you talk to ghosts?"

"No, he's not dead. He was on church business in Spain and has only now returned with the answers he sought," he said.

"So he's back in Paris." Dust in the loft seemed to rise with our voices. It smelled like old books mixed with a little something I couldn't identify. "You both know I can't leave him alone. He's a terrorist."

"He has changed. He told me himself there's no future in kidnapping and he promises never to do it again. So forgive and forget, you know."

"He took 34 people hostage in the 7th Arrondissement and randomly murdered 19 as a distraction while he negotiated the release of those Palestinian slugs."

"Yes, yes, I know all of that. He had to prove his point."

"What point was that?" I asked, suspiciously.

"Leave it alone boy, you didn't know these people anyway."

"I know one."

The man waved his left hand in dismissal.

"He knew you would be like this," he finally admitted. "He said you were stupid but becoming quite a nuisance anyway. Well, I thought perhaps you might listen to reason. But..." He shrugged.

The man raised a military knife resting in his right hand. The hilt was reversed in the palm, so the long blade pointed upward and was hidden against his forearm. It was a lethal style of close-in fighting that employed slicing rather than poking motions for a slower kill. Your opponent bled to death before he knew he was cut. With the methods taught by my Marine Corps trainer, this technique was nearly indefensible.

"His advice to me was to kill you at the beginning." He smiled apologetically.

I sidestepped around to the right, away from the knife hand. If he couldn't reach me, he couldn't cut me. The assassin made a punching movement to test the arch of the blade. I took another step.

Before he could respond, I tackled him with a wide wrestling sweep, catching the heel of his left foot. I lifted the leg over my head. As he hit the ground, I struck with a full-weight flat kick aimed at his privates, but he moved at the last instant. The impact glanced off a hip bone, and he smoothly rolled from his back to his feet.

"I'm going to enjoy cutting you into little pieces and feeding your balls to my dog."

He lunged with a right cross well out in front of the blade. I stepped back to avoid the thrust, but moved in again about a half second too fast. The tip of the blade caught my left hand as he brought his arm back. The point sliced a four-centimeter gash in the palm.

My attacker followed with another slashing motion that twisted his body off-balance. I kicked the side of his knee and he went down hard on his face. The man tried to roll away, but I landed three savage kicks to his rib cage, then one to the side of his head. Considering him for a second, I decided to football kick him on the cheek for good measure.

I ran down the stairs, taking the last six with a giant leap, and landed in the doorway before I heard him move. The woods were sixty meters across the courtyard. It was possible I could outrun him to the safety of the tree line, but if his knee was still intact, there was a fair to good chance he could chase me down and scatter body parts across the prison yard as we went.

I swung my arm and a rivulet of blood streamed into the yard in front of the entrance. I hoped I could delay his recognition that I hadn't run. Resting with my back against the exterior wall, I held my left hand up so the blood would run into my sleeve and not beside me on the concrete slab.

The killer limped heavily down the stairs, using the wall for support. He held himself in the door and looked across the courtyard. A wheezing rattle in his breath shook his body.

When he looked down at the blood in the dirt, I hit him with a roundhouse kick to the stomach. Instead of going down, he grabbed my coat and spun me back against the doorframe with such fury that I was momentarily stunned. He raised his double-edged knife to my cheek. I drove the heel of my wounded hand under his chin to push him back. The blow sent a lightning bolt of pain down to my feet, but I was hoping it hurt him worse.

I lashed out with another kick as he came at me again. The man stumbled off the porch and dropped in the dirt. My foot had caught the top of his hip but I guess it was enough. Jumping off the slab, I stomped his head several times and then aimed for his exposed ribs. By the time I lost count of the blows, he wasn't moving. I kicked him again for good measure.

Footsteps. Someone was running in the courtyard behind me. Zita was on me in seconds, pulling me away.

"Come on, love. He's dead." She saw the blood dripping from my hand. "Are you hurt? What happened?"

63

"It's a cut, I'm okay."

Her eyes never left me as she unscrewed the suppressor from her gun and put both pieces back in her jacket.

"You're late, girl," I said.

"Fashionably," she smiled. "I was detained coming through the woods."

"Check his pockets."

"What's the magic word?" she asked, in her most beautiful British accent.

"Now!" I said.

"I'll give you that for a magic word this time."

Zita rifled the dead man's pockets and came away with some papers, keys and a wad of French francs. She stuffed everything in her tight jeans pocket, then took my wrist. I winced.

Ripping open the man's shirt, Zita tore away a strip of his t-shirt.

"Hold your arm up, darling." She tied the cloth around my forearm to curb the bleeding. "Now, let's get you back to my boat, and you must tell me everything."

CHAPTER 10

Zita applied manual pressure to my palm with a damp cloth until the blood flow had nearly stopped. She then alternated between an ice compress and a sink basin filled with rubbing alcohol. My arm had been numb for the last hour. Now, I thought I was going to throw up from the pain. But the bleeding eventually stopped, possibly because my body was down two liters of blood and the flow may have dried up on its own. Zita wasn't particularly gentle as she tightly bandaged the hand, so I couldn't accidentally curl my fingers and reopen the wound.

The incision was deep into the meat where initial contact had been made and the wound tapered outward as the tip of the blade had exited. Because of the excessive blood flow, the ulnar artery ending in the hand was probably nicked, but there didn't seem to be any immediate nerve damage. The sharp pain shooting from the palm through the fingertips was a constant reminder that the nerves were still intact and working just fine. On top of everything else, the burning below the wrist was nearly unbearable.

"You need a surgeon," she said. "You could have been killed."

"I had the same thought right before you arrived."

"You certainly did a job on this hand. I'm glad you didn't attempt to block the blow with your handsome face instead!" She smiled and then turned serious again. "Now, please tell me what happened?"

Over the next hour, I recounted my latest adventure, starting in Spain a week ago when I had been reassigned to watch Luis Carrero Blanco. It was longer to tell the story than to have lived it. I found myself answering some of the questions I still had and second-guessing actions I thought had been justified at the time.

Zita interrupted several times for clarification, otherwise she listened quietly. She smiled at my descriptions of the prime minister's flying car and my sprint from the Municipal Policia later that night.

When I finished the story, Zita sat running it over again in her head.

"ETA didn't assassinate Blanco," she said, finally.

"No, but they want to take the credit for it."

"And your best guess is…?"

"The CIA is up to its nose in it. I can't as yet say how or why. And I don't know where Chaban fits, but I know he does."

"Who's watching after you, Doc?"

"I have eyes in the back of my head."

"You must also have Christopher around your neck to accompany Jude," she added.

Zita knew I wore a silver medallion depicting the patron saint of the helpless and hopeless. St. Jude had been diligently guarding me for the past year, possibly from pity and possibly because I was truly a lost cause and needed a friend. These days, Jude and I were on a first-name basis, and we spoke quite often.

"St. Christopher guards against sudden death, doesn't he?" I asked, jokingly.

"Yes, he might help you there, along with bulletproof armor on your backside. You know," she said, "if you had any mates, you might not be in so much trouble."

"Maybe not," I shrugged.

"What about our chap from this morning?" Zita asked as she

unfolded the papers taken from the dead man on Sainte-Marguerite.

"He was a messenger."

"A messenger? Was he trying to carve his correspondence on your heart with the point of that knife?"

"Something like that. He had a piece of advice from Chaban, a choice really. Before this guy tried to slit my throat, he basically said Chaban wants me to get off his trail, or die wishing I had."

"I see," she said. "We really need to find this guy. MI6 is standing ready to offer him a very long stay with Her Majesty's pleasures because of his little trick in Paris."

"I have a feeling Chaban won't be going to jail."

"What have we here?"

I followed her eyes to the papers on the table between us and immediately recognized my portrait.

"Yeah, it's posted all over Spain," I said.

"So much for blending in with the locals," Zita didn't expect an answer. "Doc, if I didn't know you had nine lives I'd say you are fortunate to be alive. Next time, your Frenchman will send someone who can do the job right. But the real question is, 'how did he know you were here?' It seems your fame has preceded you."

I was followed again, or played. With the smell of death sticking to me like tree sap and my picture decorating most of the country, it was increasingly difficult to maintain a low profile on the peninsula. Without other options, Chaban knew I eventually would need safe passage to the north, and there were very few routes out of Iberia that didn't go through Barcelona. I could have been seen boarding the overnight express, or picked up in Marseilles since I disembarked there without a disguise. Watching me was about as difficult as sitting with a sick grandmother in a locked room.

"I need to call home and report in," I said.

I picked up the telephone receiver and dialed uneasily.

"Where in the living hell are you?" The voice said through clenched teeth.

"I'm...out of Spain."

"I know that much!"

"I have a lead on Chaban."

"Didn't I tell you to suspend that operation?"

"He's back in Paris."

"I don't give a rat's right testicle where he is. I told you to stay with Blanco and let me know if I needed to worry."

"You don't."

"Yeah, he's dead. I figured that out for myself. But you, I worry about...do you have it tied up for me, then?"

"I may never find Chaban again."

"God damn it! Listen to me, boy. I need a full report on Blanco. Get your skinny ass back to Spain from wherever you are. I mean today, not tomorrow, or I'll have you back digging toilets in East Africa faster than you can say, 'President Kennedy, I love the Peace Corps!'"

The line went dead.

That's where he found me, knee deep in mud and some kind of animal crap, feeling lost and abandoned at the edge of a rain-soaked crust of ground called Tanzania. The short story was that I had joined the Peace Corps as an alternative to war. They assigned me to an initial tour in Paintsville Kentucky, just off the Cumberland Plateau and a stone's throw from the Lost World of West Virginia. When I realized they weren't kidding, I jumped at the unexpected opportunity to visit Africa. Lions and tigers had seemed preferable to dinosaurs, but not by much, as it turned out.

Enter the NSA with a slick story and three months of training. My contact had offered me unrestricted travel through

Europe, with an occasional venture into watching, learning, and reporting on terrorist activities. Well, it had sounded better than what I had at the time.

"Well, that was nasty," Zita said. "I heard him all the way over here. Your man sounded mad enough to sack you. All right then, to Spain we go."

"We?" I asked.

"Someone has to keep you safe, darling. Besides, I want to show you England one more time before you kill yourself."

We'd seen England together once before. I smiled at the vision of her sleeveless sundress playing in the light Cotswold winds west of Oxford. We had walked hand in hand for hours before settling on a shaded hillside overlooking Bourton-on-the-Water. She'd unfurled a checkered tablecloth for the fresh-mowed grass and we'd eaten fruit and cheeses with a Bordeaux that had warmed the spirit. That rare English afternoon had lasted forever, and I remembered every detail.

We had laughed and loved the time away, dancing around the curiosity of new emotions until we'd been too tired to move. We had lain wrapped around each other after that, just talking. We had spoken of many things as the sun fell beyond the hills, mostly silly things. She had told me about the tiny scar just below her rib cage and I'd asked where she had gotten such beautiful eyes. She'd asked where I had gotten such a nickname. Although I had magical hands, I was certainly no doctor.

I'd once worked for a few days in a mortuary, keeping the place clean, and my classmates had immediately begun calling me Doc. When I'd been sweeping the embalming lab near the end of the first week, one body had risen from the dead. I'd run from the basement and may have still been running if the mortician had not finally chased me down in his car. He'd explained it was all an outrageous joke, but I'd quit, anyway. The job hadn't lasted, but the nickname had.

"Now, off to bed with you," she said, interrupting my thoughts. Before my wry smile could widen, she continued, "By yourself, darling. I have some shopping to do before we leave tonight. I expect you to be resting when I return. And," she added. "Keep your arm raised on a fluffy pillow."

I crawled onto the duvet, exhausted. Every ounce of strength was gone. A major league headache was beginning and my entire arm throbbed like blood was rhythmically spurting out from my fingertips. I closed my eyes and imagined the monster's crushing grip was gone from my head, my shoulders, my back, my stomach, my legs and my feet. Then it all let go, and I fell from the edge of the abyss into grateful oblivion.

I woke with a scare when the apartment door opened. I rolled off the bed, thinking about a weapon when my bandaged hand hit the edge of the nightstand. Burning streaks of pain shot through my body. Son of a…that hurt! The late afternoon sun flooded in the west window and the bright light stabbed my eyes. It was impossible to focus on the dark figure moving in front of me.

Zita struggled to the table with two large bags of supplies, curiously eyeing me with each step. I must have been a sight. I had ended up on my knees next to the bed, holding the bandage with a grimace that must have looked like I was praying. My head sank to the duvet. She sat on the bed and gently lifted my face. My forehead was hot in her hands.

"How are you feeling, my love?" She asked.

"Not so good."

"Take two of these and call me in the morning as your American surgeons say." She shook two tiny blue pills into her hand.

"When are we leaving?" I asked.

"I've arranged a booking on the night train back to Barcelona for a fat, one-armed blind man and his nurse. We have a private sleeper compartment, so there will be no interruptions," she said.

"You are a creative one, aren't you?"

"I have a quite brilliant teacher in the art of concealment. Besides, you need to protect your hand until it heals a bit. And," she continued, "We don't need questions about your bandages when we exit France, in the event there was a witness to your little pissing contest this morning."

"Understood."

"Can you shoot accurately with your right hand?" She asked, knowing I was left-handed. "I have a small Beretta for you."

"Zita, I can't shoot straight with either hand. Besides, I don't like guns," I said.

"I don't understand why."

"Because I almost shot you in Berlin."

"Well, you better learn to love them for a while. This little lad is going to be your best friend for a few weeks and perhaps longer, if you ask me. Judging from what I witnessed on Sainte-Marguerite, your hand-to-hand skills are a bit dodgy at best."

"That's funny. Who says the English don't have a sense of humor?"

"Right, then. Let's fit you with your clothes and mask now. You must be running on a flat battery so I'll get you tucked up as soon as we join the train."

The overnight to Barcelona rolled into Cannes at 9:45 p.m. and would depart at exactly 10:00 p.m. Transportation schedules throughout most of Europe were the same absolutely and without exception. Arrivals and departures were so punctual that many people relied on airplane engines, boat horns and train whistles to reset their house clocks.

We waited in line on the platform, wearing Zita's disguises. The fat costume made it difficult to move easily, so I was assisted

71

by my truly helpful nurse. I struggled up the coach steps one at a time as an impatient queue formed behind me. The tall, thin lady at my side wore a freshly starched white frock, and her French cut hair was tucked under a cap that exposed only the front fringe. She carried two small duffle bags looped on an arm and gently pushed me with the other. Her skin was flushed pink and several times she apologized to the gathering audience.

"How does one blush at will like you did a minute ago?" I asked when we were settled in our sleeper compartment.

"What do you mean?"

The train's whistle sounded a short burst as the engine jerked into motion and slowly pulled away from the station.

"You were blushing with embarrassment out on the platform."

"Blushing?" She smiled. "My face was red from trying to carry you up the stairs."

"And what a beautiful face it is."

"Bootlicking does not become you, my love, but do tell me more!"

She kissed my lips tenderly and pushed me back on the bed.

"Let's unfasten your straps and let your arm free before gangrene develops. I don't believe there's a bloody decent surgeon on this train."

Zita unbuttoned my shirt. Two belt straps held the fat-pillow in place against my chest and stomach. She loosened the bindings and carefully lifted my arm from the underside. The bandages were showing signs of stress and seepage, so she cleaned my hand again and re-wrapped it. Zita fumbled in her bag for the bottle of pills. Straightening with the medicine, she shook two more capsules in her palm.

"For the next eight hours, these will kill your consciousness with kindness, exactly like the 1960s."

"Will I hallucinate?" I asked with a grin.

"You might drool, love, but you'll remember absolutely nil."

I swallowed the pills with a swig of bottled water and lay back. I felt the rhythmic rocking of the train and heard the light tapping of the rail joints as the coach passed over them. Within minutes, my head had melted into the pillow and my body floated away on a puff of smoke.

CHAPTER 11

"You missed him again?" The Frenchman screamed into the telephone. "How many morons does it take to kill one idiot?"

"In Pamplona, the target was not certain so the shooter chose and fired."

"And three times he chose wrong?"

"The boy was in disguise. Because of this, I used two in Cannes to be sure. I found the woman dead in the forest this afternoon. Also being an American, I thought she might…" The caller stumbled. "The other was less talented than his reputation suggested."

"I'm not spending any more time or money on amateurs! If I don't hear positive results within 24 hours, I'll send another and this time he'll be looking for you! Do you understand me?"

"Yes, sir."

"Let me explain," he said, ignoring the man's answer. "This weekend, he'll come to your country cottage. Yes, the one near Orleans. He will gut the old caretakers in your kitchen. He'll sell your wife to recover my money if she's worth anything. He'll set your children on fire to keep warm while he digs out your soul and eats it. When he finally lets you die, you will meet many others who have also failed me."

"Yes, sir. I'll go myself."

CHAPTER 12

The pounding of the rail joints woke me before dawn, but I couldn't keep my eyes open. I drifted. My body fell through the bed, through the train, and dripped onto the track. Each splash became an ineffective spike, desperately trying to hold down the rail as the wheels passed over my remains. The noise grew louder; clack, clack, clack, knock, knock, knock, bang, bang, bang. The wind peeled my skin away. The shaking ripped my bones. I was losing my grip on the ballast. I couldn't keep it together much longer.

I sat up breathing hard. The train was still, quiet except for the incessant tapping of the rail joints. Peering through the curtain, I saw a Spanish guardsman intermittently banging the butt of his automatic rifle against the window of each compartment as he moved down the train.

It was our wake-up call, on behalf of the Spanish Tourism Board and Generalissimo Franco. A platform light dimly flickered and I involuntarily yawned. Zita was already hurriedly arranging and rearranging the contents of the luggage on the seating area across from the bed.

"Good morning. I trust you slept well?" she asked, glancing around.

"I don't remember," I said, rubbing my face in the crook of my good elbow.

"That's good. Let's have a peek at your bandage then get you cinched up. We better retouch your face, too."

We stepped off the train into a growing crowd of tired travelers. A faint, reddish thread separating the horizon from the eastern sky provided the only light. I looked across the barren fields surrounding us. The Pyrenees were not quite visible to the northeast, hanging like long, low clouds above the undulating foothills. The station house blocked the western view, but the desolate southern vista made us feel desperately alone. There was no sign of life beyond the tracks, no beasts, no birds, no bugs. The border crossing didn't belong to any world I knew.

"How much farther is it to Barcelona from the end of the earth here?" Zita asked.

"It's another few hours."

"Then there's no sense waiting on a longer queue than necessary, let's get through customs," she said.

The crowd had doubled in the last five minutes. Zita steeled herself to push through the mass of people on the platform and was surprised when the seas actually parted for us. Fat, blind guys were as sacred in Spain as skinny cows were in India.

Franco took pride in his efforts to ensure the disabled were contributing members of society. The handicapped and the mentally infirm were generally provided with menial jobs like peddling newspapers or selling lottery tickets so they might feel like valuable cogs in the Nationalist machine, but mostly it was to lessen the burden on the government dole. With tickets pinned to their coats and newspapers tucked under an arm, the handicapped were free to wander the streets selling their wares and people usually moved aside, if not in need of an immediate purchase. That beat begging, but not by much.

Months ago, I had used a similar disguise to trail an informant, but it turned out to have been a little burdensome. He had inadvertently been leading me to the men who masterminded the kidnapping attempt of a West German bank executive on assignment in Madrid. Three innocents had been killed in the failed operation and I needed to find the team of perpetrators before they could make another try. As I followed the informer, however, I had been stopped so often by people wanting a lotto purchase that I had lost the man I had been chasing. But I had made enough lunch money from the sales to include a bottle of wine.

A platoon of soldiers wielding automatic weapons roughly formed the sleepy passengers into make-shift lines for passport inspection. We landed in the slowest queue behind three long-haired, unkempt hippies. Their pupils were pinpoints and their clothes smelled like weed. I knew we would soon have the pleasure of witnessing a total body cavity search.

"Where are the guns?" I whispered.

"Safe, darling. They're in your bag here."

"My bag? Are you crazy?"

"No," she said slowly. "Not according to my latest MI6 evaluation."

As the trio of dope smokers was led away for further interrogation, Zita presented our passports to the disinterested clerk. He lazily pulled mine off the counter and opened the cover. Without a word he dragged Zita's passport down beside the other. She had them made the day before, and I doubted the ink was completely dry. The customs agent appraised the documents, glanced up at us, and then re-examined Zita's photo closer. He considered her beautiful face.

"¿Este es su pasaporte?" I translated from Spanish to French for fun.

Zita glanced around dismayed. She asked the agent, "Voyez-vous une autre infirmière ici, qui me ressemble?" Had the idiot seen another nurse here that resembled her? The man looked at her blankly.

"Sí, es su pasaporte," I translated. Yes, yes, it was her document. The agent scrutinized her entry visa. He squinted and brought Zita's passport close to his face. Reluctantly, he smacked a large stamp in each book and pushed them back across the counter.

"Paso a la zona de declaración, por favor." The agent pointed us toward the declaration line for baggage inspection.

Zita placed our luggage on the low steel table in front of two armed agents. How could they possibly not find the weapons? I casually eyed the exits from behind my sunglasses, even though I knew it was lunacy to attempt escape when the crap hit the clapper. There was nowhere to run.

The first agent was inside Zita's bag in a flash and pulled out a handful of her knickers. As quickly, he replaced the undergarments without fully inspecting them and zipped the bag closed. Flustered, he slid it to the second man who placed a 10-centimeter line of white chalk on the top. That bag had just cleared customs.

The embarrassed man unzipped the next bag. There was a magazine on top I didn't recognize and I was as curious as the agent to see what it was. He slowly lifted the thick publication above his head as the centerfold unfurled.

"Playboy!" He exclaimed.

Eight guards ran toward us. Pornography was illegal under the Franco regime. It was all I could do to not raise my one good arm and assume the position against the nearest wall. At the very least, we were going to be charged with the minor crime of pornographic solicitation. At the worst, we would spend our rocking chair years spitting tobacco juice out into a dirt prison yard. They would certainly find the guns next.

The guards surrounded the counter. Instead of detaining us, they continued around to steal a memorable glimpse of the

French playmate. The agent holding the picture taut politely refolded it and glanced up at Zita who was certainly as stunning as the magazine model. She tilted her head in my direction.

"Insiste pour que les articles que j'ai lus à haute voix." Zita announced. From the look on their faces, I was pretty sure the guards had no idea what she was saying about me.

"Lo he oído. No soy sordo," I complained. I could still hear very well, you know. And having my nurse read the articles to me was not a crime!

The guard smiled as he placed the booklet back inside the bag and zipped it closed. The second man placed his chalk mark on the satchel and we were free to go. Zita swept up the two bags and led me through the far door toward the Renfe commuter train waiting for the final leg to Barcelona.

We sat in an open car, opposite a man wearing a Tam-o'-shanter and dressed in a striped polo shirt over American-style jeans. My heart was pounding like a racehorse on the last turn at Belmont, but I managed to catch the eye exchange between Zita and the Scotsman. The man opened a Spanish language newspaper, and finding an interesting article, was instantly consumed. I leaned in close to Zita.

"That was brilliant," I said.

She smiled with a mischievous twinkle in her eye. It was always the same with Zita. She moved through her day with an infectious calmness that made the world follow her lead. It was nothing she said or did, really. She was simply there, with a beautiful, suggestive serenity around her as if it were the most natural thing on earth. Both circumstance and consequence were bent to suit her, and she never worried about anything until it actually happened.

The Renfe engine left the border crossing before 8:00 a.m., dragging three cars loaded with weary, listless passengers.

Sounds of erratic breathing were heard as many tried to sleep upright in very uncomfortable seating. I dozed, listening to an enthusiastic young man enticing a child of 4 or 5 to squeal with laughter. Her volume would rise to the point of breaking glass, then slowly subside before rising again as the man made another funny face or contrived some strange noise.

Two hours later, the endless ride was over. A bowl of zombies oozed from the coaches after the train mercifully pulled into Franca Station. No one paid attention to me or my nurse, nor did anyone see which way we went.

CHAPTER 13

We were back in Pamplona before our impromptu brunch in a station restaurant had a chance to digest. The air was crisp and winter had definitely settled on the plateaus that nestled in the Pyrenees of northern Spain. It felt like snow. The wind had turned in sharply from the Atlantic, blowing over the rough coastal terrain, up over the headlands and promontories, searching the high plains for a place to rest. The weather front finally decided to stall over the city.

Still in disguise, Zita and I walked along Calle de Tafalla near the Ebro River. For all practical purposes we were simply an invalid and his nurse out for a stroll and a bit of fresh air. My hand was looped around the crook of her elbow, lightly resting on a sleeve. We were in no particular hurry, though we were late for a pre-arranged meeting with a man who would provide introductions to ETA.

As always, there was no guarantee a promised handshake could be executed, but it was my last chance to speak to the emerging terror cell. Knowing it would cause more harm than any possible good, I needed to warn them away from accepting responsibility for the assassination. The lucky few were about to be imprisoned while the core of the group would vanish into a landfill under a freshly planted forest.

As we walked, it was comforting to occasionally see the shadow of Tam-o'-shanter Man, hat now removed, as we progressed toward the rendezvous with whatever awaited us at the other end. I was used to working alone so it felt good to have some backup. I relaxed a little. My shoulders dropped, my muscles loosened and I opened the locked door holding back my fatigue. A sudden yawn caught me in mid-step and my eyes watered into tears.

We came up behind a small, very old and very slow moving woman. She stepped unsteadily along the narrow sidewalk, precariously balancing two heavy shopping bags at the ends of down-stretched arms. She could not have weighed more than 40 kilos. Her faded black dress appeared to hang from a wire coat hanger rather than frail shoulders. The old woman's legs were as thin as baseball bats and may have been made of wood too since her knees didn't bend as her flat sandals slapped the hard concrete. Her feet were deeply cracked and the heels were the color and texture of rotting potatoes. It hurt to look at them.

"Can't we help her?" I asked.

"Always the soft heart. You'll get yourself killed one day reaching for some damsel in distress." Zita shook her head with a soft smile and patted my hand at her elbow. "You're supposed to be blind. Act like it."

The old lady suddenly stopped at one of the many double doors lining the block of flats. She eased her bags down carefully. I heard the jingle of keys in her hand as we passed and a heavy door slammed behind us. We were alone again on a quiet residential street overlooking the river.

"Where is your man?" I asked.

"He's there."

"I haven't seen him in a while."

"That is the point, darling."

"The meeting's around the next block. There's a small park with a couple of benches. The guy we want will be sitting to the left nearest the water."

As we turned the corner, the park came into view above the tiny, gas efficient cars lining both sides of the lane. It was like any of a thousand other places where old men wasted their days feeding pigeons. An open space sloped up from the river still blanketed with grass and spotted with several shade trees giving cover to three neatly arranged benches. A brick mosaic semi-circle fanned out in front of each bench where audiences of birds came to worship their food gods. We saw all of this, as well as something we hadn't expected.

"Jimmy's there?!" She said.

Zita saw it before I did and bolted across to the park. Two men sat on the bench shoulder to shoulder. When I reached her, she was examining a small caliber bullet wound to the back of Tam-o'-shanter Man's head. His confused eyes stared out of a tortured face.

"Shit! Shit! Shit!" Zita swore.

The other man had been knifed in the back below the rib cage and two liters of blood had pooled in the dirt behind the bench. When I touched his shoulder, he slid to the side and toppled face down onto the brickwork. I pulled a thick wallet from his pants. This had to be the man we came to meet.

Glancing across at Zita, we both knew that I had been made again. Someone was either stuck to my butt or using my penis as a pull toy. Either way, it got our attention. Zita touched Jimmy's face a last time before standing.

We hurriedly moved away from the river past an endless row of houses on Calle de Eslava. The tiny street was quiet but the buildings were closing in on us. Zita looked back several times. I didn't know whether it was to ensure we weren't followed, or if it was for Jimmy.

As we passed an open door, someone spoke.

"Hey." The man was holding an Italian made 32 caliber

Lercker pistol manufactured during the 1950s. It was old but still very lethal. "Step inside," he commanded. "Do not draw your weapons. Leave them where they are and you'll live."

I took a deep breath and hesitated.

"Do not provoke me. If you stay out there much longer, you will surely die."

CHAPTER 14

"Call me Argala," the Spaniard finally said. "I am ETA." He put the long barreled revolver in its shoulder holster.

"ETA? I don't understand," I said. "Who was the man in the park?"

"Who knows? Wrong place, wrong time?" He shrugged. "He was dead when I arrived, so naturally I thought you had killed him, until I found..." He continued solemnly, "Sorry about your friend. It couldn't be helped." Argala hesitated.

"Who did this?" Zita asked, and again the man shrugged.

"First you must understand the oppression the Basque have had to bear for centuries. My homeland has many enemies and some live right here among us. We fight to expel any who would usurp our freedoms."

"Why...?" I asked.

"Why?" The man cut my question short. "Incidents such as these are necessary to the cause of liberty. We Basque must have our lands free. A little death now brings attention to Spanish oppression, for the larger good and the eventual independence of our country. We believe public sentiment will soon fall behind us and support our right to govern ourselves."

"I meant to say, why kill these two men?"

"Your government is very curious about what we are doing. You might ask them."

"My government isn't interested in anything you do. We both know ETA didn't commit the Blanco assassination so we'll leave you as you are, to pursue your justice with Spain. My best advice to you though is don't take the responsibility. It'll be the end of ETA, along with any chance the Basque have for freedom."

"You underestimate us. ETA has been planning this for six months, with Operación Ogre."

"I've heard of it," I said.

"How much do you know?"

"I understand it never left paper."

"That is partially true," he admitted.

"What's Operación Ogre?" Zita asked.

The man explained Operación Ogre was the name of an ETA plan that included, among other things, the assassination of Franco's prime minister. The operation had identified a small team to covertly follow Blanco. Their mission had been to determine when and where his daily routine was so precise that one could set a watch by its timing. The surveillance had concluded that mornings after church presented the best opportunity. ETA had then begun soliciting armed soldiers for an assault that would hit the prime minister's vehicle with full force frontal and rear attacks.

Early in the previous October, ETA had been approached by a mercenary who had examined the design and immediately told them there was another way. His plan was fast and clean, offering the chaos without the confrontation, and that changed everything.

The man had said he and his team would run the assignment and ETA could handle security. Two of his men posing as stone sculptors had rented a basement apartment across from the church. Once in the downstairs rooms, the mercenaries had tunneled beneath the avenue and packed the cavity with 88 kilos of explosives, which the man had also supplied.

Something must have happened, Argala explained, because

the man had executed the plan three days early. ETA hadn't been ready. They didn't have security in place. When ETA had arrived, they found themselves in the middle of holy hell. The mercenary had disappeared, leaving the highlanders holding their huevos with one hand and hailing a taxi with the other.

"But no matter, we'll bear the toils of Basque independence through the grace of God. So according to plan," he said in conclusion, "this morning, a day after our Lord Jesus Christ's birthday, ETA announced responsibility for the assassination of Prime Minister Luis Carrero Blanco."

This was not good. ETA had been tricked into taking ownership of the assassination and now the total might of Franco's army was about to crush them. Because of their hatred for Spain, they were either unaware or unconcerned with the consequences set in motion.

"Who came to you with this plan?" I asked.

"We have many supporters."

"I mean this particular supporter. The mercenary. Did he come from my friends in the U.S.?"

"We do know your people. CIA had offered a plan and the help to carry it through. It had been very tempting but, we rejected your help in the end. Instead, we chose to work with the French because many of our countrymen also live under Catalan oppression. To work with a compassionate partner seemed most appropriate. That is what's so strange."

"Strange?" I asked.

"The man who killed the two in the park is French."

"You have him?"

"Yes, of course, we have him. Didn't I say that?"

"Is he an associate of the French sympathizer with whom you were working?"

"It is difficult to say. We thought he might be one of yours, or the Soviets, but we have been questioning him so we might know by now."

"May I speak to him?"

"If he's still alive," he shrugged.

Argala led us to a windowless, three-story distribution center that fronted the Ebro River not far from the park, where two dead men were now chatting about their future. The warehouse was at least 200 years old and I thought it was pitching a little to the left. I was not certain how it remained standing, but it was remarkably still in service. The exterior was clean and we passed a modern office area which displayed the building's only window in its door. Argala escorted us down an alley to an entrance on the far side. He knocked four times.

"Stay here and I'll return with your answer," he said.

The deadbolt clicked and the door shuttered backward as the seal around the frame reluctantly released. The rusted hinges creaked loudly in protest as the door swung in. Argala stepped into the darkness and the door closed with the same troubled groan. The afternoon fell quiet except for the whistle of the wind along the river.

I pulled the dead man's wallet from my coat and stared at what was left of his world. His name was Edmond Rousseau and the address on the identification card was a few blocks east of here. I found old grocery receipts and telephone numbers on folded scraps of paper. There was also an expired membership card for something I didn't recognize but there wasn't a single family photo.

An old condom was tucked under a leather flap. The old man must have carried it since the war. The paper peeled off in my hand. The rolled prophylactic felt like a dried worm. I threw it on the ground and wiped my fingers on a sleeve. I didn't want to know where that thing had been. I sighed and tossed the wallet carelessly across the alley with the rest of his life.

"Merry Christmas, a day late," I sheepishly said.

"Happy Christmas, my dear." Zita swung her arms around my fat-pillows and gave me a kiss. "That will have to do until we can properly celebrate."

The door bumped open before I could respond. Argala stepped halfway out and motioned us inside. The warehouse was illuminated with harsh, streaking shadows and light. It was made worse by flickering overhead fluorescent bulbs filtering through the dust in the air. When our eyes adjusted to the dim conditions, five men stood in front of us and two behind, each with a semi-automatic weapon leveled at us. Thirty-round clips were locked and loaded, and the men waited for a command.

"My apologies but it is necessary. May I have your bag, señorita?" The man held out a hand.

"We are unarmed," Zita said.

I knew my Beretta was safely tucked in with my bandaged hand and was fairly safe from discovery, but the last time I saw Zita's weapon, it had been in her handbag. The man thrust a fist inside the leather tote and rooted around for several seconds, then politely handed it back to her. There was no gun.

Someone behind me gently probed my coat and pants, then stepped around to examine the front. I stood open-legged, but the man patted a few places and stopped, satisfied.

"This way please."

Argala motioned for two of his men to follow. He led the way through rows of television boxes stacked to the ceiling. We paused at a large elevator and he pressed the down button which shone brightly in the low light. The motor kicked in with a smooth hum and the door panels vibrated. Our escorts were relaxed and speaking together in reduced tones.

The huge elevator bumped to a stop. The metal doors parted

from the middle and opened to the top and bottom. We walked into an immense cavern that ordinarily transported forklifts between floors. The air was musty, and white mildew created unusual patterns on the walls. The boards under our feet had rotted dangerously thin in places. Argala pulled the strap to reseal the doors and the old wooden coffin slowly descended into hell.

The elevator opened onto a corridor even darker than the floor above. The only light came from bare bulbs hanging by long electrical cords. Chain link fencing separated locked storage bays containing expensive electronic equipment. Argala stopped at the bay nearest to the far wall. Inside sat a man, tied to a chair, and he was in desperate need of a doctor. He was covered with his own blood and the wall was splattered behind him. A single man wearing rubber kitchen gloves stood over him.

"Ahora, él coopera," said the man wearing the gloves.

"I bet he's cooperating now. He needs a doctor," I demanded.

"It won't help," Argala said. "He has some structural damage that can't be fixed and there's too much internal bleeding. See his swollen stomach? He has possibly an hour so ask your questions quickly."

I squatted in front of the dying man. What was left of his chin rested on a badly damaged chest and his breathing was barely audible. His nose had been broken several times and the air passages were completely closed. Any oxygen getting to his lungs now was coming through his mouth.

I couldn't tell if his eyes were open or closed. The aggravated sockets were puffy, discolored slits, making it impossible to know if the eyeballs were still intact. His shirt was ripped nearly off his torso and soaked red with blood.

The sadist with the rubber gloves slapped the side of his captive's head. The prisoner stirred and drew a deep breath while trying to lift his head. Large purple bruises dulled his pasty skin. He looked like he was already dead. Both ear drums were punctured and a number of teeth were scattered on the floor. Blood was mixing with his saliva and falling in long strings of drool on his chest.

"Monsieur, pouvez-vous m'entendre?" I asked. The man with the gloves raised his hand to strike again. "¡Alto! Retírese!" I shouted and turned to Argala. "Please tell him no more hitting."

He gave the order in traditional Basque and the sadist backed away one and only one step, in defiance. Crossing his arms, he glowered at me with the same hatred he displayed with his prisoner. He wanted me to know who was in charge.

"Monsieur, pouvez-vous m'entendre?" I asked again.

The man's eyes suddenly went wild behind the slits and fear replaced the dying light for a few precious seconds. His whole body was trembling as he tried to focus on me. Through erratic breathing, he formed words with cracked lips but all sound was trapped inside. It was no use. The poor man had exhausted the last bit of energy he was ever going to have. A slack head flopped back to his chest.

"Can you find out what he told your man before it came to this?" I angrily asked. "We'll wait by the elevator."

Argala questioned the sadist as we walked away.

"Where's your gun?" I asked in a whisper.

"Never mind," she replied, and then added, "I'll let you search me thoroughly tonight."

It was nearly fifteen minutes before Argala rejoined us. His face was blank, forcing me to break the silence on the elevator ride to the ground floor.

"Well, what do we have?"

"Of consequence to you, he followed you from the Riviera. He killed the two in the park and he was waiting to kill you too.

His assignment did not include us. It was personal. But, I am sorry to report, he does work under orders from our friend in Paris."

"Did he say what his name was?"

"This man?"

"No, the Parisian."

"His name is Chaban. I don't think you know him but he knows you and he doesn't seem to like you very much."

"How reliable is this information?"

"Did he look like he held anything back?"

"Is Chaban the man who financed and executed Operación Ogre?"

"That is of no consequence to you."

CHAPTER 15

As we prepared to leave, Argala was intercepted by an associate. He told us about a pair of local policemen who had been investigating a damaged loading dock door in the back of the building and had noticed a gap large enough for a person to squeeze through. They had come around to the lobby to notify management but found the doors unlocked and the offices empty. Before anyone could stop them, they had called the incident into headquarters on their car radio and two more cars had been automatically dispatched.

"They are here now?"

"Si," said the man.

"I'll speak with them."

He told us to stay out of sight as he pushed through the double doors. Zita and I crouched behind an L-shaped counter and watched the policemen attentively listening to the man in charge as he gave instructions to his team. The captain was animated, shouting orders with exaggerated arm and body movements. Finally, he slapped his hands together to indicate the briefing was over. Saluting, the men disbursed as Argala approached waving his arms above his head to get their attention.

"Tiene una pistola!" Jesus, one of the cops had seen Argala's shoulder holster under his open coat.

The captain drew his service revolver and fired once striking the ETA man in the chest. Argala was thrown back off his feet and landed motionless on the rough concrete. His body lay splayed awkwardly under a pile of rumpled clothing. In the silence that followed, all eyes stared at the dead man.

Unexpectedly, an ETA man stepped from the side of the building and leveled an Ingram Mac 10 at the group of policemen. Bullets slammed into them as blood splattered across the windshields and side panels of the small Spanish Seat patrol cars. When the chamber of the Mac 10 froze open, three lay dead, another was writhing in pain, still another was trying to stand on two shattered legs and the sixth man was sprawled on his back near his car, radioing for help.

The killer calmly pulled the empty clip free, dropping it to the ground. Snapping a new magazine in place, he re-engaged the firing mechanism and walked to the dying men. He reset the machine pistol to semi-automatic and systematically executed the three wounded men. I felt Zita flinch as each loud bang broke the silence. The man stood over the bodies without moving, the gun hanging loosely at his side.

"This won't end well," I whispered to Zita. "Let's go!"

With no good reason to do so, we remained low until we reached the rear of the warehouse, then sprinted for the back exit. It was locked. Zita pointed to a bevel in the loading dock door and the two of us slipped out into the afternoon. Turning down the alley running behind a row of warehouses, we made our way to the next street.

"You certainly know how to show a girl a good time, Doc," Zita said, after we turned onto Calle de Lezo and slowed our pace. "That's what I love about you."

A rumble like coming thunder rolled toward us and within seconds a caravan of heavily armed military vehicles came into view. A canopied jeep led the procession, escorted by four canvas-covered trucks full of Franco's elite soldiers. Two pickup trucks pulling three-inch American-made demi-cannons brought up the rear. They were moving fast, perhaps 50 km/h, too fast for the narrow street. Everything and anything was giving way to their approach as they sped toward the warehouse.

"Let's find some shelter and remove our costumes," Zita suggested.

"I know a place," I said, removing my dark glasses so I could see more clearly.

We crossed into Parque de la Taconera and out the other side where we found ourselves at a small roundabout. One of the spokes over the river wound its way up a small incline and disappeared into a maze of confusing roads. I remembered a plain bed-and-breakfast not far from there run by an old Castilian and two of his grandchildren but I wasn't totally confident that I could find it again.

As we crossed the bridge, holy hell erupted somewhere off to the right. One of the demi-cannons barked. An echo hung in the heavy air a few seconds, then fell away. There was a second and third explosion in close succession that shook the pavement under us. The siege of the warehouse had begun. Small arms fire charged the crisp afternoon and I prayed every bullet was finding its mark. I didn't want a stray round coming our way.

I hoped the ETA members had been smart enough to have left right after us but as soon as I heard the weapons fire, I knew they had chosen to remain in the safety of the reinforced building. Thinking about it, though, I wasn't certain which was worse; to wage a running gun battle through the back alleys of Pamplona or to stay in the warehouse and fight it out from there.

The distant assault continued, sounding oddly like a high-pitched musical celebration punctuated by the cannons' percussion. I imagined a small orchestra at a riverfront band shell playing a loud medley of Tchaikovsky concertos while picnicking families watched a barrage of fireworks overhead. The frenzy built to its climax, then the band and the bullets abruptly stopped. Another two short bursts signaled the end of the skirmish.

Zita and I stepped inside the wedge-shaped reception area of Mi Amigos English Style Bed and Breakfast on the corner of Calle de Arbizu and Calle de Isaba. Large windows faced both thin, threadlike streets, giving a good view of pedestrians approaching from either direction. The lobby was filled with small, white-cloth covered dining tables where guests took their meals. There was a petite young woman standing behind a rib-high counter, patiently waiting to greet us. Her smile was as broad as her face.

"Good afternoon," I said in English. "Do you have a room available for my nurse and me?"

"Yes, sir," she answered, with a slight British accent. "It is our off-season so you may have a room of your choosing."

"Ah, then the room above us will do nicely."

We slid our French passports toward the blue-eyed Castilian native. As she noted our numbers, names and Paris addresses on a registration card, I signed the guest register as Pierre-Michel la Fontain and paid cash for two days in advance. The young woman retrieved a key from a pigeonhole behind her and laid it on the countertop with an audible clunk. She announced dinner would be promptly at 8:00 p.m. if we cared to join the only other guest. I palmed the key off the counter without replying.

After a short soaking shower down the hall, Zita turned the communal bathroom over to me while she retrieved our bags from the train station. I stood under a very hot shower, letting the water run over my head and back. Leaning against the wall with my wounded hand raised above my head, the hot drizzle felt good and I didn't move until it turned lukewarm. I toweled off, glad the hotel was vacant because it was going to take an hour or more for the boiler to reheat the water.

I padded back to our room. Tossing the towel on the desk chair, I fell across the bed facedown and was asleep in seconds. My body succumbed to a deep senseless sleep, for a while anyway.

As soon as the afternoon light had faded from the room, my eyes sprang open. The darkness sat heavily on the surrounding silence. The little girl was in her coffin beside the bed, smiling at me with those haunting eyes. I sat up and pulled the blanket over my naked body.

"The door was open," she meekly said. "I came to see how you are. You've been in trouble, no?"

I tried hard to clear a woozy head.

"It's okay," I managed.

"I've asked you before, why do you do this?" she asked.

I rubbed a cheek with the back of my right hand and yawned. I wanted to tell her I saw my father in Chaban and I saw too much of my father in me. I hadn't liked it when I was a kid and I didn't like it now. I wanted him dead. Both of them dead, ripped right from my head and heart. Maybe then the weight of condemnation would be lifted from my back.

"It's easier than some things," I finally admitted.

"You're an amateur. These people will kill you too."

"Do you have room for me in your coffin there?"

"Don't throw your life away."

"I'm kidding," I said.

"You're hard-headed," she shot back and averted her face. She angrily wiped at the blood on her cheek and I thought her eyes filled with tears.

"Can you look at me, please? I…" I asked hesitantly.

"Do you think I can't see? Because your image of me is like this doesn't mean I don't see you exactly as you are."

My request had come out wrong and the room quietly fell

into a desperate nightmare of rage and regret. I felt guilty and I didn't know what else to say.

She sighed finally, "I came at the wrong time."

"I'm sorry." I held up my hands. "I promise I'll be more attentive."

"Don't do it for me. I'm already dead, remember? Anyway, I didn't come for this. I was concerned and you didn't seem well. Perhaps you need to see others and seek comfort there."

"You are the only one I can see," I said, softly. The silence sucked the oxygen from the room. "Help me. I need to find him."

"You are on a road with no exits."

CHAPTER 16

Zita re-dressed the half-moon slash on my palm. The incision was red and raw but the line was clean. Although the wound continued to throb when the hand dangled at my side, I could tell it was getting better. Zita's drugs were keeping pain down and infection from taking hold. I could move my fingers with little distress, with the help of the other hand. Regardless, I wasn't wearing that fat suit again.

"Were you followed from the train station?" I asked.

"Of course, they should be here any moment." I rose slightly, with a start. She continued. "Three lads and a pair of old geezers were smitten. You know the boys can't resist me. They must be searching in the road below by now."

"Okay." I gave up. My head dropped back to the pillow.

"You are the one, my dear, who has a knack for inviting your enemies to every party. I'm going to tie you to the bed tonight. It's the only safe place for us both. Tomorrow I'll teach you something about surveillance evasion."

State-sanctioned news coverage about the warehouse shootout was all over the television that evening. The newscaster reported on an incident earlier today where the subversive terrorist group ETA murdered six unarmed policemen outside a warehouse. The police had responded to an anonymous call describing an unconfirmed disturbance along the waterfront. After being lured to the location, they were ambushed by cold-blooded killers and two unknown associates.

Our esteemed National Police Force responded quickly, trapping the band of butchers inside the building before the cowards had an opportunity to flee. During the ensuing battle, three of the terrorists were killed and five more were captured. These surviving rebels will be questioned regarding their involvement in today's action. Additional evidence was found further implicating this group in the senseless murder of our Prime Minister Luis Carrero Blanco last week in Madrid.

Authorities are still searching for at least two unknown accomplices, believed to be providing funding to the group and having possibly incited today's insurgency. They are also wanted in connection with an unidentified dead man found beaten and tortured on the lower level of the warehouse. The pair slipped through our police net and escaped apprehension during the gun battle. They are described as a heavyset man in his fifties and a young female accomplice. They were last seen near the river and a full-scale search for them has been initiated in the area.

Three guardsmen were slightly wounded in the conflict when falling debris hit them as they rushed the warehouse entrance. All three were treated, cleared for active duty again and released back to their units to continue serving our Great Leader, Generalissimo Francisco Franco. This insult to Spain and el Caudillo will not be tolerated and the perpetrators will be swiftly and severely punished.

The bastards had given us up.

"We need to change rooms," I said. "Can you pick a lock? I'm afraid I need two hands."

"Yes, darling. Anyone just beyond daft can pick a lock," she hesitated then added with a smile, "Present company excluded, of course."

"I missed the class on how to pick a lock with your teeth." I grumbled.

"Doc, you missed all of the classes."

Zita pulled a small pouch from her handbag and disappeared into the dark hallway. I took a long, tired breath and packed the duffels one-handed, deliberately leaving aside the fat suit and the nurse's uniform. That clothing was no longer safe to wear. If I could have burned them, I would have, but after having torched half of Tanzania a year ago while trying to start a campfire, matches and a one-armed man were probably not a good combination right now. Zita returned as I finished packing.

"Ready?" She asked.

Zita took the two bags, and I grabbed the rest. Switching off the lamp, I swung the door closed with the heel of a shoe. She led me up two flights to a room at the back of the third floor landing. No light would be seen from the front of the building and the added distance might give us precious time if the soldiers decided to search door to door.

Zita tossed the duffels on the bed and pulled the heavy window dressing closed. The already dark room went pitch black. I dropped the nurse's uniform at the base of the door to catch escaping light and switched on a lamp. The 25-watt bulb illuminated a small area circling the bed.

"We should be safe enough here for the while," she said.

I curled up on top of the duvet and let my head sink helplessly into a pillow. Zita held on to me for warmth until she dozed off. I lay awake for an hour or more while she slept soundly. Listening to her rhythmic breathing, I finally faded away but my rest was not as peaceful.

Agitated, I woke every five minutes believing I heard people talking around me, and other times I thought I heard footsteps in the hallway. I turned every night noise into major danger. There was a ticking clock in my head that wouldn't quiet.

But then it came. I heard a real footstep in the corridor. I was certain. Grit crunching on tile. It happened only once, but it was distinct, distant, somewhere below. A soft clicking sound was followed by a creak, then a rush of feet. I sat up. Zita stirred in her sleep and settled again. At the door, I kicked the dress away and opened it a crack. It was dark and quiet. I waited. Nothing. Then I heard low voices. I lifted the Beretta and listened again.

Zita touched my shoulder. Her face reflected how tired I felt. Blinking to clear her eyes, she forced a smile. I pointed to the gap in the door. There were confused feet on the stairs. Two men started up.

"No están aquí. ¡Vamos," a voice barely above a whisper came through the white noise. Boots reversed down the steps and everything fell dead silent again. In the street, a faint rumble echoed as a truck engine turned over. I lowered my weapon and put it away.

"They think we've already left the hotel."

"We have to separate for a while," she said. "They'll be expecting two of us to be traveling together."

"Another hour or two of sleep first," I sighed. "They won't be back before morning when they can't find us elsewhere."

I fell on the bed and rolled to my back. Zita gently lifted my bandaged hand and laid her head on my chest, wrapping my arm around her. We slept until the early sun peeked through a slit in the east-facing curtains and split the room in soft reds and yellows. I woke as soon as Zita slipped from under my arm. She was sitting on the edge of the bed with her face turned down.

"Right," she said at last and stretched both arms high above her head before standing. "Meet me in Paris in two days' time."

"Paris?" I asked a little surprised.

"Tell me you're not going there, dear, and I'll be much relieved."

I thought I must have become as easy to read as a first-grade primer. Zita had grown to know me better than anyone during the past year. She always seemed to know what I was thinking.

"I guess I'm going to Paris," I answered, flashing a grin.

We emerged into the lobby where freshly laundered tablecloths covered the breakfast tables. The young woman with whom we had spoken the previous afternoon was changing the last of the linens. Her huge smile faded to a blank stare as she recognized us. I placed the key on the counter with a smile. She remained motionless and just watched as we walked through the lobby.

"How much time do you suppose we have before the soldiers arrive?" Zita asked.

"I'm not sure she'll be calling anyone but if she does, I'd love to hear her explain where we were last night."

"Give me your weapon, these will go into the river," she said. I handed over the gun, suddenly feeling like a man forfeiting his wallet to a mugger. "I'll bring another for you to Paris, love. French customs are not nearly as easy to fool, or as forgiving."

We turned west along the river and Zita tossed the weapons into the water while we walked. As we approached the bridge back to the south side, I gave her a long kiss and said, "I'll see you on Saturday."

"Doc, please come alone this time."

CHAPTER 17

I caught a ride on a fruit truck coming out of Pamplona. The farmer was returning home to Ejea de los Caballeros after selling his load in the open market and offered me a lift as far as his orchards. The road was rough going through the mountain passes, but the old farmer kept my attention from the narrow passages and sudden drop-offs by serving as proud tour guide for his beautiful country. The panorama was breathtaking, winding its way from the high clouds down through the blues and the grays of the highlands to the valleys below.

The road eventually shed the mountainous terrain of Navarro and opened onto the fertile, high plains of Aragon where Ejea de los Caballeros rose in the near distance. The land around Ejea became much more arable and productive farmland after the aqueducts were built in the 1960s to bring a constant flow of water to the region. The farmer told me he could not complain about his life since then. It was hard, back-breaking work, but he and his family were making a good wage.

The fruit truck slowed to a stop at the farmer's turnoff. The engine rumbled loudly and exhaust fumes filled the cab. I thanked him for the ride, turned to open the door and stopped. He had both hands on the steering wheel when I faced him. The morning sun was still low enough in the sky to hit us full in the face.

"¿Consideraría usted llevarme a Zaragoza, donde tengo más posibilidades de otro viaje, por favor?" I asked.

I needed to go all the way to Zaragoza, otherwise there wasn't a snowflake's chance in hell I would ever catch a lift from here. The man looked at me with one eye closed. He suddenly looked exhausted.

"Tengo 1,500 pesetas." I offered him $50 USD and pulled the cash from my jeans. The farmer stared at the money and considered it a long time. Finally, he folded the bills into his shirt pocket and shifted the old truck into first gear.

He didn't say another word for 75 kilometers until he dropped me near the bus depot in Zaragoza. Embarrassed about taking the money, the farmer tried to give it back as I jumped to the ground. I told him he earned it and closed the door. Throwing my backpack over a shoulder and putting a pair of steel-rimmed glasses on my nose, I walked away. The old truck didn't move for a long time but finally it made a U-turn in the middle of Calle de los Predicadores and headed toward home.

Before leaving Pamplona, I had negotiated with the clerk at an early morning pharmacy for my current student disguise. I was hoping the glasses and backpack were good enough to get me out of Spain. Walking past a group of guardsmen as I entered the bus depot, however, I suddenly wished I could have also grown a mustache overnight. They stopped talking to glower, but no one moved to detain me as I stepped inside.

I checked the schedule in the lobby for the next express bus to Barcelona. It wouldn't leave until four o'clock. There was a bus to Tarragona that left in an hour and I decided to hop on that. It would take me within 80 kilometers of Barcelona. With any luck, I could catch a ride there and be back at the train station by mid-afternoon. I bought coffee and a dry baguette at a kiosk and sat to wait with a discarded newspaper.

Like many modern Iberian cities, Zaragoza had its origins with the Romans and changed hands a number of times over the centuries. The Goths ruled the city for a while around 500 A.D. Afterward, the Berbers and the Arabs controlled the region and Zaragoza grew to be the largest Muslim city of northern Spain. Even the great El Cid was well known here. Zaragoza was the home of Francisco de Goya and Ferdinand II of Aragon who, with his wife, Queen Isabella I of Castile, sponsored a small Italian's voyages to the New World.

The bus pulled out of the station onto Av del Castile at precisely 11:00 a.m. but the schedule went south from there. The engine coughed and sputtered, then quit. The driver cranked the key as the bus slowly rolled downhill in neutral and the motor came back from the dead with a lurch and a loud roar. Unlike the European rail system, Spanish buses were not known for their punctuality or reliability so there was no guarantee we would arrive on time, or at all.

Skirting the old city, we cruised by a Moorish palace built during the second half of the eleventh century. Its ramparts and outer shell were just about the ugliest thing I'd ever seen but I'd heard its real beauty was on the inside. The bus bumped across the cobblestones on Puente de Piedra and ran alongside the Basilica of Our Lady of the Pillar, a Catholic Church believed to have been the first ever dedicated to the Virgin Mary, sometime around 40 A.D.

The driver dropped the throttle to the floor in anticipation of the open highway. The bus was not quite one-third full so the passengers had spread out after boarding. I inspected the face of each person now, remembering what Zita had said about my being easier to follow than an 18-wheeler on a two-lane highway.

I was a little paranoid. Instead of wondering if I was being followed, I found myself assuming one of the passengers had to be trailing me. I moved back three rows to an open area. No one noticed except a lone man in the last row who glanced at me over his newspaper. I leaned back for the two and one-half hour trip to Tarragona.

I wondered how Zita had fared after entering the train station in Pamplona. Military vehicles had lined the surrounding area when we approached. Soldiers had milled about the building and the platform area had been thick with patrols. She had let her hair down, unfastened a button on her blouse and widened her bright blue eyes a bit more. Instead of trying to sneak by the guardsmen, we had thought she might try the opposite and cause a little scene.

She had breezed past the leering soldiers and walked inside the tiny station for a ticket to Barcelona. She had settled on a bench midway down the platform to wait for her train. Within seconds, three men had propositioned her. If any of them had joined her on the train, she was going to have an interesting trip. I seriously doubted any of them would have made the full journey alive. I grinned, pitying the fool who tried to touch her and praying Zita didn't make the evening news.

The engine noise and the hum of the bus tires lulled me to sleep with a smile on my face. I dozed on and off for the better part of 100 kilometers thinking about her. I had first met Zita when she was fresh from a security detail during the aftermath of the Munich Olympics and I was fresh off the boat. She was two years younger but so much wiser than I could ever hope to be. I had been charmed at first sight, enchanted really. I couldn't say what she saw in me, but we'd been fast friends and lovers ever since.

The sound of the air brakes startled me awake. The bus slowed, veering to the right of the Tarragona depot where the passenger disembarkation island offered plenty of room for weary travelers to step down and collect their luggage from the belly of the bus. I glanced at my watch. We were less than an hour late,

107

not as bad as it could have been.

I waited for everyone to exit before gathering my belongings. With a small tug, my backpack fell from the overhead rack. I noticed the Spaniard from the back row watching me as he walked to the terminal. Our eyes locked briefly as he looked back one final time before disappearing inside.

Passengers were still searching the open undercarriage for their luggage when I dropped to the ground. I headed for a row of dumpsters at the edge of the building. Pulling a cardboard box from the trash, I ripped off the end flap and wrote the word "Barcelona" on one side.

It wasn't long before a woman in a red convertible Ferrari swung into the curb at 50 km/h without braking until the last second. The car stopped on a dime and I had a vision of the driver being thrown through the windshield, but she held firm with a cool smile on her face. I tossed my bag in the back and hopped over the door, landing in the passenger seat just before the afterburners kicked in. The car slid smoothly back into the light afternoon traffic on Avinguda de Roma. In the passenger mirror, I caught a glimpse of the Spaniard from the bus tracking the car as we pulled away.

My chauffeur was the daughter of an American diplomat out on a jaunt for the day in Tarragona. The city hadn't lived up to her expectations, so she was returning early to Barcelona where she lived. The old Roman outpost was too creepy, she said, and she was excited to get back to the city for a night of clubbing.

"You should join me," she said.

"Sorry, I need to be in Paris by tomorrow."

"I have tons of friends and we can hang out. They would love to meet you and listen to your backpacking adventures through Europe. I hear it's all the rage now back in the States. Everyone is planning an excursion to backpack or bicycle or something around Europe. I'll tell you what. Why don't you stay tonight and tomorrow I'll personally drive you to Paris. By the way, my name is Karen."

"It's nice to meet you, Karen. Your offer's very tempting."

"Okay, it's a date then. Have you finished college or are you still in school? What are you studying? My father says the only thing worth studying is world economics. Boring! What do you think? I'm starting college in the fall at University of Barcelona. I'm going to have to find a way around this economics thing, though. I'd rather keep partying, you know, keep my options open for whatever comes along that's not world economics. Hey, what did you do to your hand?"

"I cut it shaving," I answered.

"Oh, I thought you were going to tell me a story about a drug deal going bad, or maybe espionage. I've always wanted to meet a spy. Can you imagine living like James Bond? Always outwitting the Russians or whoever, visiting exotic places like the Riviera and what about those gadgets? Now, that's the way to live! God, I love those movies! I'm not sure about this new guy but that Sean Connery is a dream!"

It was like that for a solid hour. Karen talked non-stop, emphasizing words with a flip of a hand, sometimes both hands as we drove the coastal road to Barcelona. I was able to add a few words to the monologue, but I'm not at all positive she heard a syllable of what I said. Truthfully, I was more interested in staying on the zigzagging racecourse, than anything she said. My heart was floating in my throat, which was a little too close to my gag reflex.

Karen swerved off the road and skidded to a stop in front of Franca Station with the practiced ease of a Hollywood stunt driver. Her eyes flew open in mock surprise and she grabbed my arm. Before she would release it, I had to promise three times to call her as soon as I arrived in Paris.

"I'll be there by Monday at the latest so I'll need to know where you're staying. Please expect me then and save all of your time for me. You're so interesting to talk to."

As she rocketed away, she left a long strip of rubber on the asphalt for my pleasure. The brake lights flashed on three-quarters of the way down the block as the Ferrari decelerated to zero. The car sat in the middle of the boulevard idling for a long time, as if the girl was considering coming back. But as quickly as she had stopped, the car sped off and vanished around the corner.

Happy she decided not to turn around, I stuffed her phone number in my jeans, forgot about it and walked into the station lobby. The schedule board was spinning faster than fan blades set on high, but when it eventually stopped, an evening express to Marseilles caught my eye. It would arrive by 11:15 p.m. From there, the morning train to Paris would work perfectly. If all went well, I would be there by dark tomorrow.

Before buying the ticket, however, I sat in the corner of an open-air coffee shop watching travelers come and go. The terminal was busy and noisy. People were everywhere, moving in twenty directions at once. There was no semblance of sanity. I really needed that lesson in counter surveillance from Zita because I had no idea what I was doing. Finally taking my chances, I went to the ticket counter and bought a one-way fare to Marseilles.

CHAPTER 18

"Do you have the blueprints?"

"Yesterday." The handsome Spaniard slid the packet across to the man with the stone gray eyes.

"Any problems?"

"None, in fact, the engineer gave us a bonus."

The bartender checked their glasses.

"Refill, mates?" He asked.

Gray Eyes looked down at his beer and waved the man away.

"What do you mean a bonus?"

"There's a way to use less explosives and make it look like an accident. That might keep them guessing until we can disappear," the Spaniard added.

"I don't care what it looks like as long as they all die. I want to see bodies dropping from the sky."

"You will. Instead of dynamite, he suggested we get some of what the Americans have started using in Vietnam."

"Yes, C4. Not right for Blanco," he mused. "But it does solve the problem of getting close with fifty kilos of dynamite. Run another test to see how it works. There can be no survivors."

"He said a little in the right place and gravity takes over."

"What about the courier?"

"There's a small problem with him."

"I don't think I heard you correctly." His stone gray eyes burned holes through the man sitting beside him.

"Well, more of a complaint," the handsome Spaniard

hesitated. "We're meeting in Marseilles later tonight and I'll get it sorted out."

"Do what you have to do. I need those schematics. The blueprints do no good without them."

CHAPTER 19

The morning train out of Marseilles left at the civilized hour of 9:00 a.m. I caught a fair night's sleep at a dingy, overcrowded youth hostel off Rue Sainte near the wharf. Youth hostels in Europe were tantamount to camping on a crowded, noisy beach, except you usually didn't have to dig a hole to pee in if you were willing to walk down the hall.

Anyone following me would be sleeping in equally uncomfortable quarters somewhere nearby. The waterfront was lined with hostels and pay-by-the-hour hotels; not a Ritz in sight. I was looking forward to finding someone hobbling along behind me, nursing a sore back.

I showered early before anyone stirred and left the hostel by 7:30 a.m. Gare St-Charles was a kilometer's walk from the waterfront down Cours Belsunce and over on Rue des Dominicaines. I found an outdoor coffee shop on the way that served a continental breakfast of baguettes with jam and butter on the side.

Standing at a tall table with a sandwich-sized roll in my hand, I watched a well-dressed man heading toward the café carrying a small satchel. His eyes were set on me even as his head swung back and forth through traffic. Does he know me? I pulled my backpack close, ready to run.

When the man was closer, I saw that he acted as anxious as I felt. Maybe he had coffee shakes, but he kept looking back at me. Sipping from his cup, he pretended to watch the traffic and glanced at me again. I stared at him menacingly.

The man paid his bill with coins he nervously dropped on the counter. I heard one roll and clink against a saucer. Turning, he almost ran into me. His eyes averted to the ground as he hurried away. Crossing the avenue on an angle, he took long, quick strides. The man looked like he wanted to run but his shaky legs wouldn't bend at the knees.

I kept my eyes on him until he was lost from view, thinking that could have gone better. Where was Zita when I needed her? Unable to tell the difference between someone following me and someone following the smell of coffee was disheartening.

Now I was feeling bad too, having scared the bejesus out of a Frenchman for no reason except possibly the sheer fun of it. I should have known better than to think he was following me. This guy was well-rested, with no sign of a backache.

I stayed another fifteen minutes before grabbing the rest of my baguette and setting off down Rue des Dominicaines toward the train station. Cutting through the park, I had to drop the rest of the bread for a gang of menacing birds in order to escape with my life. They'd stopped following me by the time I reached St. Theodore's Church. I hoisted the backpack higher on one shoulder and picked up the pace.

In the church gardens across the way sat a man removing the paper from a sandwich. He looked up. It was the guy from the coffee shop. He stood as we stared at each other. The paper fell from his hand, revealing a small revolver. He raised the weapon and fired.

The bullet hit one of St. Theodore's angels sitting on a perch four meters above and to the right of my head. Cement chips rained down as I ran under the protection of the church's porch. Taking the six stone steps in two strides, I bounced off a startled priest who appeared in the doorway.

THE HOLLOW MAN

I moved quickly down the center aisle of the nave and off to the right at the altar, where I noticed the basement access. I considered finding what was left of St. Theodore in a dark corner of the lower level and hiding with the remains, but three steps down at the first landing was a side door that opened onto a narrow causeway behind the church. Harsh daylight flooded into the dim interior as I stood in the opening waiting for all hell to break loose, but the tiny parking area was empty.

Behind me I heard a sudden raised voice and momentary scuffling. I slipped through the door. Crossing to the other side of Rue Saint-Théodore, I followed the curve around to the north, where it intersected Rue Francis de Pressensé. A lone car cruised past. I walked against the traffic on Pressensé, glancing back every few steps. I became distrustful of everyone.

Paranoia jumped on my back and seized my head. I found myself looking for clues to validate every fear. Danger was hiding in doorways and suspicion outlined strangers' faces. Any of these people might be working with the gunman. It was someone pretending not to notice me; someone cool, nonchalant. On a station bench, a man was intently tapping his foot. A woman was fussing with a baby stroller.

I wasn't going to make it to the train. My legs were stiffening and I could feel my insides about to curdle. In a panic, I willed my feet to move. Move. Move! Slowly at first, then I started to run and I couldn't stop, too afraid to look around.

By the time I reached the platform, my spine was a river of sweat. It hurt to climb the coach steps but within a few seconds I was settled into a second-class compartment on the Paris train, seated so I could see passengers approaching from the terminal. As far as I knew, no one suspicious followed me on board; as if I had a clue what suspicious looked like. Most important though, I didn't see the coffee drinker.

115

We began rolling so slowly I had to look at the ground to be certain we were moving at all. The train sailed through the north end of Marseilles at 30 km/h then doubled its speed as we hit the outskirts. The ride was smooth and quiet except for an occasional jostle from an uneven track.

Outside Marseilles, we hit the foothills and climbed west, away from the blues of the Mediterranean. The gray hilly terrain, though not very great in altitude, was enough to block any remaining view of the sea. We were leaving behind the coastal paradise made famous by the beautiful people. Settling back, I knew the rolling landscape would not change much all the way to Montpellier.

The town was built on extremely uneven ground, ten kilometers inland on the River Lez. Legend has it the name of the city means 'naked hill' because of the poor vegetation found here. Whether or not that was true, I can tell you the city's undulating walkways took full advantage of the erratic countryside. Many of them were narrow and steep. I heard people say those attributes gave the city an intimate charm. I had been here before and intimate did not come to mind. The word I used was claustrophobic. Nostradamus went to university in Montpellier and I'm pretty sure this place had spawned some of his more nightmarish predictions.

The engine sat idling at the station while several cars were pulled off the back of the train and another was added. Near the door of each coach on a European train was a small rectangular sign which identified its final destination. I wondered how many unsuspecting tourists over the years had boarded a train thinking they were bound for one destination, only to end up in a different city, or even another country, because of the coach they chose. A traveler would make that mistake only once.

The train was as eager as me to be on the move again. The

hydraulic brakes blew off steam in anticipation. The engine shook the coaches to ensure couplings were tight. The conductor finally secured the ramp steps and locked the coach doors. At long last, everything was ready to go and once again the train rolled out of the station at a snail's pace. Buildings outside the compartment barely moved, but the engine's increasing speed soon blurred my near vision.

The usual rail route to Paris from the Riviera circumvented the center of France in favor of a westerly arc through the countryside. It was perhaps not the most expeditious way to get from point A to point B but this was definitely a ride not to be missed. The French were in no hurry when the circuit was designed, believing travelers would in turn not feel rushed to reach their destination. So, the track curved out toward the Atlantic and 308 kilometers to the west northwest lay Bordeaux.

The jagged, pitched hills along the coast smoothed into rolling mounds covered in moor grass sprinkled with purple and gold wild flowers. Pockets of grape orchards began spotting the land, separated by rough rock fencing that created odd designs across empty brown fields. Too small for commercial production, these vineyards were barely large enough to supply a single family with wine through the winter.

Eventually, endless vineyards covered the hills as far as I could see. Groomed terraces followed the contours of the land, flowing like strands of hair in the wind. Although mostly barren this time of year, thousands of vines hung on row after row of wood and wire in anticipation of the spring growing season.

We were entering the Bordeaux wine region, where an average vintage of 700 million bottles of wine, 60 different varieties, were produced yearly and shipped to markets worldwide. A limestone base made the soil rich in calcium and the Atlantic offered an oceanic climate perfect for growing grapes. A number of rivers crisscrossed southwestern France, providing one of the best natural irrigation systems in Europe and some of the most scenic views any passenger could want.

I grabbed an early lunch in the dining car and walked toward the front of the train. Most of the compartment drapes were closed as I strolled along the corridor. That was fine with me; less distractions and less chance of being seen. I found the diner four coaches up the train. A waiter was dreamily leaning back against the bar as I entered and sat at the counter.

"Oui?" he asked.

I yawned, not wanting to think about a foreign language right now.

"Anglais?" I asked.

"Oui."

"Can I have a ham sandwich and a Coke, please?"

"Un sandwich de jambon et un Coke," he said to himself and turned away.

While he made the sandwich, my attention was drawn to the large picture windows behind me. A lone chateau stood in the distance, growing in grandeur as it grew in size. Spreading across a hilltop, the chateau towered three stories above the outbuildings that surrounded it. The expansive gray-topped structure was a magnificent example of eighteenth century architecture with its white stone shell enhancing the corner parapets and rising spires. A lone child stood in one of the floor-to-ceiling windows at the second level and waved as the express train flew past.

"Oh, and cheese, too," I said.

"Oui, avec fromage," the man repeated absently, without turning around. He carefully arranged the plate and glass in front of me and poured the Coca Cola from a freshly opened bottle. "Voila!" He said and set the empty bottle by my hand.

The ham sandwich consisted of a split baguette smeared on

both inside surfaces with butter. The ham, one thin slice folded over, was laid on the butter and on top was a transparent slice of cheese. I wasn't positive what kind it was. French cooking yielded some of the most delicious food in Europe, but they could use a few lessons in the art of sandwich-making. Ham and cheese is what actually made it a ham and cheese sandwich, I thought. Otherwise, it's just bread and butter. Even so, the sandwich tasted great on an empty stomach.

I ate in silence, occasionally sipping the warm Coke. Shortly after arriving in Europe, I quickly acclimated to drinking beverages at a customary room temperature. Ice was simply not provided unless specifically requested. I forgot to ask more times than not so it became easier to drink the beverage as served. Now I was used to it.

"Not many students join us this time of year. Are you studying in France?" The waiter asked.

"Yes, at the Sorbonne," I replied.

"You are going all the way to Paris then? Do you know that we go to Lyon from Bordeaux? Another dining coach will assist you into Paris." He checked the time. "We are due into Bordeaux presently."

As I made my way back, I could feel the engine braking slightly and its speed decreasing as I walked. Entering the coach before mine, I noticed a compartment door jarred open several centimeters and the curtain covering the window was in disarray. I instinctively peeked inside. A man was sprawled against the coach window with his head tilted back, sleeping.

I stopped a step beyond the door. I knew this man. It was the coffee drinker from Marseilles. I took a longer look. He didn't appear at all well. His skin was pasty and I wasn't certain he was breathing.

I thought about choking him to finish the bastard off but

119

searching him for identification and rifling his satchel might be a bit more useful. I should have stolen a knife from the dining car. A weapon would have boosted my confidence and made me braver than I felt. I decided to risk it anyway, knowing that I could always run if he stirred.

Moving into the compartment, I didn't see the bag he had been carrying. It wasn't on the cushion beside him, on the floor or in the overhead. I folded back his coat to lift his wallet and saw his shirt was soaked with blood. The hole in his chest was still leaking into his tucked-in shirt, and there was a sack of blood pooled at the back of his waist. I reached into the inside coat pocket.

His hand suddenly snapped up and caught my wrist. I tried to pull back, but his grip was amazingly strong for a dead man. The wallet flew from my fingers, bounced off the window and landed at my feet. I couldn't loosen his hold and I was starting to panic when he exhaled a long, audible breath and the hand fell away. With my chest filling like a water balloon, my eyes didn't leave him as I bent to retrieve the wallet. I didn't want any more surprises.

A voice started begging me to run and keep running. Another was screaming that I was crazier than first imagined. Listen to me. You're not coping very well. Sanity isn't reasonable in this situation. You're shaking. Don't think. Run; do something. Dammit! We're not finding common ground here, are we? Let me do the thinking for you. Get up and run!

In less than two minutes, I was back in my compartment, but it took much longer for my heart and pounding head to return to normal. The train stopped in Bordeaux to make coach changes and take on new passengers. Policemen patrolled the platform but none were moving toward the coaches yet. The first time one blinked in my direction, I would be off the back of the train and gone. I'd rather not be wanted in two countries before I turned twenty-five. I could live without ever going back to Spain but France was altogether different.

When we finally left the depot, I realized I had been holding my breath. What in the living hell was going on? Somebody had killed the man who tried to kill me. Was the assassin helping me or hurting me? I had no idea what was going on, but it had more to do with me than I wanted.

CHAPTER 20

We were an hour on the other side of Bordeaux by one o'clock. I opened the dead man's wallet and found approximately a thousand francs in ten and twenty franc notes, the equivalent of $250 USD. I folded the bills into my jeans. An inside pocket contained photographs of two different women. On the back of the picture featuring a smiling blonde, was an address neatly written in a feminine hand. It was a flat in the 6th Arrondissement on the Left Bank.

The name on the driver's license was Jean Le Roux and the address above his signature identified a place in the 8th Arrondissement. I was familiar with that area of Paris. Le Roux lived on the north side of the Seine, a short walk from the Arc de Triomphe.

Napoleon had built the triumphal arch 150 years ago to honor those who had fought and died for France in its Revolution and Napoleonic Wars. During his time, the arch had strategically lain just outside the city's edge so his victorious armies could reenter the city through its portal. Now the 8th Arrondissement was central to Paris and was a very busy commercial center containing one of the world's most well-known street names, Av. Des Champs Élysées.

The train reached its top speed of 110 km/h and we settled into the smooth glide of an endless porch swing. Lost in thought, I gazed into the hollow space outside the window. I didn't notice the passing vineyards, the occasional tractor tilling virgin fields or the stone walls and tree lines that defined the boundaries of land ownership. I didn't feel the sun warming my face. And I didn't hear the compartment door as it slid open and softly closed behind a lone figure.

I straightened abruptly when I realized a young woman had moved into my field of vision. Without hesitating, she sat on the leather bench across from me and smiled softly. She was perhaps eighteen or nineteen, barely above five feet tall. Her brown hair was shoulder length with bangs that almost covered her eyes. When she spoke, she pulled the hair back from her face with both hands.

"American?" she asked, in a thick Eastern European accent. There it was again. Somehow my nationality preceded me. I nodded.

"I think so," she continued. "I hope you don't mind I join you. I am in compartment over there by an old Brit who will not shut up. He is so rude and his ears stick out to here with more hair than his head." She motioned with her hands. "I think the creepy man is going to drive me crazy. Then he say he wants to show me Paris like no one else can show me! He is not even French. I do not know what that means. He think I am in the loo now. God, I hope he does not seek to me."

"I don't talk much," I said and turned back to the window.

"You are going to Paris, ya?" Again I nodded. "This is my first time there."

"Mine too," I lied.

"I am on holiday from my school. I come to experience the revolution."

I searched her face curiously.

"What revolution is that?" I asked.

"The sex revolution," she said, innocently. "I think it is in Paris."

Coming up from the south of France, I wondered why she hadn't gone directly to Paris from her country. Possibly, the girl had gotten lost somewhere along the route from Eastern Europe, or perhaps she was not ready for Paris until now. As scary or exciting as the City of Light may be for someone, there was a certain flirtatious dance that always romances us from the temptation to the take-up. This sort of thing consistently took time and when the stars lined up, we realized we were ready. I didn't have the heart to tell her she had probably missed the revolution altogether.

"I wouldn't know," I said.

"Of course, because you do not go to Paris yet," she responded, with a spark in her eye. "I have seen this in the underground newspapers in my city."

"Where is your home?"

"Prague. Where is your home?"

That was a good question, I thought. I had heard once that home was where people would open their door to you and they would have to let you in, no matter what. The trick for me was getting someone to open the door in the first place.

"Chicago," I said.

"Gangsters! We see the movies. It is dangerous there, no?"

"Not really."

"Our government tells of murders and capitalism in America. They say your cities are very bad. We know many killings with the machine guns in your Chicago. This is what happens with too many freedoms."

"Those are movies you are seeing, make-believe. Don't you have make-believe in Prague?"

"Yes, we have theater." She was defensive. "We sneak also to the university to watch American movies. I do not understand them sometimes but they are not so bad. They make me dream and now I am here."

"Will you go home at the end of the revolution?"

"I do not think so," she hesitated. "Besides I will not until our people are free again. I hate the Russians for many reasons and wish them all to leave us alone." She brightened. "So until then, I see the world."

"And Paris is the first stop." I smiled.

"Yes, Paris is the place I begin."

She lapsed into thought. Her eyes were moving rapidly in a strange, waking REM sleep. She was already in Paris, feeling the sun on her face, walking among the artisans, tasting world renowned cuisine, seeing beauties never before seen and adding her own small mark to the long history forever infused into the eternal City of Light.

The train slowed its approach into the outskirts of Nantes. Clouds rolling in off the Atlantic grayed the afternoon and brought a soaking rain to the city. The storm stalled on top of us. For a moment I was back on the colorless, deserted streets of central Madrid. Through a water-streaked window, the debris from Calle de Coello oozed down a canyon of broken buildings and washed away under the train as we passed over it. The next street was the same. The same. The same. The same. Thunder clapped with a sharp flash of light and I jumped upright as the engine jerked into the station.

The Czech girl stared wide-eyed at the people on the platform as the train awaited passenger exchanges. She was curious about everyone and everything. Why did women wear nothing on their heads, how can the people afford such nice clothing, why was everyone smiling and where were the soldiers? She had not seen any soldiers in France, though she knew they must be here somewhere. Thoughtfully, she sat back as the train left the station.

Personally, I had been searching exiting passengers for anyone who might have killed Le Roux. I wanted him off the train. I could do without that stress all the way to Paris but it looked like I was destined to worry about that too.

"You know, there are no soldiers here," I finally said.

Her head suddenly snapped in my direction as if she had been slapped.

"No soldiers?" Her voice echoed in the small room. She smiled, briefly embarrassed.

"No one much cares what you do in France."

After a moment she said, "Well then, I do it all."

"Just don't kill anyone and you'll do fine," I said. "Please excuse me for a moment. Would you mind watching my backpack?"

Standing, I stretched and walked to the door. The girl turned back to the window. Both hands were clasped around a crossed knee and a lone foot was bouncing to the rhythm of something in her head. I stepped into the corridor and closed the compartment door.

CHAPTER 21

Somewhere between Bordeaux and Nantes, I had decided to get rid of the body in the next coach. Before the train reached Rennes, Le Roux needed to take a short walk off the bottom step at the carriage door. After my recent rise to stardom in Spain, law enforcement would be beating up old ladies throughout Europe to find me, and it would be for more than my autograph. I knew I was being paranoid, but I was certain I'd be the prime suspect if the police found a dead man and me on the same train.

Le Roux had to leave through the door. It wasn't a choice. He was too large to squeeze through the thirty centimeter gap in the dropdown compartment window. The chances of my being caught with a body in the corridor were 80-20 against the luckiest kid in the world. But I was partial to wine and women, both of which were highly restricted in prison. Twenty percent would have to do, it was him or me.

Before moving to the next coach, I stopped in the restroom and emptied the paper towel dispenser. It was three-quarters full and I hoped it would be enough to soak up the blood before I moved the body. I laid the stack on the edge of the sink and stared at my reflection in the stainless steel mirror. I searched for a clue as to what in the living hell I thought I was doing.

Tapping lightly on the Frenchman's compartment, I pushed the door open and locked it behind me. It had been a few hours since I was here and the vague smell of decay now hung in the air. I dropped the window and let in the fresh breeze. Hauling the man forward, his weight fell on my upper body. With a free hand I jammed half the paper towels behind him in the sofa crack.

I pulled the polyester shirttail from his pants and the congealing blood plopped on the paper towels like an uncooked egg. I thought I was going to throw up down his back when the yoke burst and spread across the seat. I laid him down and shoved my head in the open window where I let the chilly wind shake me from this dream. Breathing deeply, I gripped the window ledge with white knuckles and held the oxygen in while I fought the urge to vomit. It would have flown back in my face anyway.

Sucking in a huge breath, I turned back to the body. The heart had stopped pumping long ago so all the blood that was coming out had already oozed down his back. I put the rest of the towels on top of the bloody mess. Gingerly bunching the towels into a loose ball, I thought about chucking the bundle out the window but immediately imagined people in the next compartment seeing blood splash across their window, or worse if it was open. I decided to walk the remains back to the restroom and dispose of them there.

Standing over the toilet, I dropped the towels and flushed. The blue-colored water rose slightly then the bottom cover released, dumping the contents onto the tracks below. Blood had spattered on my bandaged hand. Not knowing if it was mine or the towels had leaked, I peeled away the gauze and flushed that too. The blood wasn't mine but my palm looked as pasty as I felt and the skin seemed to be lifting away from the bones.

I walked around the bathroom partition to the coach door leading off the train and tried the handle. It had been locked by the conductor and there would be no picking this one. Locks on French trains were secured with a special heavy-duty railroad key whose barrel fit over a spindle that guided the teeth into the tumblers. I shook the door in frustration, which helped nothing but it felt good. With the pinch bars, I slid the glass down to waist-high. The opening would have to do. I went back for Le Roux as a hurricane howled after me.

My plan was fairly simple. I would support the dead man with his arm around my neck and my arm around his back. If anyone entered the corridor unexpectedly, I would explain my friend was drunk, and I was assisting him to the restroom.

I'm not sure what I was thinking because it didn't exactly play out that way. I hoisted the body up and secured a good grip. He was damned heavy and his legs weren't cooperating at all, dragging uselessly behind us. I wrestled for a new grip around the midsection and pulled as I struggled backward. Now, I would have to tell anyone we met that my friend was dead drunk, and I was dragging him to the restroom.

Fortunately, we ran into no one. At the stairs down to the door, I was careful to get in front of Le Roux to support his weight as I maneuvered to the bottom. If he slipped and fell, I would have never been able to lift him out of the stairwell. I walked him down, face to face. Each step went faster than the last and at the bottom I hit the door so hard I thought it might fly open and take us both off a passing bridge.

I tried lifting the body from that position without success. His weight was bending me through the opening too, so I shifted and lay the dead man's torso in the window with his arms hanging out. Grabbing his dangling legs in a bear hug and lifting, I was surprised how easily the wind sucked Le Roux through the hole.

Staggering back to the bathroom, I vomited three times and was barely able to keep my head from dropping into the toilet water. After washing my face in cold water, I had another round of dry heaves and needed to freshen up again. I sat on the toilet with my head in my hands. That was a mistake. I was going downhill fast.

While I still had the strength, I crawled on hands and knees to the door and pulled myself up to open the latch. I tried to stand straight, but the best I could manage was a sort of quarter bend with my head drooping toward unsteady feet. I hung my head out the same window that had taken Le Roux, letting the crisp air bite into my ears and scrape my face raw.

When I opened my compartment door, I was unbelievably weak and my legs were still not working right. The Czech girl was sitting with her knees pulled up and her arms wrapped snugly around her legs. Snapped from her daydream, she smiled as I sat down. I tried to smile back as I ran a hand instinctively through wet, unkempt hair and glanced away. My palm was itching unmercifully. I wanted to scratch it but I didn't want to rip the incision open with my nails. I gently rubbed my fingers together.

"What do you do with your hands?" she asked.

I stared at them. I almost told her I'd done a great many things with my hands but I stopped short because that story would have filled a dozen train trips to Paris.

"A few weeks ago, I cut my palm on a broken Coca Cola bottle," I said, instead.

"I like Coca Cola." Then she said, "You are ill, ya?"

"Yes," I explained. "I threw up."

She was confused so I imitated a circular motion from my stomach to my mouth. She nodded.

"That is bad. I feel sorry."

The young girl lowered her legs from the couch and placed her folded hands in her lap. She gazed sharply down then jerked her face toward the window. The closer we got to Paris, the more nervous she became. She bit her lip several times and I wondered what she was thinking. Was she afraid to let herself imagine what was coming?

"Do you have money?" I asked.

Her face was blank. I reached into my pocket and pulled out the money I took from Le Roux's wallet. Reaching for her hand, I curled her fingers around the notes. I wanted no more to do with him.

CHAPTER 22

It was dark when the train reached Paris' Gare du Nord terminal. We stepped off the coach into unintentional chaos as people hurried past in every possible direction, throwing apologies in their path to clear the way. Some passengers were anxiously seeking the correct platform with children, baggage, and apprehension in tow. Others were pleased to be home from a stressful trip. With more than 40 active platforms, Gare du Nord was the busiest train station in Europe.

The girl from Czechoslovakia stopped after a single step and tried to back up when she saw the confusion, but there was no place to go. Her eyes grew wide and panic flushed her face. Wrapping an arm around her, I placed my head close to hers and led her out into the concourse where the crush of people dissipated. We walked slowly past the kiosks, the shops and the ticket counters. We were two reunited lovers on our way home.

We wandered into a short taxi line and slowly separated our heads. With my arm still around her waist, I whispered, "Are you all right?"

She nodded.

"I am afraid," she said.

"You're safe now. Do you have a place to stay?"

"Yes, I stay with family near university."

"Here is our taxi," I said.

She protested but I guided her into the back seat and climbed in beside her. I asked for the address and gave it to the driver. The lights of the city were coming up and neon signs illuminated the shops across from the station. Sitting forward on the seat, she turned to the window as the taxi jumped into traffic. A horn blared behind us.

"My name is Kamilla Prochazka," she said, without turning toward me. "But it is easier to call me Kami, I think. My mother does not like it but I do."

We crossed the river toward the Left Bank at Pont Neuf and despite its name, it was the oldest bridge still in use across the Seine. Construction had been completed at the beginning of the seventeenth century and it had been Paris' first stone bridge that did not also support housing in addition to a roadway. The bridge had been an immediate success, carrying heavy traffic from the start and judging from the backup we encountered, some of the original congestion was still in the way. As the taxi began to move onto the western tip of Île de la Cité, I pointed out Notre Dame Cathedral.

"Have you seen pictures of Notre Dame before?" I asked. "You must walk back here tomorrow in the daylight. I understand the stained-glass windows are beautiful with the morning sun coming through."

A slight smile broke the side of her face as she stared at the cathedral. Her hand unconsciously went to the window ledge.

The taxi turned left on Quai des Grands Augustins and we paralleled the river for a few blocks, coming closer to Notre Dame before turning right onto Boulevard Saint-Michel. Kami's eyes didn't leave the Gothic structure until it passed out of sight. I wondered what she was thinking when her attention turned back inside the car.

"I see pictures in my school but they are not like this." She was in total amazement. Kamilla Prochazka, I thought, welcome to Paris.

I explained to her Boulevard Saint-Michel was the scene of innumerable clashes between French underground and German occupation troops during WWII. The street still carried many of the scars from the fierce resistance fighting. The buildings remained pock-marked in many places where bullets from heavy arms fire chipped the concrete and stone building faces. The French never repaired the structures so the stone would always bear the reminders of their fight for freedom.

"Like my country, only..." she hesitated, summoning something that did not want to be remembered.

Kamilla must have been one or two years old during the 1956 student riots in Prague. She would have no memory of that time, but I was certain she vividly remembered the occupation and protests only a few years ago even though the Soviets had officially relinquished power back to a mostly non-communist government by 1970. The evolution was very slow and experts expected the passing of many years before fully democratic elections could occur. The Czech revolt had been called the Velvet Revolution by the western press, but for those who had lived through the overthrow, it was anything but a soft, fuzzy transition.

Off Rue des Ecoles lay a block of student flats that reminded me of walk-up brownstones in New York. We stopped at the third building after the taxi turned left onto Rue Laplace. I passed the fare to the front and the driver accepted it over his shoulder with a curt "merci." A pair of reading glasses perched on his nose as he began writing the destination in his log book. I handed him another twenty francs. He glanced at the money, then scratched out the address he was writing and wrote another somewhere in the 10th Arrondissement, several miles closer to the train station.

"Merci beaucoup," I said, as he took the bill and shoved it in his money pouch.

Standing on the sidewalk, Kami peered up at the building, then at the paper in her hand and back at the building. She took a deep breath. For a moment, I thought we were at the wrong address. Behind us, the taxi accelerated away, and she turned to me, surprised.

"Don't worry. I'll walk from here. My hotel isn't far." I waved vaguely in the direction of the Sorbonne.

"Thank you," she said, "for things you do." I nodded and hoisted my backpack to go. "Will I see you sometime?" she asked.

"If you're not too busy with your revolution, I may stop by for dinner soon."

She stayed fixed on the sidewalk until I disappeared around the corner. From the shadows, I watched as she reluctantly mounted the steps and rang the buzzer. Within a few seconds, the door opened and an older woman stepped out and kissed Kami on both cheeks. She said something then took the girl's hand and pulled her inside. I waited, hoping there would be no problem that would send her back out on the streets.

Walking west along Rue Descartes, I stumbled upon a well-hidden bed-and-breakfast offering only four rooms. I almost missed it. Lost in thought, I was reveling in my impromptu plan of using Kamilla Prochazka as my lover to make myself a little less noticeable. If a tracker was searching for a single college student at Gare du Nord, I hoped the ruse had fooled him. I was delighted that a bit of Zita had rubbed off on me.

Hotel Villa d'Estrees Paris was an old converted estate house, squeezed in between a row of stone-faced walk-ups. Unusual for this neighborhood, there was a small manicured lawn that covered a razor-thin side yard. A new wrought-iron fence with a push-to gate offered a small amount of privacy without hindering the building's charm. Dutch lace curtains hung on freshly painted windows and plant boxes with blooming flowers adorned both sides of the door. A porch lamp glowed dimly in the evening light, signifying there was a vacancy.

The proprietress gave me a room on the top floor, where the ceiling angled down with the roofline. There was a partial view of the backyard, and a large skylight made the room feel open and airy. A single bed was pushed against the opposite wall and a desk stood next to the door. From the Spartan décor, I knew I was in a student's room.

I stretched out on the bed without switching on the light. It was only eight o'clock, but it felt like two in the morning. I needed to go downstairs for a shower but I thought I might close my eyes for a few seconds. My breathing relaxed, quickly settling into a deep rhythm. The room was warm, and I drifted off.

Sometime during the night, I woke softly from a foggy dream. My eyes opened, and I found myself staring at the ceiling like something up there mattered. When I finally rolled my head toward the window, the shadow of a wispy figure was fluttering in the dim light. I blinked instinctively a few times to clear my head, though I knew it wouldn't make a difference. She was sitting in her coffin midway between the bed and the window.

"I knew you would come back to Paris," she said, still not quite focusing on me.

"I have this thing about justice and playing by the rules."

"Do you? No one else cares. Why should you?"

"That's my dilemma, isn't it?" I smiled, thinking about the irony. "I admit having no rules is more fun. Yet, here I am always trying to fix things. Make everything right, somehow equal and fair. But honestly, I don't know the difference between right and wrong anymore? Everything's messed up. I feel like I'm being tested, ya know? Is this my chance to choose a side? Because I could go either way right now."

"You need to find out who you are. What you are, deep down. Then you will know."

"I'm not sure I will know until I'm sitting safely beside you." My voice came out small. "I guess I just want to make a difference to one person."

She wiped at the blood on her face and waved her hand in nearly the same motion. The movement made me feel like my compassion was not needed or wanted and, at any rate, it was a trite offering. I never felt so disregarded, though I knew she didn't mean the gesture to be callous. The memory of that feeling did not pass for many years.

"This man is psychotic, a danger to others. I need to understand how he thinks then I can find him before he does this to anyone again," I said, trying to change the subject from me.

"And you believe I know how he thinks?" she asked.

"Yes."

"Well I do not," she said. "I'm happy that you have returned to Paris but I am also frightened for you."

"I'll be fine. I have you to help me," I said, as the smile faded from her face.

"He is cruel and unpredictable. I cannot help you with that."

"Can you just tell me where he is?"

"I do not know in terms of time and space, but your paths are destined to cross."

"What do you mean?"

"You will soon see. I cannot say more."

The girl gradually faded like an image on an old television picture tube. Her body turned gray, then milky and finally transparent as black took over the room. I replayed the conversation, trying to understand what she meant, but I had no clue. I never had a clue.

There wasn't a thing I could use to find my way except what

was in Le Roux's wallet; a few addresses and a single picture of a beautiful woman. Tomorrow, I would start there.

CHAPTER 23

"The courier was holding out for more money," said the Spaniard.

"You should have slit his throat on the spot."

"We saw the American arrive in Marseilles on his way here and it spooked him. So for fun, I told him if he popped the kid I'd give him what he wanted," he said with a smile. "I even supplied the gun. It would've been worth it."

"The American's coming to Paris? You didn't think that was important enough to tell me? When were you going to say something?" Calming himself, he said, "The little bastard is persistent, and resourceful. I'll give him that."

"Well, I thought we might get lucky. They could have killed each other." The words came out reflexively before the Spaniard could stop himself.

"I told you to leave the kid alone. He might kill you before we're done here, and if he doesn't I might. Either way, you'll get what you deserve. I'll take care of him when I can take care of him. He's been nothing but a distraction so far and I need to refocus on business. I want those schematics and I don't have time for any more games, yours, his, or Le Roux's."

"I have them, and Le Roux's dead," he assured the man with gray eyes.

"That's not good enough!" The man was suddenly furious. "Send the man from Reims. I want him erased from the planet. I want his house burned. I want his property sold to African immigrants. I want his ancestors dug up. I want his kids ground into sausage. I want everyone he ever knew slaughtered."

"Yes sir," he said after a long silence. "I'll take care of it."

"And spread the word. Nobody robs me."

CHAPTER 24

By nine o'clock the next morning, I was standing in front of Jean Le Roux's apartment building in the 8th Arrondissement. It was a short walk from the Saint-Phillipe-du-Roule Metro stop, two blocks north of Av. Des Champs-Élysées. The Rue d' Artois address was a refurbished industrial complex recently converted into upscale loft accommodations above a row of storefronts. The building's brick had been sand-blasted to reveal its original rustic color and style, throwing the block back in time a hundred years.

I crossed the street between the last of the rush hour traffic and pushed through a glass entryway between a music store and a jewelry boutique. There were two mailboxes in the small foyer, one for Le Roux's apartment on the first landing and one for the floor above. I pressed the top buzzer, prepared to explain it was Jean and I had locked myself out again. My breath rattled in the dead air. I waited without an answer.

I examined the security door as I reached into my coat pocket and extracted the lock tools. Dropping to one knee, I inserted two picks and started humming Elton John's new song "Daniel," while I played with the tumblers. The song had debuted on the radio that morning and I couldn't get it out of my head. It was about a guy's brother who went to Spain. I wasn't sure why. Either I missed the reason or Elton didn't say. I had been to Spain too, and the last time hadn't turned out so well. I was hoping France might be better as the mechanism released and the knob turned.

Le Roux's apartment door was steel with a single lock in the handle. No deadbolts. It amazed me how people equated a metal barrier with increased security. Europeans would have a difficult time feigning safety in the States behind a door like this. Five Chicago cockroaches can pick a similar lock in twenty seconds. One good-sized New York rat can eat his way through in less than three minutes. It took me somewhere in between to open the door.

The apartment was laid out as one large—no, one really large—room, and I immediately saw I was alone. As I watched translucent ribbons of sunlight stream in the undressed windows and dance with submissive shadows on the hardwood floors, I found myself wishing there had been a divider or two to add a little suspense.

The toilet and shower were open all around. A pseudo kitchen stood against the far wall and a living room ensemble arranged in a three-sided square was near the center of the 3,000-square-meter floor. I had never seen a loft apartment before. I wondered if this was the style or if Le Roux had spent all of his money on the purchase price and there was nothing left for either privacy or furniture.

The sofa was a pull-out. I extended the bed to search between the mattress and the spring mesh. I wasn't sure what I might find. A slip of paper with Chaban's name and address would have been nice. But there wasn't a thing of consequence, so I put everything back together and walked the parameter of the room looking for hiding places, loose floorboards or slots cut in the wall.

An open rack serving as a closet stood near the bathroom. I swished the clothes back and forth, then pushed them together with both hands, listening for the crinkling of paper. Moving each garment separately, I felt for heavy objects. A small cedar dresser rendered the same result. Nothing.

I moved on to the kitchenette. The appliances were immaculate, and I was beginning to think Le Roux hadn't fully moved in yet. Plates, saucers, cups and glasses were all put away neatly in separate see-through, head-high cabinets. I climbed on the sink to get a better view. The china was evenly spaced and the shelves were spotless. There wasn't a trace of lint from a drying towel, no fingerprint smudges and not one speck of bug matter anywhere. I jumped down and grabbed the dish towel from the oven handle to wipe the shiny surfaces I had touched.

After hanging and readjusting the towel, I opened the oven door on a whim. Inside the tiny bay were two cast-iron skillets. I carefully examined each, but in the end they were exactly what they seemed to be. As I replaced the pans on the rack, my eyes drifted to the roof of the small enclosure. A manila envelope was taped to the top. Inside were passports providing three new identities for Le Roux. There was also a list of six telephone numbers and a set of initials beside each.

I tamped down the envelope and put it in an inside coat pocket. Slowly turning in a full circle, trying to determine if it was worth a more comprehensive search, I decided to let it go. If we needed a closer inspection, MI6 could come back for a professional toss.

Listening briefly at the door, I was on the stairs halfway to the ground floor before realizing I hadn't relocked the apartment. Breaking stride for a half-second, I decided it didn't matter much to anyone except Le Roux and I figured he wasn't going to be too upset. He had a bigger problem at the moment.

I pushed back through the outside door and walked north along Rue d' Artois in the same direction as traffic, toward the center of the business district. I turned onto Rue de Berri. The morning chill had burned off and I was sweating in my long coat. I should have left it back in the room. My thin sweater was more than enough for the afternoon. I needed to find a cool, quiet place to examine the phone numbers I'd found.

A sudden explosion rocked the ground. The noise echoed from everywhere through the urban canyons. My ears were ringing, and I was back in Spain. People were running. I stepped against the building to get out of the way. Where was the blast? Were these idiots rushing toward the explosion or away from it? I couldn't tell. Wait. An acrid smell mixed with the wind. There, to the left. Panicked people were scattering behind me. Dammit, it was Rue d' Artois.

Walking against the flow of pedestrian traffic was difficult and hurrying became a lost cause. I weaved a serpentine path through the maze and eventually turned the corner back onto Rue d' Artois. Smoke was billowing from the roofline about mid-block on the same side as Le Roux's apartment.

Son of a bitch! Don't people shoot each other anymore?

The windows of his loft were blown out and flames were leaping up beyond the next floor. Fire had already reached the roof. Part of the brick facing crumbled from the force of the blast and I thought the building might collapse. Le Roux was having a bad couple of days.

The familiar sound of emergency vehicles drifted across the crowd. Wheee ooooo wheee ooooo wheee ooooo. The Prefecture of Police arrived first with a team of men. They formed a wedge and cleared a path through the throngs of onlookers, but people merely closed in behind them again as they moved along the street.

Fire trucks crept forward into the crowd. The curious onlookers paid no attention until the lead truck bumped some of them. Unwillingly, the ranks parted and finally gave way. A hook and ladder moved in as close as it dared. The extension rose and two firemen heroically jumped on for the ride. One dragged a hose up with him as both men climbed to the top. The first fireman disappeared on the roof and the second shouted for water.

I felt someone approach from behind. The person stood very close to my right shoulder and didn't make a sound for a disturbingly long time. Getting annoyed, I thought a spectator was crowding in for a better view. A Parisian's personal space bubble was only slightly greater than that of the Japanese. It wasn't much of a bubble, actually; more like a thin film of oil to which a surrounding flat slice of air might cling.

"Hello darling."

I spun quickly.

"Zita! Jesus, you scared the crap out of me! How did you find me?"

Stepping around front, she gave me a kiss with her eyes closed and smiled again before reopening them.

"You are about as hard to find as a Frenchman in Paris, my dear. I look for trouble and I know you aren't far away."

She gazed up at the burning building.

"Is this your doing, love?" She asked.

"Not exactly," I said.

She eyed me curiously.

"And specifically how 'not exactly'?"

"I wasn't anywhere near here," I protested.

"Down the block?"

"Around the corner." I admitted.

"Am I going to want to hear this?"

"Probably not."

"Is anyone dead?"

"Not today." I couldn't look at her directly.

"Well, that's certainly an improvement."

CHAPTER 25

We sat at a sidewalk table outside a coffee shop on Rue Balzac. Although Zita and I were less than a hundred meters from Av. Des Champs-Élysées, traffic was unusually light heading away from the normally busy street. The commotion from the explosion and fire had dissipated, even though the smell of smoke still lingered above the fumes of the city. Zita sipped a cup of Earl Grey and I opted for a mug of stiff coffee from some former colony in French Africa. We shared a plate of orange-poached pears.

When the dessert was gone except for the remains of the light orange sauce, I leaned both elbows on the tabletop and waited. Her attention was focused on a couple, locked arm in arm, slowly meandering along the sidewalk. I watched her as she drank her tea. Zita was a very proper young lady, holding her teacup daintily gripped in one delicate hand while the other rested palm up in her lap. She looked at me over the rim of the cup.

"What is your connection to the exploding building, then?" She asked. All I could do was blankly stare at her.

I opened my mouth several times to speak but stopped as my mind raced backward over the past few days to find the right place to begin. In retrospect, I should have started the story when we parted in Pamplona. I put another packet of sugar in my coffee to cut the bite of the African bush which still lingered after the grinding process. Zita waited patiently.

"The man who used to live on the first floor there took a shot at me in Marseilles. He followed me onto the Paris train."

"Where is he now?"

"I found him dead in his compartment so I put him off somewhere on the other side of Rennes."

"Found him dead or made him dead?"

"Found," I said. "I thought I lost him in Marseilles."

"That I believe," she said. "Who was he?"

"I'm not sure, exactly. Jean Le Roux is the name on his driver's license. There's not much else to go on. I don't know who he was, what he wanted, why he tried to kill me or how he fits with Chaban, if he does at all. He didn't act like CIA though I wouldn't put it past them to assign a rookie to pop me for the experience. He was uncomfortable, like he'd never fired a weapon before. It turned out, thankfully, he hadn't. He aimed for my head but the kick took the bullet high."

"Well, darling, if you made him, he was strictly an amateur," Zita finally said.

"Oh, that's funny." Trying to change the subject, I said, "I found a telephone list and a few passports in his apartment."

"I'm just having a bit of fun. Don't be cross. You know I'd accompany you through the gates of Hades and right out the other side. That's mostly because you're so easy to follow," she smiled. Zita loved to remind me of my knack for dropping bread crumbs, so any half-blind Hansel and Gretel would have little trouble seeing in which direction I went. "Besides, we have to get you out of this mess into which you have inserted yourself. Let's see the phone numbers. I'll have our gents trace them."

"There are country codes from France, Germany, Belgium, Spain and Italy. This one might be Czechoslovakia?"

"It's Poland," Zita corrected.

"My first thought is they're clean numbers, places he can turn when he needs safe passage from wherever he might be stranded."

She glanced through the passports. "These are new, never used. We'll run them as well. I'll pass the lot to someone who can help."

Zita folded the paper twice. She slid the numbers and passports into a fitted jacket pocket.

"In the meantime, let's pay this lady a visit," I said.

I handed over the photograph of the blonde woman from the dead man's wallet. Zita scrutinized the woman's features. Finally, she turned it over and read the address.

"And you got this how?"

"It was in Le Roux's pocket."

I turned toward the waiter to get the bill. He was inside chatting with a customer, in no real rush to get back to his job. I managed to get his attention by waving and he was none too pleased seeing the demanding foreigner. Americans were all impatient and refused to slow down even on holiday. Striding to the table with an arrogance only a French waiter can muster, he asked, "Oui, Monsieur?"

"L'addition."

The waiter examined the empty dishes and pulled his ticket book from a side pocket. Counting to himself with some internal calculation, the man wrote a single figure on the ticket and waited while I fished thirty francs from my jeans. The waiter walked away with the money held out in front of his chest to avoid my odor.

A faint smoke cloud still hung in the sky over Le Roux's building as Zita and I strolled along Rue Balzac toward the George V underground stop a block south on Av. Des Champs Élysées. The last of the water runoff followed us downhill until the gutter took an outward turn just before we descended the empty stairs into a dimly lit metro lobby. I disturbed a lonely clerk for a pair of tickets.

On the first landing down to the trains, a student was playing an acoustic guitar. Singing the old American country-western ballad Stand by Your Man, his voice was twangy and a bit too loud for the confined space of the passage. As we stepped around the open guitar case, I noticed a nice pile of coins and notes scattered across the bottom. Though the sound was mildly irritating for a number of reasons, singing in the subway seemed to be fairly lucrative.

We came out of the Metro at Notre-Dame des-Champs in the heart of the Left Bank. The buds on the park trees were already sprouting, and the grass was flecked with shades of yellow and light green even though it was still January. It had been a mild winter across much of northern Europe and there had been no snow all season in Paris. Temperatures had averaged 10oC for the previous few months, which was unusually mild for the upper valleys of France. As a result, cities as far north as Amsterdam were expecting an early spring.

Thinking about it, I don't remember ever seeing snow in Paris. It must have snowed or at least flurried sometime, but for the life of me, I couldn't recall when. Some places were like that. Always perfect weather, no matter what. When I was there, no rain fell in London, no smog settled in the valleys of California, no hurricanes destroyed the islands and no snow blanketed Paris. I hadn't spent a bad day in any of these places. Always perfect weather.

"Did you research the neighborhood or this woman?" Zita asked.

"I don't do research. I act on impulse," I answered.

"If I thought you were serious, I'd shoot you right here."

She peered at me without a smile. After all this time, it was still difficult for me to understand British humor. Was Zita being funny or was she serious? Either way, I decided not to turn my back on her for a few days.

"She lives about half way down a block of flats," I said. "Top floor. No security. No back exit but there's roof access which will get us as far as the next street over if we need it. There isn't much traffic but enough to mention. A few dog walkers, a couple of kids.

"We should act like we belong as we approach since the neighbors seemed fairly nosey. Early this morning, two old men were already out playing dominos on the stairs a few buildings down from the one we want. They eyed me carefully. It's Saturday so there may be more people wandering about this afternoon. How was that?"

She eyed me seriously. I decided the shooting reference was famous British humor, known everywhere in the world but understood in few circles away from the old commonwealth. I decided I'd still keep her in front of me for a while anyway.

Rue Madame cut through a quiet neighborhood a block west of the Luxembourg Gardens. During his early days in Paris, Hemingway frequented le Jardins du Luxembourg, often spending many afternoon hours simply admiring its beauty. It was purported that he regularly wandered the park around the Medici Fountain in leaner times, pushing a baby carriage. While no one was paying attention, he would grab and strangle a pigeon, tossing it inside as he strolled. Though a pigeon wasn't as big or as tender as a chicken, this illegal act no doubt added a tasty main course to a meager dinner table.

We entered Rue Madame at the far end, walking hand in hand like lovers out for a breath of fresh air. For a weekend afternoon, the neighborhood was unexpectedly empty. The activity I saw earlier had vanished. There was not a single pedestrian, child or dog on the street. Even the old men playing dominos had retired inside for softer seats and a nap. I checked the time. It was almost one o'clock, the traditional start of lunch in Paris, but it didn't explain the ghost town we encountered. It was eerie.

We climbed the steps of the woman's building and entered the public foyer.

"One man's sitting in his car reading a newspaper," Zita said.

"There's another standing in a doorway," I added. "We have about two minutes before they follow us in."

"I'll keep the stairs clear to give you perhaps another minute, love. We'll need to exit via the roof. The front door's no longer an option."

CHAPTER 26

We sprinted up the stairs surrounding an ancient steel-framed elevator. Zita pulled a West German Heckler and Koch P9 from a small handbag and checked the magazine. I heard the cocking mechanism lock in place.

"Do you have one of those for me?" I asked, still a little breathless.

"Sorry, darling, you're on your own with Madame Butterfly there. Let's hope she was trained as a lady and went to charm school. If she has a pistol in her hand, she's not going to be happy to see you. You now have two and a half minutes."

"Right," I agreed.

I was inside the apartment in seconds. The living room was open and alluring, with the early afternoon sun beaming through large west-facing windows. The décor and furniture reflected a definite woman's touch. The apartment was furnished in classic Louis XIV and there was an original oil painting or two on the walls. A lingering hint of perfume hung in the air but there was no sign of the woman.

I knocked on the wall to announce myself and cautiously moved toward the bedroom.

"Mademoiselle, je suis de l'entretien de batiment," I said, acting like I was the janitor on an emergency call. No answer came. There was only the hollow silence that echoed my voice back through the short hall. "Mademoiselle?" I called a little louder.

I walked past the bathroom and glanced in. The tile in the shower was dry, and the sink was as tidy as a third-grader's school desk. A cupboard stood partially open where extra towels and linens were stacked neatly on three shelves.

I stepped into the bedroom. An immaculately made double bed jutted from the middle of the far wall. There was a small writing table to one side and an ornate clothes armoire beside me with several pairs of high heels tucked beneath it.

At the glass doors opening onto a petite balcony, I peered through the transparent drapes. The street was empty. The men watching this building were already inside. I was running out of time.

I turned back to the room and was struck by how neat and polished the surfaces looked. The apartment was more like a hotel suite than a place one might live. The homey touches and personal items one might expect were missing. There wasn't a comfortable chair. There wasn't a framed photograph, television, radio, stack of magazines, book or notepad, and the wastebasket was empty and clean.

Lifting the latch on the armoire, I found a rack of hanging clothes. I brushed the mostly nighties and lacey underwear from side to side. I checked under the bed, between the mattresses and finally rummaged through the desk drawers. Nothing. I was surprised there wasn't a Gideon's Bible open on the pillow.

A shot exploded in the hallway. I ran back to the front where Zita was positioned in a shooter's stance, half in and half out of the apartment door.

"Behind me, upstairs now!" she shouted.

I raced toward the roof access. Heavy footsteps were pounding up the stairs. Sensing Zita right behind me, I crashed through the door into brilliant, blinding sunlight. My vision was still adjusting to the stark afternoon when I heard another report

153

from a handgun. Panic jolted my system and I recognized the edge of the roof just before I ran off into the air.

I headed north toward the next building where there was a low roof divider. We hurdled it without slowing, but the second was much taller with broken glass cemented to its rim. I hit the top of the ledge with a glancing roll, letting my body absorb the impact. The thickness of my coat cushioned the rotation across the ledge, smashing down the big shards as I went over. I landed on all fours as a pair of legs sailed over my head. A little taller than me with the very long, lean legs of an athlete, Zita vaulted the barrier and me in one stride.

I caught her as she reached the end and found the fire escape. She risked a quick peek over the side to see what was waiting for us. Zita threw a leg over the side and I heard metal clang under her shoes as her head vanished from view. I was right behind her.

Popping up to see where the gunmen were, I was surprised to see a lone overweight man stopped halfway across the rooftops. He had given up the chase and was leaning on a roof barrier, trying desperately to catch his breath.

"One's on the ground," I yelled.

Zita picked up the pace on her descent. She hit the ground with a spring in her legs and crouched in a firing position until I also jumped free.

"This way," I said.

As I sprinted around the corner, the second assassin stepped from the shadows of the alley and we collided hard. The man's chin clipped my head at the hairline and we both went down. He lost his grip on the weapon. As he tried to shake off the stunned feeling, Zita delivered a crushing blow to the left kidney. He went limp.

"Damn it! That hurt!" I winced, holding a hand against the huge welt rising on my head.

"I think it hurt him worse," Zita said. "Help me get him into the alley before we have company."

"Thanks for the compassion. I'm going to have a headache for a week."

"Guinness is on me tonight. That'll put the Mickey in you and you'll forget all about your poor head."

We each grabbed an arm and dragged the unconscious man thirty meters down the alley. Each step increased the pounding in my head. We dropped him behind a dumpster and I kicked his legs out of sight. It hurt too much to bend over. I hoped he'd understand. With the makings of a knot on my scalp the size and texture of a peach pit, there wasn't any way I could hold my head that it didn't hurt and my right eye was not focusing very well.

"Wait. I know this clown!" I said. "He was in Spain last month but I can't think where. Do you have any aspirin?"

"Do I look like a bloody chemist?" she asked, glancing down the alley to the street. "Turn around. I'm happy to rearrange a kidney like your friend here if it'll quiet you down."

"If I knew you wouldn't leave me with him, I'd say 'go ahead'."

"I may do it anyway if you don't stop wasting time we don't have. Stop complaining." Zita looked back down the alley again. "Where did you see him?"

"It was Madrid, near Blanco," I said. "He and a woman were in the courtyard where Blanco landed." I opened my eyes wide to clear my vision. "Does he have ID?"

Zita was already rifling the man's pockets. She tossed a wad of folded French francs on the ground, along with car keys and a wallet. I pulled out his driver's license and read the name before shoving the whole thing into a slit in my coat lining.

"Can you wake him?" I asked.

She shook his coat lapels without reaction. Dragging his

dead weight halfway up and leaning him against the alley wall, she slapped him twice on the left cheek and once on the other.

"Is he dead?" I asked.

"No, but he does have a ruptured kidney. He's having a bit of trouble breathing and he's wet himself. Blood has seeped through his pants at the crotch."

"So, he'll wish he was dead when he wakes up."

"I'm afraid so, my dear." She slapped him again, and he slowly regained consciousness. I leaned over him no more than a finger's length from his nose.

"Monsieur Shaller, do you speak English?" I looked at Zita. "Christ, I don't think he can hear me."

"Qu'as-tu fait de moi?" His words were barely audible and his eyes remained closed.

"Rien. I haven't done anything to you but you're very sick. Vous êtes très malade. Vous pouvez mourir. You've lost a kidney and there's nothing else we can do for you. I've sent for a priest. Do you want to confess?"

"Non, ma vie est terminée." He was struggling to speak.

"Great, I envy you. Your life's complete, but you don't want to take so many others to the grave with you. Innocent women and children are involved. They've done nothing to you."

"Ils sont tous en train de mourir pour ma cause," he said, through closed eyes.

"What cause?" I asked, incredulously. "Quelle cause?" He didn't answer. My frustration was growing to the boiling point. I wished the whole world could speak the same language. "Where is Chaban? Où?"

"Vous ne pouvez pas l'arrêter," he coughed. "Chaban est trop proche de la réussite."

"What?" My voice echoed in the alley. "I saw you at the Blanco bombing. What were you doing there?"

"Blanco a été un test." The man shook his head and spoke through the spasms racking his body. "Cette fois, Chaban sera célébrée. Le monde se souviendra de lui."

Now he was scaring me. The assassination of Prime Minister Blanco was already something we'd never forget, and if the truth was ever known, schoolchildren would learn how Chaban tried to single-handedly restart the Spanish Civil War. If that was a test for something bigger, then God help us if he succeeded.

"What is Chaban planning? Here in Paris? Ici, à Paris?"

"Oui, où d'autre?"

"Quand? I need a date, damn it, I need a date."

"Bientôt, et bientôt vous vous joindrez à moi." We had just run out of time.

The man bent over with severe cramping. I thought he might throw up, but he just lay there in the pall of the dumpster and slipped into unconsciousness. Zita rolled him to his back. We slowly stood, and I staggered slightly. It felt like every drop of blood in my body had rushed to the top of my head and was trying to punch its way out. The rhythmic hammering suddenly turned into the drum solo from In-A-Gadda-Da-Vida and I realized that the genesis of the song was not drugs after all, but pain.

Staying close to the wall, we made our way to the end of the alley. Zita held her weapon ready, searching the shadows for movement; a man, a woman, anything that didn't belong. Expecting to see the out-of-shape man from the roof, we were surprised that no ambush was waiting. Where was the fat man? Where was his backup? It didn't make sense.

We hurried steadily north for two blocks, then cut over to Rue de Rennes, blending with the afternoon foot traffic. We slowed our pace and followed a group of tourists off to the left toward the Saint-Sulpice Metro stop. Zita paused at the entrance to search again for the second gunman.

Settling into a nearly empty coach, Zita appraised my head. She tenderly drew her finger across the lump.

"I'm afraid you'll not live to celebrate your thirtieth birthday, Doc," she said.

"What do you think he meant when he said we can't stop Chaban now?" I asked.

"Something epic is about to happen in Paris," Zita answered, wearily.

CHAPTER 27

"Tick...tock...tick...tock. Are you there, Doc?"

Hearing her voice again brought me back from the heart of hell. Rubbing my hands across a tired face, a finger caught the bump on my head and I grimaced. I tried to rise twice before my elbows would support my weight.

Zita was in a deep sleep next to me. She was lying on her stomach and her shoulders gently moved with each breath. Her dark auburn hair had fallen across her face and she slowly brushed it back. She turned away from me, lost in her own dream.

The little girl was sitting in a chair by the window, no coffin, just a frail child wound up in a seventeenth century armchair. Moonlight from the open window spread through her translucent body, sending prisms of pale color across the room but she cast no shadow beyond the opaque illumination that lay loosely on the parquet flooring.

I had the impression the light was seeking something. It flickered on the wood designs by the bed. I felt the cold air seep under the duvet like invisible hands and grip my bare legs. I wanted to move, I wanted to hide too, but I couldn't do either.

"How do you know my nickname?" I asked.

"I know many things now," she answered, distractedly.

The girl's chin tilted up slightly. It appeared she was focused on a corner of the ceiling above my head. She was agitated, fidgeting nervously with her fingers. She continually wiped at the blood on her face. Her body was softly vibrating, like she was

159

hyperventilating, but she wasn't. My small friend hadn't breathed in ten months.

"What is it?" I asked.

"Did I tell you that I personally know Georges Pompidou, our president? He is like a grandfather to me."

"I don't believe I know anyone like that," I said. "Does it mean they have to know you personally, too?"

"He'll soon be joining me." She ignored me.

"Do you know the future?"

"Know it?" She hesitated. "No, it's more like a feeling."

"Is that what's worrying you?"

"It's his time. He's very ill."

"Then what is it?" I asked, confused.

"Do you know I disregarded my studies that day and I was on my way to visit Georges? I wanted to ask him for a new pair of shoes my papa wouldn't buy for me. Papa said I already had too many. I was very upset with him. What girl has too many shoes?" She paused. "I was cutting through the courtyard when the gunmen came. I could have walked on but I noticed the one you seek with a pistol at his side. I was curious."

The little girl stopped again and cocked her head like an obedient dog listening to her master's voice.

"He saw me following and placed an arm around me. He was nice. He told me we'd have a little party for a while, that's all. You know, hang out and have some fun. I thought this was a good way to make my father worry. Many people gathered in a large room and he gave us food and water, anything we wanted while he spoke with authorities. He let people leave when they asked. Well, I thought he let them go," The girl wiped the blood from her face.

Chaban had taken control of the British Embassy in Paris and demanded the release of six Palestinian terrorists from English

160

prisons. The consequences for refusal or delay had been swift and irreversible when he began killing hostages. To demonstrate his sincerity, Chaban had released three captives prior to the first telephone contact with negotiators.

As they had walked down the sidewalk toward safety, they were executed in full view of the television cameras. Subsequent to each unsuccessful call, three additional hostages had been killed and one freed. It hadn't taken long for Britain to acquiesce. The Palestinians had been flown to Syria and released to the wind.

After the embassy doors had opened and the remaining hostages led to freedom, the terrorists inside had surrendered, but Chaban hadn't been among them. The building and grounds had been thoroughly searched by elite forces but no trace of the man was found. He had escaped in the confusion and eagerness to shuttle the captives to safety. Walking out with the prisoners, looking rattled and exhausted, Chaban had been treated and he vanished before police could question him.

"Why are you telling me this?" I asked.

"Because it's my fault!" Her voice was raised.

I peeked at Zita. She hadn't stirred.

"What's your fault?" I asked.

"This whole mess is my fault."

I shook my head.

"You didn't cause anything and you could have stopped nothing."

"Don't argue with me! I was afraid after he killed the first people. I told him that I know Georges Pompidou and he would come to save me. It made him laugh until he realized I was serious. He demanded to have the president come to the embassy but Georges told the terrorist he wouldn't come. The man put the telephone receiver away, smiled and shot me without saying a word. I don't know what I did but it must have been very bad. He let the rest of the people free then and he went away with them."

"You didn't do anything. He's a bug-crazy nut-ball who'd kill his own mother for money. No one can predict what crazy will do."

She continued to stare at the ceiling without moving. I thought for a moment she left and it was only her heat trail I saw. Finally, she wiped at the blood again. I wanted to say so many things to her, but nothing came out as she slowly dissolved into the pallid moonlight.

I lay flat again and stared at the ceiling where the little girl had focused, thinking I might be able to see what she saw. Zita awakened a little after dawn. She rolled onto her back and rubbed her eyebrows. After taking a deep, half-yawning breath, she turned her face to mine and smiled.

"How is your head, dear?" she asked.

"Better."

"Have you been awake long?"

"A while."

We showered and dressed in silence. Zita was ready for the day before me. She had a natural beauty that needed little if any makeup and was blessed with rich, straight hair that was easy to manage. She was pulling long fingers through wet hair when I sat on the bed next to her.

"I can't avoid it any longer. I have to call home and it's not going to be pleasant."

At the window, I looked down on Boulevard Saint-Michel and watched the early morning traffic begin to back up because of an accident near the corner. The delay had incited several altercations and one full-on fist fight. As much fun as it was to curiously voyeur other people's problems, I had to make the call now.

"Do not tell me you're in Paris, boy," the man said, in disbelief.

"I'm in Paris," I admitted.

"Talking to you is like jerking a dead donkey uphill. The only thing saving your smart ass is that three days ago five ETA members were arrested for Blanco's assassination. You might as…"

"They didn't do it." I cut him off.

"They… How did I know you were going to say that?" he asked, in exasperation. "All right, let's have it."

"It was Chaban. You know I tracked him to Madrid. He was there when the bomb went off. Yesterday I ran into a guy here who swears on his left kidney Chaban planned and executed Blanco's assassination as a test for something much bigger in Paris."

"How reliable is this?"

"Very."

"Any idea what the bigger thing is?"

"Not yet."

"Okay," he sighed strong enough to blow smoke through the receiver. "Either way, Blanco's on ice for the moment. What do you need?"

"Some help?"

"No can do, son. The CIA is already making my skin flake off about you being in the field. I told 'em you were only doing some research and I'd bring you in as soon as I could. But if I don't hear from you again, that won't be possible if you get my meaning. And not talking will probably make both of us feel better. I know I already do just thinking about not talking to you. When you see a company agent, run. Otherwise, I don't know you. How much time do you need?"

I had no answer for him.

"Look," he sighed again. "We don't exist. You don't exist. There's nobody I can send. We aren't issued weapons. We're just a bunch of analysts. We observe and we learn. That's all."

The telephone line crackled in the silence between us. I had nothing to say.

"Fine, keep your head down and your ass behind you, kid. If your ego gets shot off, well, you can probably survive without that but I have to tell you, it wouldn't be the same. Frankly, you've already lasted longer than I thought you would. Just find out what Chaban is doing. A target, a date and we'll turn it over to Interpol or MI6. Call me when you have it done. Don't call me if you're dead. Godspeed."

The line went dead. Still holding the handset to my ear, I gazed across the room.

Nice, I thought, real nice. Does the saying 'come back with your shield or on it, I'll await your return in Sparta' mean anything to you? I was on my own, with nothing but a handkerchief for armor and my balls for ammunition. I should have asked for a bottle of raw ether, a prostitute, and a knife in the heart. Death would have been quicker.

In the end though, I knew he was right. The NSA couldn't admit to sanctioned operatives in the field since the agency's work was limited to the capture and analysis of communications, not human intelligence. That would have been in direct conflict with other security organizations like the CIA and FBI. So, if an NSA field agent somehow did exist, he would be forced to Never Say Anything.

In my case, I was off the books, picking up cash at American Express whenever I needed it. Effectively, I was simply a tourist whose prime mission was to explore Europe's underbelly on the government's tab. If I happened to observe an illegal act against my country, I would have no alternative but to report it as my patriotic duty.

I replaced the receiver in its cradle. Zita was watching me, smiling.

"I don't want to know about that conversation, do I?"

"It's better that you don't know the details, I guess." I answered. "The bottom line is I'm cleared to find him."

"It's good to have you with us, officially," she smiled. "We Brits aren't so bad in a pinch."

I had to smile too.

"I've pinched a Brit from time to time," I agreed.

"Right, how shall we play this since you're a step ahead of us?"

"Let's find Bobby."

CHAPTER 28

Bobby was an American expatriate living in Paris and he was, without a doubt, the most enterprising and accomplished panhandler I'd ever met. I had once witnessed him, armed with only a wheelchair and a homeless sign, approach a young military captain in full-dress uniform. Within a short time, Bobby had the young Frenchman convinced the down-on-his-luck vet had commanded the final French unit to leave Vietnam two years earlier.

A stray Communist bullet had shattered his spine during evacuation, as he had ensured the last of his wounded men were securely on board the chopper. Returning home, he hadn't been able to find a job because of the disability. Bobby had rolled away with four crisp 100 franc notes even though France had not seen action in Vietnam since April of 1956 when the grifter was only eight years old.

Having lived on the streets for most of his time here, Bobby knew the city better than the best taxi driver. He knew where to be, what to do when he got there and how long to safely stay doing what he came to do. The man didn't have his finger on the pulse of Paris; he gave it life. Six years into a one-year experiment to take Europe by storm, Bobby ran comfortably with fringe members of society who made the rest of us very uncomfortable. The feral network that absorbed him outpaced Ma Bell as the best communication link going. Bobby was a part of the unseen soul that observed, studied and learned to live off this collectivism we call civilization.

If Bobby didn't know about it, then it had never happened, nor would it ever happen in Paris. But finding him was always a problem. Bobby was everywhere in the city and he was nowhere. He was pure granite in the face of every defenseless victim and when he needed to be invisible, he was Windex-clean glass.

We spent the morning putting word on the pavement that I needed to talk to Bobby. Hitting the typical tourist attractions frequented by panhandlers, pimps, prostitutes, parasites, grifters and gangs of children, Zita and I talked to too many of these migratory workers with the same result. No one knew Bobby or exactly how to get in touch with such a person. But slightly before noon, a small, balding man well under five feet pulled me from the crowds accumulating around the base of the Eiffel Tower and offered to read his tarot cards to help give my immediate future some meaning.

I turned over the gypsy's fee, and he turned over the cards. The small man laid out seven cards in a V-shape turning each face up; the Moon, the Magician, the Five of Cups, the reversed Queen of Cups, the Eight of Wands, the Four of Pentacles and Death. He slowly moved his fingers over the cards as he studied them in great detail. The diminutive gypsy's hand went to his chin and he thoughtfully rubbed the stubble between his thumb and forefinger. It was quite a show.

"Mmmm. This is interesting," he said, perusing the figures on the mystical cards.

"What is?" I asked, playing the game.

"I see you will be in Montmartre this afternoon near the base of the Basilica. Monsieur, do you have an appointment today at Sacre Coeur?"

"No."

"Well, the cards never lie. I suggest you be there at 1:30 p.m.

The Magician you seek can be found near the steps." Without warning, the little man jerked upright, grabbing my wrist at the same time. "Sir, there is more. You'll need to know this. The other is the message but this is what the cards truly tell me." Our eyes locked.

"Okay," I said. He released my arm and slowly turned back to the cards. Only then did our eyes separate.

"I see an unknown man, lost and alone in the Five of Cups. He has wandered into an unfamiliar world of secrets and lies. Much is hidden from him by Death's black cloak. Though Death is all around this man, he is not Death's chosen. If he wants to know where the secrets are hidden, we must ask the cards close to Death.

"Death is at the bottom of the V so that means the cards just above it; the Four of Pentacles here and the Moon here. The Four of Pentacles represents the truth he seeks but the Moon creates deception and confusion for him. The Eight of Wands over the Moon carries news of an important event but this information is in opposition to the man's success. Be very careful. Our Magician may provide the direction, but, the unknown man's destiny lies with Death."

"And the Queen?" I asked, pointing to the top on the left side.

"The Queen is an illusion who hovers above the unknown man. She is watchful but no match for his monsters."

I thanked the little gypsy with another token of appreciation and rejoined Zita, who was mesmerized by a tattoo-laden street performer. He was juggling fire and using parts of his body, including the tongue, to transfer a flame from torch to torch. I noticed two girls pushing their way through the captivated audience.

"Qu'est-ce qui arrive ici?" asked one girl, straining to see.

"Juste un autre gars mangeant le feu," answered her friend. I smiled and repeated her answer to myself. It's just another guy eating fire, as if it were an everyday occurrence in Paris.

"I hate to spoil your amusement," I whispered in Zita's ear. "But I've found Bobby."

"Wait a bit. One doesn't see this sort of thing every day," she protested.

"Apparently, one does."

I took her hand and gently pulled her away.

We grabbed a light lunch at an outdoor café which afforded one of the many world-famous views overlooking the Tower. Zita picked at crêpes filled with cherries simmered in a Kijafa wine sauce while I told her of my exchange with the bantamweight fortune teller. She sipped at the Campari and orange in front of her.

"He will be at Sacre Coeur, then?" she asked.

"He'll be somewhere close to there," I answered.

I cut into my own peanut butter, banana and honey crêpes and forked a huge bite into my mouth.

"I hope your man can tell us something we don't know."

I swallowed hard and put my utensils down. I hope he can too, I thought.

My attention drifted toward the ticket concession tucked under one leg of Gustave Eiffel's creation. Across the expanse of grass, perhaps twelve hundred people were queued in a snaking line running away from the entrance. Tourists were waiting along a cinder path for an opportunity to ascend to the top and experience their own moment of awe.

"If we don't get onto him soon," I said, "my fear is that he'll succeed in murdering thousands this time and again vanish in the wind. Before that happens, I want to get so close to him I can smell toothpaste when he breathes."

I squinted at the iron lady once more. The Eiffel Tower had originally been built as the gateway centerpiece for the 1889 World's Fair. Since then, its familiar light-brown likeness had become one of the most recognizable images in the world. In its time, this Tower was the tallest man-made structure on earth and today still remained the tallest in Europe. I understood it was the most visited, paid monument anywhere. Millions of tourists each year either climb the stairs or ride the lift to take in the beauty of Paris.

"I know what it is." Zita turned to me curiously. Without returning her gaze, I asked no one in particular, "How many people do you imagine are on or around that tower at any given time? I would estimate two thousand in the winter and potentially three times that many as the weather grows warmer."

My eyes didn't leave the Tower. I was trying to imagine the damage a hundred kilos of explosives would cause on a busy spring afternoon. Thousands would be killed and injured. If Eiffel fell, the earth would surely tremble from its impact. Alongside math and science, our children would study the many worldwide effects created by this one act of terrorism.

"He'll want an escape plan," Zita considered what I was saying. "It'll be something foolproof, conceivably a delayed detonation. He'll want to be safe but close enough to ensure success."

"Close enough to see people die," I added.

My heart slowed and finally stopped beating all together. I felt the collapse of my own desperation and weakly watched as hopelessness filled the void. There was no longer any reason to breathe. The already dim light in my soul went dark and shrank into its own blackness. If human can think to do this to human, then a new kind of monster had crawled from our latest state-of-the-art slime and now walked beside us forevermore. The world had just changed and the innocence we thought would always live to protect our children was now dead.

CHAPTER 29

We emerged from the Metro at the Musée de Montmartre stop two blocks from Basilique du Sacre Coeur and walked against sparse traffic on a one-way avenue that doglegged to the left up an incline. Montmartre had fallen into disrepair since the artist community had dried up. The streets were now a dingy gray that seemed to soak up the sunlight, turning the brightest day into dark shadows.

We hiked up Rue du Mont Cenis past rows of small tourist shops selling unusual knickknacks for the neighborhood. The shelves of one outlet displayed hundreds of Napoleonic busts of varying sizes and likenesses, swords and antique pistols. Religious artifacts adorned another window, including wall-mounted crosses with inset clocks and the word Paris stamped beneath Christ's feet. I was betting this shop also had a crate of 2,000-year-old relics stashed under the counter for every true believer who would have otherwise left the store empty-handed.

The base of the climb to Sacre Coeur came into view as we turned onto Rue Azais. A pair of wide stone steps separated by a manicured lawn marked the start of the pilgrimage to the top. At the edge of the near walkway stood a rather unorthodox priest with long, unkempt hair and beard. The man of God was preaching to a small gathering of Basilica visitors.

"The Sacre Coeur Basilica was designed by Paul Abadie," the priest said. "Construction began in 1875 and it took almost forty years to complete. But due to the onset of World War I, it was not consecrated to the Sacred Heart of Jesus until after the war in 1919. Sacre Coeur is one of the most beautiful and sacred places to celebrate Roman Catholic catechism. It is located at the summit of butte Montmartre, the highest point in the city. From the top you may admire all of Paris in its grandeur, humbly lying at your feet. We urge you to make the pilgrimage to the basilica if you have not already done so. We also ask that you help us preserve its beauty for your children and their children. Let us pray."

Two nuns passed through the spectators in search of donations as the priest lowered his head and raised his arms.

"O Heavenly Father, bless these pilgrims who have come to visit your shrine today. I thank you for bringing your flock to us in our time of need to care for your holiest of places. Please ask each of your children to share a small token of their belief with us now so we can continue our work in your name, Christ Our Lord. Amen."

The priest slowly raised his eyes to the spectators, ensuring he was the last to end the prayer. He crossed himself.

"On behalf of Basilique du Sacre Coeur, we thank you for your guiding wisdom."

I waited for him to approach us, knowing his scam might not be fully concluded. He shook a few hands in appreciation and waited for them to leave. As the audience dispersed, Bobby saw me smiling. He conferred briefly with the nuns before joining us.

"Hola, amigo," he said, giving me a bear hug. "I heard you were in Spain. What're you doing back in my hood, which I don't care, and who's this beautiful lady, which I do care?"

"This is Zita. We're working together."

"Well, I wouldn't mind working with you too. Don't let these solemn duds fool you."

"They don't for a minute," she said.

"Ah, that's the story of my celibate life. It's the one thing I miss about my current state of affairs, you know, classy women. Once in a while, I do receive a little manna from heaven by way of one of God's servants there." Bobby pointed toward the stairs where the nuns had disappeared. "Well, they're not really nuns."

"Bobby, we need some information."

"I'll do my best, brother, for you and the lady. What do you need?"

"Chaban."

He stared at me as the smile dropped from his face.

"Heard the stories, seen the results, but I ain't never met the man and don't want to," he finally said.

"I know he's bad. I need to find him."

"Do you have a death wish, brother, cuz the guy's crazy dangerous?" Bobby was shaking his head. "If I give him up, my black ass will be grilled in beurre noisette, given a fancy French name and served with papas to fat tourists over on the Left Bank. It's goodnight, John-Boy."

"He'll never know who dropped the dime."

"Man, I've made a career out of staying away from Chaban."

"Is he in Paris?"

"Hell yes, he's here."

"What's he planning?"

Bobby sighed. His eyes darted to the left before settling back on me.

"I don't know for positive. Shit, man. I've been thinking of booking it to Italy anyway. You know, new scams to run, better-looking women...hell, I'm kind of digging this religious direction I'm heading. With all those Catholics in Rome, I'll make a killing." His face revealed a little of his pain. "I hear there are a lot of dead people coming out of this. I don't want to be one of them, you understand me?" He said.

"What do you mean?" I asked.

"Word is the man has set something heavy in motion. I don't know what it is but it's rolling hard already. And, that's more than I want to know. We hear this guy's coming and we know it's going to be bad. I back away, man. Shut my eyes and back away."

"I need a place or a date. Something."

"There's nothing, man. He's got a few wackos on board and that's all one ride can handle. It's a closed session and ain't nothing getting in or out, you know what I mean?" He hesitated and licked his dry lips. "Look Doc, I would love to help you, brother, but I don't know how I can."

"If you don't know, who does?"

"If I didn't owe you... I'll see what I can do. No promises, man." Bobby exhaled.

"Find out if his target is Eiffel or another tourist attraction. Can you do that without getting your butt in a sling?"

Bobby hesitated.

"I know a couple of cheese weasels who'd give up anything or anybody for that matter, including themselves, for fifty francs. Do me a solid, man, front me some bread." I handed him everything in my pocket, about 1,000 francs. He tucked it away in his robes without glancing at it. "I might be able to round up something for you. I'll be in touch. Peace, brother." He added with an exaggerated bow, "My lady."

Bobby crossed himself again, turned and disappeared up the steps toward Sacre Coeur.

"He knows more than he's saying," I said.

CHAPTER 30

Atop the only hill in Paris, the white, travertine stone monument loomed over its gentle slopes like sitting royalty. Those standing at the base of the dome, 237 steps above the floor of the basilica, had a magnificent view of fifty kilometers in any direction. According to Parisian folklore, one could surely see Rome if the Alps weren't in the way.

It would have been impossible to follow Bobby up one of the two long, open staircases to the summit without being seen by everyone. It was the only way up or down for pedestrians, so we slipped into a cutlery shop opposite the basilica to wait. The large storefront gave us a clear view of people leaving Sacre Coeur.

"Puis-je vous aider?" the clerk asked. He was a very tall, thin old man who tugged self-consciously on a mismatched toupee. The man removed his glasses and smoothed his mustache. Obviously more interested in me, Zita turned to the window and concentrated on the stairs across the narrow road while I distracted the shopkeeper.

"Oui," I said. "Je cherche votre couteau pliant meilleure qualité."

"Ah, you are American. Our quality knives are in the showcase here." The salesman removed several folding knives of varying sizes from beneath the glass and laid them on a thin, felt cloth open on the countertop. I took my time examining each.

"Might I suggest this one, sir?" He lifted the smallest and opened the blade in a single motion, handing it to me butt first. I reached for the knife with my left hand and the shopkeeper saw the red, crescent-shaped mark of the newly forming scar.

"Oh," he said. "You are more of an aficionado. In that case, I recommend this other." He took the knife back with a tug of his hairpiece and presented me with an alternative from under the counter.

"It is palm-sized, easily hidden from your opponent when folded and can be opened with one hand. The knife is very effective for close-in fighting. Its blade retention is excellent. This particular steel will maintain its sharpness after many uses. It will not break when thrusting and is also balanced for throwing." The salesman spread his palm out toward the tool. "This knife is Laguiole, proudly made in Thiers, in the central country of France. See, here is the distinctive bee symbol at the bolster, carried on every knife produced. And this is a numbered edition for your benefit," he added.

One of Bobby's nuns walked down the stone stairs. With deliberate actions, she casually smoothed her habit, glanced up and down the street, looked back up at Sacre Coeur, purposely turned away from us, and haltingly walked down Rue Azais. I glanced at Zita with a question on my face. She dismissed me with a shake of her head and I turned back to the shopkeeper.

"Do you accept American Express?" I asked.

"Yes, of course, with pleasure."

The man took my card and stepped to the register. I moved close to Zita and raised my eyebrows slightly.

"Decoy," she whispered. "Be patient, love."

I signed the payment slip while the clerk wiped fingerprints from the knife with a soft cloth. He held the blade to the light to be certain it was clean before closing it. Slipping my purchase in a tiny paper bag barely large enough for the knife, he handed the pouch to me but held onto it for a half-second too long. He was smiling.

"Thank you, sir. Your business is always welcome," he said. "Come back to see me here anytime."

As I joined Zita, a second nun came down the stairs and scanned the street uncertainly. When she reached the sidewalk, she turned quickly in our direction and crossed in front of the shop window.

We followed at fifty meters until the nun reached the corner. Stepping into a doorway, we watched her glance back before turning left onto Rue Chappe toward the Moulin Rouge. She gathered her habit in one hand as she disappeared.

"You stand farther back. I want to catch up a bit," Zita said. "She may have had a fair look at us together but she won't recognize me alone. People just don't pay that much attention to their surroundings."

Slipping out of my coat, I threw it around my shoulders and perched my trusty coke-bottles on my face. I crossed to the other sidewalk and lagged enough to intermittently keep Zita in sight. She moved steadily, closing the gap on the nun.

I watched a master at work. When she was forced to slow her pace, she pretended something caught her eye in a shop window. When she wanted a closer look, she closed the gap. Zita overtook the woman once and entered a lingerie boutique, while the young woman maintained a deliberate gait southward. She emerged carrying a small bag and continued her pursuit at more of a distance.

As the nun crossed an alley, she abruptly stopped and turned toward the blind corner. She took a step back in surprise and said something, pointing farther down the street. In that instant, an arm reached from the cover of the building and grabbed the woman's habit, pulling her into the shadows. A muzzle flash lit the alley and the nun collapsed on the pavement.

Zita ran with weapon drawn. I sprinted after her, catching up as she came back out of the alley and dropped to her knees over the woman. A saucer-sized blotch was spreading across the nun's upper torso. Blood had given the material a rich black luster.

"Check her pockets. Do they have pockets in these things?"

"How do I bloody know? I'm looking!" she snapped.

"Well, you talk to God more than I do," I snapped back.

"Praying is not exactly a conversation. Besides, the subject of pockets in a nun's habit never came up."

"Who would kill a nun, for Christ's sake?"

"She's not a nun," Zita was distracted. "But she's definitely dead."

"Let's go. We need to find the shooter."

"Right behind you, dear."

We raced down the alley toward Rue d'Orsel and emerged on a busy open boulevard. I hoped to spot a man hurrying away. If the shooter had a car waiting or if he even ran to the next intersection and turned off the street, he was long gone.

"Nothing," Zita said, looking to the left.

"Nothing," I started. "Wait, there!" I jerked my head in the direction of an older couple down the block who appeared flustered. The man was dusting his partner's coat as he examined her for injury.

"Pardonnez-moi, monsieur. Qu'est-il arrivé?" I asked.

"Un hippie a attaqué ma femme comme il passait."

What the hell? I thought he said a hippie punched his wife.

"Pourquoi aurait-il faire cela?"

"Elle aurait pu dire quelque chose," he said.

It turned out that she had called someone a name as he ran past and the man irritably threw a roundhouse punch that landed on the old woman's forehead, knocking her to the sidewalk.

"A qui ressemble-t-il?" Zita interrupted, bringing us back to some sanity.

"Comme lui."

"Sir, do you speak English?" I asked.

"Yes, a little. He resembled you, only not so short. Not so young," and eyeing me again, he said, "Perhaps not so blond."

Great, we were chasing a man who looked not so much like me.

"Anything else? Long hair? Short hair? Beard? What about his clothes?"

"Not so long as your hair. His coat was not so gray."

Wonderful, there's another set of revelations.

"Which way did he go?" Zita asked, urgently.

"He went there, to Rue des Martyrs." The man pointed to the west.

"Merci beaucoup," I said.

Rue des Martyrs was a major north-south, one-way avenue that intersected the Boulevard de Clichy at the end of a long block. We had an even chance of at least seeing our man before he reached the busy cross street and was gone forever in the foot traffic near the Moulin Rouge.

A northerly wind whipped at our backs, reminding us to hurry. Searching for someone not much like me certainly didn't eliminate many people, except perhaps a few teenage girls, but there he was about a hundred meters ahead of us.

I recognized the dull brown color of his coat from the alley. The killer was walking with both hands in his pockets and his shoulders were pulled up around his neck. He was nervous, unsteady on his feet. His entire body swiveled when he looked around.

On his fourth or fifth swivel check, the man spun enough to see us and he went slack. His hands came out of his pockets, but he wasn't wielding a gun. There were a few seconds' delay when the three of us were thinking about what to do.

Zita and I started to run. At full steam, we easily closed the gap to less than fifty meters. The killer hesitated a little longer. His legs instinctively carried his body several steps backward. He tried to right himself. Stumbling as he turned, he fell to his hands and knees but was up again and reaching racing speed in seconds.

His head swung back and forth, searching for a way out of his predicament. Both sides of the street were lined with gated, medieval-styled courtyards now used primarily for automobile parking. I hoped they were all closed and properly locked, but dammit, he found an opening. The man tried to change directions abruptly and hit the frame hard as he steered into the corridor. We ran up breathlessly right after the gate banged shut and wobbled back ajar.

Zita raised her weapon and braced her back against the loose door. She softly backed into it and swung the gun down in front of her as the gap grew. The passage to the courtyard was dark and smelled like a cemetery on a damp night.

The gate stuck on something when I leaned against it and wouldn't swing any wider. I pushed with more strength. It banged against an uneven cobblestone and bounced back at me. With my shoulder on the edge, I chanced a peek behind. The recess was empty except for an old, fat-tire bicycle that was hanging by the rear wheel.

Zita was almost to the courtyard, lingering in the shadows of the overhang. I joined her. We scanned the enclosure. Stone walls. No windows. The only door was padlocked. Trash cans lined the nearside blind wall. He was in the courtyard, but where? We were totally exposed once we left the safety of the overhang. I opened the blade of the knife. It was my contribution to the gunfight.

Duck-walking around toward the left, Zita focused on what

was in front of her while I protected the rear as well as I could. If the guy still had his gun, we were in trouble. My knife was useless against anything but a death run at her. I wasn't very good at throwing a knife. Not enough practice. I threw a knife once at a madman coming at me. The hilt bounced off his chest and he stopped to pick it up. He was crazy and now he had a weapon.

Zita crouched between two trash cans to check her position. She swept the courtyard. Nothing. The man had vanished. Was there another exit? She moved another meter.

The gunman was crammed back against the wall, shaking so badly I'm surprised we hadn't heard him. He was an odd-looking fellow, not much like a killer at all. Oblong eyes that were squeezed tight punctuated a drawn face. Spongy, swollen lips moved almost imperceptibly. Something in his throat made his breath erratic and shallow. Zita slowly lowered her weapon to within centimeters of the man's forehead. He didn't see or sense its presence.

"Où est votre arme?" she whispered to the man as I walked up. "Do you hear me? Your weapon, where is it?" He didn't move. "Oh, bloody hell. It's your turn. I'm too tired to deal with him."

"Regardez-moi, s'il vous plait," I said. "We only want to talk. Do you understand me?" There was no response except for the endless mumbling. I knelt next to Zita and reached for his arm. He flinched like he'd been shot but finally opened his eyes. The lids were puffy and I wasn't certain he was seeing any reality beyond those glassy slits. His nose was running and it smelled like he had thrown up on his clothes.

I lifted his wrist without resistance and shoved the coat sleeve up his arm. Son of a bitch, I thought. Needle marks created a bizarre design along the veins. I dropped the arm heavily to the ground.

"Where's the piece, man?" I was afraid to pat him down; afraid I would get stuck with a needle and end up with hepatitis or possibly hooked on whatever was killing him.

"I need some blow," the addict finally said in English.

"You need to answer me. Why did you kill the nun?"

"She wasn't no nun, man," he stammered.

"Why did you kill the girl?"

"I didn't kill nobody," he said. "The guy said all I gotta do was point her out 'cuz he didn't know her. I needed a fix, he promised me a Lady for the lady. I done stuff for him before. Figured it was okay, you know. I didn't know he was going to shoot her, man. I got scared and ran," he said, through chattering teeth.

"Who shot her? What's his name?"

"I need a hit to clear my head."

"Think. What's his name?"

"I don't know, man. I need a drink. I'm dry, I can't talk no more," he moaned.

"I need a name and you can drink yourself to death for all I care."

"He's les Espingouin, you know, Spanish. Balderón. Calderón. Something like that."

"What did he look like?"

"I don't know, man," he complained. "He's just a guy, you know?"

"Why did he shoot the woman?"

"He said they was going to talk. He had a message for her. I don't know nothing else," he whined. "I'm going to be sick."

The addict abruptly threw up with such force the vomit vaulted his curled-up knees and the splatter almost hit us. The smell was God-awful and I involuntarily moved back. I couldn't imagine what this guy put in his body along with the heroin, because that stuff didn't remind me of any food I'd ever eaten. Maybe that was good. I thought there was still hope for dinner. Zita moved in closer.

"He's not doing very well," she said.

"Shoot him and let's go."

"Whoa!" The addict came alive, pumping both hands repeatedly in the air. "I didn't do nothing!"

"Come on, Zita. We can't get anything out of him until he dries out or we give him the blow."

"I'll be along directly," Zita said.

I walked back to the sidewalk and took my first deep breath since entering the courtyard. The chill in the air stung my throat, but I didn't care. I couldn't get enough oxygen in my lungs.

My faintness rapidly turned to anger. I was suddenly furious that we'd chased the wrong guy while this Spaniard quietly strolled the other way. Dammit to hell! He knew we were watching the nun, and he was watching us. The bastard shot her on purpose, so we'd chase this junkie.

A gunshot boomed behind me as loud as I had ever heard. I turned as Zita came through the gate.

"Did you kill him?"

"No, but I did scare the life out of him. I told him if he's lying, I'd come back with my 9mm lady and personally shoot him up. I fired into a rubbish bin to emphasize my point. He'll be daft and deaf for a time, instead of just daft."

CHAPTER 31

We spent the first part of the evening calling hotels on the Left Bank where the Spanish were known to stay. Standing inside the entrance of a public telephone café, I discreetly relieved a neighborhood directory of its hotel listings while Zita paid the 24 franc fee for a quarter-hour local dialing privileges at two telephones. We settled into adjoining stalls separated by a narrow pane. I handed Zita half the directory pages and spread the remaining pages on the tiny platform below my handset.

We began to dial. I inquired about a registered guest named Calderón and Zita requested Monsieur Balderón. Each penciled 'X' across a hotel name brought new worries and I began to second-guess the junkie's Swiss-cheese brain. This was the only thing he had remembered, and it was entirely possible that his sporadic recall had both names wrong, but it was the best we had until Bobby decided to resurface. I hoped my panhandling friend had not abandoned Paris and was already burrowed deep in the fringe underground of Naples or Milan.

"Puis-je parler à votre invité, Monsieur Calderón?" I asked each time a desk clerk answered. I said it was a family matter.

"Je suis désolé, Mademoiselle, nous n'avons pas un invité avec le nom." The response was always the same. Miss, we have no one with that name registered at our hotel.

I had long ago given up correcting people on the telephone. Because of a high-pitched voice, I was invariably mistaken for a young woman more times than not. As a result, I soon realized I actually received more amicable responses when the listener imagined me as female. Other than an occasional request for a date, which I pleasantly discouraged, I was treated with more sensitivity and compassion.

The telephone work was tedious and slow. I returned to the counter twice for coffee refills and four times for extensions to our original 15-minute request. The clerk smiled with each exchange before quietly returning to her book. I scanned the café each time as I walked back to my telephone. No one seemed the least bit interested in me or what I might be doing.

I sipped the coffee and dialed again. Every call increased my frustration. When I was ready to give up and start murdering everyone in the shop, my luck suddenly changed. I found him; or rather, I found his hotel. A wide smile creased my lips, and I took a deep, silent breath.

The clerk confirmed that Marcus Calderón was a guest at Hotel abba Montparnasse.

"Ah, très bon," I said.

He tried ringing through but there was no answer.

"Voulez-vous laisser un message?"

Thanks, no message. What I'd like to do is surprise him.

"Je ferai un tour demain pour lui faire une surprise. C'est notre secret," I said.

"Comme vous voulez, mademoiselle."

I hung up and excitedly dropped the receiver back in its cradle. Circling the listing for Hotel abba Montparnasse several times with my pencil, I pressed the directory paper against the glass between us with a smug grin. Zita cocked her head and smiled.

A short while later, we hiked out of the Metro near Boulevard Raspail on the east side of Cimetière du Montparnasse. One of four major cemeteries in Paris, this 190,000-square-meter burial ground in the south of Paris, was still only the second largest behind Père Lachaise Cemetery in the eastern part of the city.

Montparnasse Cemetery was the indefinite home of France's intellectual and artistic elite. The writer Guy de Maupassant and Frédéric Bartholdi, sculptor of the Statue of Liberty, were buried here. It was fairly tranquil in the daylight, containing 1,200 trees and countless benches where visitors might relax while searching for the grave of their favorite dead person. But in the growing darkness, the cemetery became a scary realm of unsettled spirits and the walking dead.

We entered a northeast gate and walked with a lively step through a miniature city of marble houses laid out in a structured design of parallel lines and right angles, very atypical of the French. The sun was long gone now and the gravel path disappeared when the remaining illumination from the city faded to a cataract vision of reality. Not far into the park, the sounds of Paris also fell away and the local residents began to talk to us.

My biggest fear was that I might encounter the little girl standing in the path, blocking my increasingly hesitant gait. Though I knew Montparnasse was not her forever home, I wasn't discounting the chance she may be visiting a new best friend or simply browsing through vacant real estate opportunities. Like any other piece of property in Paris, if relatives didn't continue to pay the rent on your gravesite, you'd lose it, so plots were continually becoming available. In any case, I could live without an accidental meeting with her this evening.

Eventually, the streetlamps from Rue de la Gaîté could be seen coming up from beyond the edge of the cemetery and everything returned to normal. As we emerged from the west gate, I wondered how an avenue that ran alongside a cemetery had been named Gaiety Street. Maybe it was because people were happy to be passing in a car instead of a box. Personally, I thought a more appropriate name might be Boneyard Boulevard.

"I am hoping you do not tell me we need to 'stake out the joint' as you Americans say because I'm not going back in that cemetery tonight," Zita said.

Number 20 Rue de la Gaîté was slightly off to the left, about mid-block. Albeit a four-star establishment, the old Montparnasse Hotel did not have a particularly beautiful exterior. The building was a plain, five-story stone-faced structure like so many in Paris nowadays. In typical French style, frills were not wasted on exterior decor, including the simple, small lobby which owned most of the light emanating from the front of the building.

"Do you know where we are?" I asked.

"Paris," Zita replied.

"Okay, it was a silly question but a rhetorical one." I gave her a sideways glance. "I was going to say, we're less than half a kilometer from where we left kidney man."

"Your point is, dear?"

"Great timing, girl," I said, noticing a couple turn the corner and slowly walk the walk of lovers toward the hotel entrance. "There is my point. I meant we were close to her apartment."

It was the pretty blonde from Le Roux's photograph and I was betting she was escorting Marcus Calderón back to his hotel room. The man walked with a macho swagger, looking at nothing in particular. His coat was draped across his broad shoulders. Calderón had opted for fashion rather than warmth because it was already cold enough this evening for frost to collect on our pumpkins.

The woman rested her head at the edge of his chest, curled into one bare arm. She was somehow smaller than I had imagined, maybe the height of a good-sized rake handle though definitely much healthier. She was built like a Barbie doll and in the fading light, I thought her blonde hair might be natural. The lovers entered the hotel lobby, oblivious to their surroundings. We followed in behind them.

We all strolled onto an old-fashioned, open-air lift. Calderón and his companion stood to the back of the tiny compartment after pressing the button for the third floor. I barely had the outer gilded bars closed when Zita crushed against me and her hands began roaming my body. Between kisses and fingers unbuttoning my shirt, I struggled to latch the inner crisscrossed gate so the elevator would engage. We began a painfully slow ascent.

As the lift bumped to a stop at three, I pushed Zita back and tried to straighten my clothes and hair. She was smiling mischievously, with a glint in her eye I had seen only once before. I pretended to search my pockets for a room key as Calderón loudly pushed the double gates aside and stepped off the platform. He reached back for his date and they brushed past us with a rude sigh.

"Pardon monsieur, mademoiselle," the lady said.

The couple stopped in front of Room 307 and opened the door.

"Better hurry, love. I get paid by the hour," Zita said. "Whether you're digging for your room key or getting a leg over, it's all the same to me."

I slammed the gates and punched the button for the next floor up.

CHAPTER 32

Zita and I were back at Room 307 in under thirty minutes. Figuring they did what they came to do, I wanted to catch them with their defenses down in a moment of weakness. If Calderón's thoughts were elsewhere, we might have an initial advantage and possibly take him without incident. I put an ear to the door. Quiet. I went to work with my lock picks. Zita stood with her back pressed to the wall and her weapon at shoulder height.

A faint click echoed in the hallway when the locking mechanism released. I cranked the knob and kicked the door with the force of a rhino. The swinging door shook as it slammed into something immovable about three-quarters of the way back and lurched forward again with tremendous force. Zita was caught solidly going through the opening. She bounced off the wall and went down hard, holding the shoulder of her shooting arm.

In the darkness, a hand clasped the door from behind and shoved it toward Zita. She blocked the thrust with a straightened forearm. Calderón exploded from behind the door and ran straight at me. Zita caught an ankle and his head shot forward, punching a cannonball-sized hole in my chest. I was thrown backward and hit the carpet with a concrete thud, knocking the wind out of me.

My breath came in ragged gasps. I was breathing in but it felt like my lungs were full of cotton. It was too much work for the result I was getting. Calderón was struggling to get off me. He pushed his body up using straight arms against my stomach. The precious little air in my lungs was forced out.

"Did you think I wouldn't recognize you?" He sneered.

As Calderón brought his face up, I smashed his nose with the heel of my left hand. Pain erupted through my still tender palm and a shockwave carried down the arm as I heard cartilage give way and bone snap in the man's face. He screamed.

Calderón and I rolled opposite ways onto hands and knees. I managed to lift my head for a split second. Blood was streaming from his nostrils and he shook his head like an old dog that had been handed his butt in an alley fight. I'm fairly certain we both looked like a couple of half-dead mongrels because I was still expecting to suffocate any minute. I was lightheaded and needed to get up but Calderón moved first.

He scrambled to his feet and pushed by me as he ran for the exit. I found myself staring at the ceiling again and I couldn't turn over. I needed oxygen, but now it hurt to breathe. Coughing to clear my windpipe, I spat a wad of phlegm on the carpet. I had to get up. I don't think anyone has ever suffocated while standing, though I could have been wrong there.

Eventually rolling onto my stomach, I finally managed to stand with hands on my knees for support. Fear of dying kicked in and I started to take on oxygen, like I was storing up for space travel. I decided to follow Calderón when Zita touched my bicep. I straightened.

"He's mine. See what you can get out of the woman," she said.

"Are you all right?" I asked, shakily.

"Slightly better than you, I imagine. If you're going to vomit, please do so before I return."

Zita had disappeared down the hall before I felt well enough to get through the door. My breathing was marginally improving by the time I reached the center of the room. The woman was sitting against the headboard of the bed. Her knees were pulled up and her arms were wrapped around her legs. She made an insincere effort to cover her naked body and I clearly saw she was indeed a natural blonde. There was a slight smile on her face.

"Miss, do you speak English? Anglais?" I gasped.

She stared blankly at me, running her eyes over me like warm hands. She glanced once at her purse on the table behind me, paying no attention to the clothes strewn on the floor.

"I speak English," she said, with a hint of British cadence coming through a heavier French accent. "I have nothing to do with this man. I met him tonight. May I please go?" Her words ran together as she spoke. There was a practiced innocence about her that was very effective. The little-girl routine may have worked if she hadn't been the centerpiece of Le Roux's photograph.

"No, you may not," I said.

There was a momentary spark of defeat in her eyes but it was immediately replaced by the wistful innocence she originally displayed. She smiled self-consciously and glanced away with feigned shyness. The woman licked her lips and stole another peek at her purse.

"What's your name?"

"Therese Bertrand."

"Ms. Bertrand, who's the man you were with?" Nothing. "Where did you meet him?"

"At Chaud," she said, vaguely and turned her face to the window.

Chaud was a well-known party club in the Latin Quarter catering to the dance-style rhythms of jazz, salsa and samba. Known as a discothèque, this type of entertainment venue played recorded music by disc jockeys through a PA system, rather than hosting a live band, which was still the popular format in American bars and nightclubs.

Here in Paris, these clubs accommodated a growing subculture of third-shift partiers, beat junkies and assorted vampires who awaken with the setting sun, dancing and drinking until the morning light once again cast ugly light on their beautiful, dark world. To these creatures, the night offered an alternative universe that was too incomprehensible to most diurnal earthlings. Consequently, these all-night clubs opened after 10:00 p.m. and didn't get hot until after the witching hour had come and gone. The clock on the nightstand displayed 8:47 p.m.

"Chaud isn't open yet."

"I work there," she quickly added, gesturing with her arm. An ample breast jumped briefly from its hiding place.

"And...?" I urged her to continue.

"And he came there. He is here on business and someone told him about me."

"What kind of business?"

"I don't know." She shrugged.

"What did he hear about you?"

The woman slowly unfolded her arms and lowered her legs. She stretched above her head in a sultry pose I was certain would ignite the duvet within the next few seconds.

"This is what I do," she said.

"Try again. My friend used that one. She'll be back in a moment and she's not as nice as me. She doesn't like stupid women, whereas I could be persuaded to make an exception for you." She glared at me but said nothing. I waited while she curled back into her ball. "Okay, let's try something different. Who is Jean Le Roux?" She raised her eyebrows in curious surprise.

"A pest and a fool. He's an errand boy who came into a sum of money two months ago. Lately, he fancies himself a spy."

"Now, he's dead."

"What?" Genuine shock cut several creases in her face.

"Do you want to talk now?" She blinked but said nothing. "Miss, you're into something very dangerous here and you may not be able to get yourself out of it. You're caught between us and them and we both want something from you. We are nicer and there's a good chance we'll let you live. Now, what do you know about these men?"

She folded her arms across her breasts and stared at me. I wasn't able to separate lies from any truth she may be telling me. I was no doubt asking all the wrong questions but her non-responses and short, evasive answers were grating on the little patience I had left this evening.

I didn't normally start even my best day with a lot of composure and this wasn't my best day. Most mornings, I filled my back pocket with some calm and self-control when I could find my pants and that was it for the day. When it ran out, it ran out. Maybe the British Secret Service could squeeze something out of her.

She glanced at her purse again.

"What is so important about your purse?" I asked, in total exasperation.

I turned to pick up the tiny handbag. As I released the snap, Therese Bertrand delivered a savage kick above the small of my back. I smashed against the mirror, cracking it diagonally. There goes the last of my luck, I thought. I already had one ass-kicking in the last fifteen minutes, and I was about to get another. At this rate, I wouldn't live seven years until the bad luck wore off.

The woman ripped the purse from my hand and the contents flew everywhere. I caught her wrist as she came back at me. Bertrand was still naked, presenting a major distraction to getting angry and focusing on the matter in front of me. I completely missed the other hand as it swung around from the blind side to clap my ear. The impact of the airtight slap caused my head to ring and eyes to water.

As she struggled back from the wrist I was holding, I lashed out with a sidekick that landed with a glancing blow above her right knee. I felt the joint hyper-extend and she went down, pulling me on top of her.

Normally, this wouldn't have been an altogether unpleasant position but I didn't want to risk her leaning into me with a knee to the privates or something worse. I hit her with a close-in arm punch to the jaw and it was enough to end her day poorly. Her eyes rolled up in the sockets and she was soon dreaming about fairy-tale romances in a land of wishes and rainbows. I rolled off her and lay on my back, continuing to breathe unsteadily.

"I hope you didn't just add necrophilia to your list of crimes?" I squinted at the figure silhouetted in the doorway. Zita was smiling.

"She's not dead," I panted.

"Rape then, unless you were introduced and fell in love while I was gone? Fainted with ecstasy, has she?"

"I can assure you Madame that I've never managed to make anyone pass out from ecstasy. I punched her lights out."

"Need I ask if you got anything from her? No, let me rephrase that. Did she tell you anything about Calderón or Chaban?"

"Not really," I said, sitting up weakly. "Perhaps your team can do better. Where's Calderón?"

"Gone," she replied. "I followed him as far as Atlantic Garden where Monsieur Calderón went through the park and I lost him altogether. It's impossible to find any sort of blood trail on grass in the dark, especially without a torch." She bent over the unconscious woman. "Help me get her packed up and I'll escort the lady to the interrogation agents."

"Therese Bertrand."

"I didn't know you were on a first-name basis with Blondie here. But in case either of you have a modicum of decency left, I will dress her."

We lifted Bertrand's dead weight onto the bed, leaving her legs hanging off one side. Not wanting any further conversation regarding my interview techniques, I collected the woman's clothes from the carpet and left the dressing to Zita. I helped only once, lifting the inert torso to enable the short dress to slide down over her head.

Zita made a call on the room telephone to arrange for their arrival at the safe house.

"They're sending a car. Please sit her up," said Zita. She removed a bottle of scotch from the minibar and placed the open flask under the unconscious woman's nose. "Come along, dearie. It's time to go," she said.

Bertrand smelled the liquor and frowned. With her eyes still closed, she reached for the bottle to push it away.

"You'd better drink this, Ms. Bertrand. It's going to be a long night for you." Then she said to me, "I'll meet you under the arch by noon tomorrow."

We helped the lady to her feet, but it was obvious she couldn't stand alone on the injured knee. Zita supported her with an arm around the back and the duo limped down the hall to wait for the lift's slow ascent to the third floor. Therese Bertrand was quietly sobbing as the two women struggled into the lift and I suddenly felt sorry for her. There would be no permanent damage to the leg and in a week her face would be back to its beautiful self, but it made me feel bad all the same.

Before I left the hotel, I collected the contents of the handbag scattered across the room. I was curious why Bertrand had been so interested in keeping me from whatever was inside. It was too small to hide a gun. What was it?

I found the purse. It was a single-pocket evening accessory, covered in soft calf-skin with a pale blue silk lining. A fat roll of money was still tucked inside. Judging from the top few bills, there might have been 5,000 to 10,000 francs in the bundle. It was an expensive evening for Calderón and he didn't even get to spend the night with her.

A tube of Lancôme Pinkalicious lipstick had rolled under the bed. Curious, I removed the cap to check the color and smell the scent. Making a mental note to get a tube for Zita at the next opportunity, I had a sudden urge to disappear for a few days with her and the lipstick. An image flashed in my brain of a villa overlooking the Mediterranean, the three of us relaxing in the sun on a single deck chair. Not 30 seconds into the fantasy, I was already wearing more Pinkalicious than Zita.

A lone apartment key lying near the nightstand brought me back to reality. As I bent to retrieve it, a folded scrap of paper behind the door caught my interest. It was a section of napkin and could have been on the floor for a while; it was hard to tell. I tossed it in the trash basket, but immediately plucked it out and sat on the bed.

Straightening the heavily creased paper on my thigh, I saw a code of some sort written on one side in black ink. I recognized the scrawl of a left-handed writer. The penmanship was sloppy, and the ink smeared before it had time to dry.

I found nothing else belonging to Bertrand or Calderón. Carefully placing the small pile I assembled back in the purse, I shoved it into an inside pocket on my coat and eased the door closed behind me.

CHAPTER 33

Marcus Calderón stepped into a recessed row of storefronts, just off Rue Jacob in the Latin Quarter, and nervously glanced at his wristwatch. It was coming up on noon and he was not looking forward to this meeting. The Frenchman was going to ask about something the man no longer had. Something he had lost during the encounter with the American.

He stared into the shop window and pulled the collar of his trench coat up around his face, even though the wind had fallen away under the small overhang. He suddenly wished there were more cars driving past. The street noise had dulled to a soft roar and he could now hear his own heart banging against its rib cage. He didn't like feeling so afraid.

"What happened to you?"

Though he was expecting him, Calderón was still surprised by Chaban's abrupt appearance. Needle pricks punctured his face and chest.

"Nothing!"

The shorter man carefully eyed the edge of Calderón's coat collar.

"Yeah, that nose looks like nothing."

"I said, it's nothing."

"You ran into the American, didn't you?" Chaban asked with a grin.

"Yeah, so what?"

"The so what is, I told you to leave him alone!"

"I'll take care of it," Calderón grumbled. "I already have people on the street looking for the little…"

"You're done with him! Do you understand me?"

"I'm going to…"

"I said you're done! You're going to do exactly nothing. It looks like he kicked your ass and your ego, and I don't want to hear another word out of either of them." Chaban's stare drove a stake through any thought that might be forming in Calderón's brain. "Besides, I'm starting to like this kid. He's as persistent and stubborn as I was at that age. Maybe more."

"He's dead!"

"Don't press your luck. Calm down or you'll die right here."

Calderón turned back to the shop window as new traffic noise flooded the alcove. He looked at his feet.

"Do you have the code?" Chaban asked.

"I'm working on it."

"When?"

"Tomorrow, or the next day."

"It better be tomorrow. I don't need any more delays.

CHAPTER 34

A cup of hot chocolate steamed the cool air around my face as I lifted it to my lips and sipped at the whipped cream topping. Slowly wiping the sugar mustache away, I watched two winter tourists try to traverse ten lanes of traffic on Place Charles de Gaulle, focused only on the Arc de Triomphe at its center. The duo hopped the small chain barrier separating traffic from the tiny sidewalk café where I sat and now stood squarely in the outside ring, waiting for a break in traffic.

The wagon-wheel roundabout was a literal nightmare this morning. Tour buses cut across traffic without fear and deranged drivers wielded small cars like torpedoes as fenders scraped against fenders. No one stopped. No one ever stopped in the rotary.

There was a rumor in Paris that a confused driver had once panicked in the inner lane and driven around for seven hours before he could exit onto Avenue Hoche. The truth is the car had probably been flattened within twenty minutes and trampled to dust before the end of the first hour, without a single person slowing down or taking notice. Today, there would be no break in traffic for the tourists.

A small, heroic Frenchman sporting one long, thick eyebrow under a flat, black beret vaulted the chain onto the motorway and pulled the protesting pair back to the safety of the sidewalk. Their savior tried to explain to the clueless tourists it would be much safer for them to use the underground passage to the Arc de

Triomphe. The Frenchman was as jittery as a subway rat. He waved his arms and spoke three languages at once, none of which the couple understood.

Finally, I whistled sharply and the trio turned toward the sound. I pointed to the sign above their heads and to the entrance of the underground passage that loomed up behind them. Heads bobbed in recognition and the Frenchman's arms shot out in the direction of the stairway. I heard him say "voila" as I went back to my hot chocolate.

"I wondered if you were going to let those poor people perish."

Zita sat down beside me and leaned to kiss my cheek. Her lips were chilled and her face was flushed to a beautiful glow from her brisk walk down Av. Victor Hugo. She studied the roundabout, expecting to find the remains of other brave tourists I might have sent not so quietly into their good night.

The early breeze had died down, and the day was warming nicely. Zita ordered her usual morning cup of Earl Grey before settling down to business. She was smiling curiously, and it was difficult to say what news she had. I just hoped it didn't start with something about your girlfriend.

"You won't believe what your girlfriend told our men," she started.

Great, how long would I have to live with this? Zita was not the jealous type, but she was also not about to let me forget last night so easily. She would continue for some time to tease me with her version of my Therese Bertrand interrogation. I hadn't been chatting up the lady as Zita implied, but English humor was after all, mainly based on sarcasm and a built-in desire to take the piss out of anyone who might be the unfortunate subject of their fun. She sipped her tea as she peered at me over the rim of the cup. I pretended to pay no attention to the underlying tone of her comment, so she continued.

"Well, where to start?" she asked herself. "The lady gave us quite a number of insights in the end."

Zita closed her eyes for a few seconds. She was building suspense at my expense. I sat back, folded my arms, and gazed at six people standing atop the Arc de Triomphe. It was a grand 360o view of the city. One of the tourists was pumping an arm toward the Eiffel Tower and the others were gathering close to see. A tall man with long hair and a beard organized the group for a photograph.

"Your Therese Bertrand was uncooperative at first," Zita began. "She didn't realize into what sort of trouble she'd fallen until our man explained it to her. Beauty and feigned innocence did not translate to having her way in this case."

"Gas, grass or ass. Nobody rides for free," I commented.

Momentarily speechless, Zita tilted a wrinkled brow toward me. I simply meant there was no free ride any longer. Nowadays, life's hitchhikers have to pay for every ride. Something for something, as the Romans used to say. Ms. Bertrand was trying to use her charm to get an easier interrogation. I made a motion with my hand for Zita to continue.

"She is exactly what she says she is, a tom girl," she said.

"Do you mean she climbs trees and plays cricket?" I asked.

"No, dear," she laughed. "At last, I have you with an English colloquialism. She gives comfort to weary travelers for a price and a very high price I might add."

"Is that why she attacked me? She thought I was stealing her money?"

"Quite. You are a shifty character and she did leave without the handbag."

I pulled the small purse from my coat and handed it to her.

"It's all there," I said. "Count it."

"Oh no, Angel, you'll want to return this yourself but it may be difficult at the moment as your girl is on an extended holiday far from Paris."

"She's not my girl."

"I'm not so certain, judging from the moaning and heavy breathing when I walked in last night."

"Funny, did she say what this was?" I reached into the handbag to remove the napkin containing the code. I immediately had Zita's serious side. She read the numbers, first to herself, then aloud.

"T1 S5 G17 9151. Where did you get this?"

"I found it on the floor near the door. What is it?"

"I have no idea and Bertrand didn't mention this. I'll ask our woman keeping her company just now. If Ms. Bertrand knows, she'll tell us. In the meantime, she did talk quite a bit concerning your traveling companion from Marseilles."

"Le Roux?"

"Indeed, he was an amateur, my dear, at least at assassination. Why he tried to kill you is still a mystery. He was a courier, plain and simple so he was no doubt in Marseilles to pick up a package. It appears he transported items from one place to another."

"What sort of items?" I asked.

"Money, people, documents."

"He had a satchel with him that was missing when I found him on the train. It may have been what the killer was after."

"Perhaps. About two months ago, Le Roux showed your Ms. Bertrand blueprints for the Eiffel Tower during one of his comfort sessions. They were in a very old book actually, called The 300 Meter Tower, it contained Eiffel's original drawings. He was so excited about delivering this book to a friend that he almost forgot the comfort session altogether, which she said would have been fine with her. She thought nothing more about the book until we discussed Le Roux in chambers with her. We now have men guarding the Tower around the clock."

I noticed a homeless man meander into view from Av. Foch. Slowly, he made his way around Place Charles de Gaulle, patiently waiting for each traffic signal to change. He used the time to pander himself to passing tourists. Most invariably shook their heads or pretended not to notice the unwashed indigent, but occasionally his patience was rewarded when a few coins were dropped into his waiting palm.

"What happened with the list of telephone numbers I found in Le Roux's apartment?" I asked.

"Those numbers were connected to regular pick-up points for Le Roux. They were not safe houses, nothing so glamorous. It took some effort to close them all down and question the flat owners but they recognized Le Roux from his passport photo and confirmed they gave him packages to deliver from time to time. To the man, they were told what to provide and when by telephone. Le Roux appeared with the agreed money and the packets were exchanged. None knew of a destination. Apparently, only Le Roux could say where the packages were to be delivered, and to whom."

Lost in thought, my eyes settled on the panhandler again. He stopped to forage through a trash bin. Finding something of interest, he carefully placed the object in his pocket. If it were inevitable a person must be homeless somewhere in the world, I could think of no better place than Paris. The weather was generally mild, the city was relatively flat and one could exist on handouts of baguettes and cheese for years.

"Did she mention Chaban at all?" I asked.

"The lady admitted Le Roux had dropped his name several times but she didn't know the man. Evidently, he was never on her calendar. Calderón, on the other hand, was a regular. He's been coming to Paris for several months. He told her he was a consultant working with a French concern in Madrid and now the company had a little work for him here. Calderón was quiet, never said much. She liked him because he was a good tipper."

The vagrant finally made his way around to Av. Marceau, where we sat at the Café de la Paix. He didn't seem aware of his surroundings and it was obvious his mental navigation had run aground long ago. The beggar muttered to himself as he ambled toward the café. Rubbing his face with one hand, his eyes went into rapid-fire blinking before eventually focusing on our table. He walked unsteadily on an angle toward us.

"Pardonnez-moi, monsieur," he said. "Avez-vous de la monnaie? J'ai très faim."

"Sorry, but I don't speak French," I lied.

"Um, give money," he said.

The man held a filthy hand close to my face. It was shaking badly and the smell forced me to sit back in the chair. I reached into Therese Bertrand's purse and blindly pulled a hundred franc note from her roll. I was positive she wouldn't mind helping a fellow countryman in need of food and a good bath.

"Merci beaucoup." His voice croaked.

The man pulled a half-liter whiskey bottle from his coat pocket, unscrewed the top and took a long, refreshing swallow. He offered us a drink, but receiving no immediate answer, he shrugged and tried to reseal his flask. The cap twisted out of his hand and bounced on the pavement. Slowly he tried to follow its fast path along the ground, but lost sight of it as the lid rolled somewhere behind him. Unperturbed, he tucked the bottle back in his pocket before returning to the traffic signal at Av. Marceau. The homeless man looked like he was standing at the last intersection before he entered his own personal Twilight Zone.

"Is Calderón a regular at the Montparnasse Hotel?" I asked.

"Unfortunately, no," Zita answered. "We were lucky to find him this time. Ms. Bertrand says he takes her to a different hotel each time so I'm afraid we've lost his trail for the moment."

"Calderón is the key to finding Chaban. We're running out of time and options."

I spotted several mourners across Place Charles de Gaulle praying at the tomb of France's Unknown Soldier. The sacred ground was usually decorated with fresh flowers laid inside a low chain that outlined the memorial. An eternal flame and coat of arms were set into the stonework in honor of the nameless, fallen World War I hero. I wondered if I would also slip into my own eternity as an anonymous box of bones whose only remaining legacy was that I had died, nearly 60 years ago.

"What's that?" Zita asked, curiously.

I followed her gaze to something on the table. Snatching it up, I turned it over in my hands. It was a small, dirty envelope with the flap tucked in, not sealed. There were no markings on the outside. I pulled a note from the envelope and read it.

"It's Bobby," I said, as I reread the words a second time.

"I suppose the bum was not so daft after all," Zita said.

"Perhaps not but Bobby took an awful chance relying on that space cadet to deliver anything but disappointment. Knowing him though, he probably sent the same note with two dozen of his mates thinking one might actually find me."

I looked in the direction of the homeless man. The sidewalks were full of people, but he wasn't among them. Paris had swallowed the vagrant, absorbing him into its long and storied history.

"He wants to meet. I reckon he didn't jack to Italy yet."

"Would you mind translating that into the Queen's English?"

"It means that Bobby didn't run like a jackrabbit as I thought he might."

"Darling, you do have a way with words, though I'm afraid sometimes I clearly don't know the language."

CHAPTER 35

A well-dressed, middle-aged businessman walked out of the Galeries Lafayette Department Store at 40 Blvd. Haussmann, two blocks from the Paris Opéra in the 9th Arrondissement. His long black coat was open, revealing a dark charcoal, pin-striped suit, white shirt and a blue silk tie that accentuated his eyes and the silver-gray hair around his temples. The man stroked a light-brown mustache as he strolled to the Chaussée d'Antin Metro entrance, never noticing the dishwater-blonde woman following him.

He stepped into the first car of the two-coach train. With the metro system carrying more than four million passengers per day, it was rare to find a seat on first entering a train and today was no exception. The man walked to the front of the crowded car and stood focused on the small front window and the tunnel beyond it. His gloved hand stretched up high on a passenger support pole as the train smoothly rocked its way down the track. Unlike subway traffic in the United States, which was noisy and rough riding, Paris underground coaches rode on a cushion of air inside inflatable tires much like those designed for trucks and buses.

The train stopped six times before the inanimate man stirred and realized where he was. He double-checked the underground route map above the door. The Cité stop on Île de la Cité was next. Passengers queued in anticipation of the doors opening and the businessman fell in line behind them.

As the crowd filed out, the man felt his stomach growl. Early in his career, an esteemed older colleague told him no superior would ever thank him for missing a meal. The businessman never forgot this lesson and made a point of not skipping lunch or dinner because of work. He decided to find a café near his destination for something to tamp down the twinge of hunger.

The early afternoon was overcast and the temperature had dropped several degrees during the short subway ride. The man pulled his coat closed against the wind but didn't button it. He never properly fastened his coat, no matter what the weather. This was his personal protest against early spring's cooler days. He absolutely knew it was harming only himself with this stubborn behavior but it had become habit. It was a continuing battle between one man and his nature.

The businessman cut across the island on Rue d'Arcole. Spotting a small, open-front coffee bar, he stepped in for a café au lait and a snack. The man wolfed two flaky croissants, trying to wash them down quickly with gulps of hot coffee. He was in a hurry, but stood his ground at the counter long enough to drain his porcelain cup. Asking for a 'to go' container, not that such a thing existed in 1974, was tantamount to an unholy reckoning with the devil to any Parisian. Even barbaric, irreligious foreigners had to respect centuries-old rules of European civility.

The man rejoined foot traffic on Rue d'Arcole. He stood momentarily on the narrow sidewalk, studying the surroundings from habit. With an irrational fear of being struck from behind by an automobile, he automatically glanced a second time in the opposite direction before starting out.

He impatiently weaved through the tourists until he was caught behind a slow-moving Italian couple. Both were animated, talking a bit too loud. They never looked back or thought to yield the path. The man finally lost them when he turned left on Rue Chanoinesse. He picked up the pace.

When the road curved toward the park behind Notre Dame Cathedral, a gunman abruptly stepped from a courtyard and grabbed the businessman's lapel. He shoved a 9mm Beretta against the man's cheek. Roughly pulling his captive inside the entryway, he slammed him against the wall. The businessman stared at the hand holding the weapon to his face.

"Did you think this cheap disguise would confuse me?" the man asked, in English.

Actually, I had. This was my best stab at deception to date. The ensemble had cost almost sixteen hundred francs and for that price, I had been convinced the middle-aged businessman's camouflage would have made me invisible in any city in the world, but apparently not in Paris.

The man slowly released my coat and almost lovingly ran his hand along the soft wool at my chest. I hoped he was thinking 'I have to buy one of these for myself' and not 'I'll take this one from his dead body when I'm done here'. Without warning, he clutched my throat and wrapped cold fingers around my windpipe. With incredible strength, the man pushed me up the wall until my feet dangled uselessly. The pressure of the gun made my face ache.

"What do you want?" I struggled to speak.

"It's not what. It's who," he said. "I want the black kid and you know how to find him."

"Where did you hear that?" I asked, acting clueless.

The man replied by increasing his grip on my throat and pressing the weapon deeper into my cheek. Realizing I didn't have the best bargaining position, I answered the question with more or less the truth. I coughed.

"The last time I saw Bobby, he was panning for a lift out of here. I'm certain he's found his way to Vienna by now."

"Is that right? Are you jerking me? I don't like people

jerking me unless I want them jerking me. Am I paying you to jerk me?" He renewed the pressure of the Beretta against my face. His voice rose, "I don't think I'm paying you but in your case I might make you do it for free."

"Let me down. I can't talk if I can't breathe."

The man very slowly relaxed his hand, and I slid down the wall until my feet touched the pavement again. I felt the blood draining from my head.

"Can you loosen the gun too?" I asked. "My teeth hurt."

I straightened my clothes, feeling better about standing on solid ground. For a minute, I thought I was going to have to kick this guy's ass from up in the air. The gunman stared at me.

"Better?" He asked, an unfriendly grin stretching his mouth.

He patted my jaw three times. The man was about my size, but bulkier, and he sported short-cropped, curly black hair and three-day stubble.

"Now to business. Where's your friend?"

"I wish I knew because he owes me money."

"Curious," he said, ignoring me. "That either makes you a liar or the bum I beat to death. Which is it?"

The gun waved dangerously back and forth in front of my nose.

"You beat a bum to death?" I asked, disbelievingly.

"I crushed him with my bare hands because his bones were brittle from eating crap his whole life. Oh, he told me what I needed to know but I beat him anyway because blood excites me. He screamed and pleaded for mercy. I guess he thought I had a heart, but I don't. I just love the color red. I kept hammering him and it felt fantastic! Blood dripped from his face. I watched it run through my fingers." The smile suddenly faded. "So, let's talk about Bobby."

The man had his palm on my chest, pinning me to the alley

wall with a straight arm.

"I told you. I don't know where he is."

"Then you better start dreaming up some believable shit. I need to find him so we can have a little chat."

"What's he done to you?"

"To me? Nothing. He poked his long black nose into someone else's business. Now that someone wants him dead." He shrugged. "The man gives me money, so Bobby's already in a shallow grave outside of Rouen, only he doesn't know it yet. With you, the man is less concerned. He leaves your life with me. So tell me, where...is...Bobby?"

"I can't tell you what I don't know."

The man hit me on the temple with the flat of the weapon.

"Are you sleeping in there? Wake up!" He hit me again with the gun. The man's lips curled into a thin smile. He holstered the Beretta with one hand and said, "I'm going to squeeze every drop of blood out of you and drink it in front of you. You'll be begging me to put a bullet in your head."

The man cocked his arm like a baseball pitcher and threw a fastball at my head. I snapped my face to the right in anticipation of the impact. The blow clipped my ear and his fist slammed the bricks solidly beside my head. I heard bones shatter. In that stunned instance, my attacker loosened his grip on my chest and I smashed the heel of my hand up under his chin and followed with a hard left cross to the exposed throat. The man staggered back gasping for air through a crushed windpipe.

I side-kicked his knee and the defenseless assassin collapsed to the ground. My brain flashed on endless movie fight scenes where the hero always hauled the bad guy to his feet to punch him again. Fair play. But equal wasn't part of the equation growing up on the streets of Chicago. I didn't want to break a hand on his hard head and I was no hero. Fair only happened in make believe.

I kicked the man again and again. With each assault, I thought of the nameless bum, this cruel man senselessly murdered. Eventually, the gunman dropped into unconsciousness and stopped trying to roll away. I gave him three more slashing kicks to the head for any other helpless people he had tortured. People who don't provide pardon and mercy don't deserve it in return.

"Do you still like blood when it's your own, you son of a bitch?" My voice was raised, crazed. I kicked him on the side of the face again. "Now you have some. Does blood still make your dick hard?" I kicked him in the groin. Zita pulled me back off my feet as I wound up to kick him in the stomach. Instead, I wound up sitting in the alley.

"Enough, darling. You made your point, whatever that may be," she said.

"Where were you? I could have been killed."

She bent to examine the killer.

"It appeared you had things well under control. However, I was hoping you might save something of him for MI6 but that now appears out of the question. I'm afraid we'll be talking amongst ourselves for the next several months waiting for this bloke to wake up."

I almost felt sorry for the lifeless bastard across the way; almost.

"From the position of that right arm, he should have no problem scratching his own back when the urge arises." As an afterthought, I added, "I like your hair with the highlights."

"Only you could think of a thing like that at a moment like this. Don't get used to the blonde tint because it's not staying for long. I actually like my natural hair color, unlike your American women. Let's get you to your feet. I must call in this mess, and then we can meet your Bobby."

With Zita's help, I stood and gingerly dusted off my clothes. There was a rip in the coat sleeve, the shirt and tie were stained and my shoes were covered with gore. The dark gray wool of the pants was soaked with blood spatter, leaving them looking like I had waded in muddy creek water.

"Let me know if you think of a story I can use when I return these clothes," I said.

Zita's eyes widened in disbelief and finally in horror when she realized it was possible I wasn't kidding. I straightened my mustache with a small grin.

"Come on, I know where we can find a telephone and a washroom."

Zita glanced at the unconscious man and decided he wouldn't be mobile for some time. She reluctantly followed me out of the alley.

CHAPTER 36

The park that lay behind Notre Dame Cathedral was dedicated to Pope John XXIII about a year after his death in 1963. A beautiful grassy area covered more than 1,000 square meters, segmented by walking paths, rows of shade trees and wooden benches. In the center of the garden stood the still functioning three-sided Fountain of the Virgin, honoring Mary and the Christ child. It was circled by a half-meter high wrought-iron fence enclosing a magnificent year-round bed of red and yellow flowers. Tourists often came here to contemplate the meaning of life or the history of Paris or simply nothing at all, amid the scenic views of the flying buttresses, the river bridges and the dark, still waters of the Seine.

When I reached the tree line on the east side of the square, Bobby was moving quickly across the manicured lawns toward the walking bridge of Pont Saint-Louis. He had passed the fountain and looked like he was walking straight at me with his head down. I wasn't positive he had seen me.

Sitting on a bench, I watched Bobby for another twenty meters, wondering if he was playing 'if I can see no one, then no one can see me.' I whistled a sharp high-pitched tone somewhere in the range of dog hearing. Bobby slowed considerably by the time he reached the bench. He sat on the far end and bent to tie a shoe.

"You're late, brother. Where've you been?" Nodding at my pants, he asked, "Have you been playing Jesus and trying to walk on the Seine again? Forget it. I don't want to know. I thought the man finally capped you so I was leaving for parts unknown."

"I was delayed. I ran into a guy who wanted to talk to you."

"Shit, I knew it. I'm a dead man!"

"Bobby, what's going on?" I asked.

"He's put a hit on me and there's no place to hide in Paris, man. This place's crawling with people who want to pop a cap in my ass."

"Who?"

"Chaban, man!"

He glared out at the lawns, but his eyes were focused on another time and place. He rubbed his hands together, then wiped them on his pant legs. For a man who lived comfortably beyond the edge of society with drug dealers, pimps, thieves and murderers, Bobby was scared. His knees bounced like the pistons on a 429 V8 engine as his feet pumped nervous energy down into the hard-packed path.

"I got to go," he said. His legs stopped drumming.

We sat without talking and Bobby's knees started pumping again. Even though the temperature was not more than 10oC, sweat was beading on his forehead. He swallowed hard and his hands went flat on the bench like he was ready to jump and run. Incessantly, he scanned the walk either for something familiar or something frightful; it was uncertain which, maybe both. He was making me nervous too. I glanced up and down the way.

"Why was this guy looking for you?" I asked, quietly.

"Because of you, man," he blurted.

"Me?"

"You wanted me to find out what I could about Chaban without getting hung up on something sharp, so I did, and I did. Now peril and menace be following me and I can't shake 'em. I'm screwed, blued and tattooed." He shook his head with resolution.

"We'll get this guy, Bobby." I tried to reassure him.

"Maybe in your dreams, my brother, but this space cadet is gone and I ain't coming back to Earth until I know he's been dead a year. Somebody better be showing me the stake that went through his heart too."

"Tell me what happened," I said.

"I was looking into what you asked, you know? Hanging out in a pub over in Saint-Germain-des-Prés in my blind guy outfit, having a Belgian and edging up behind these two guys, you know?"

"What pub?" I interrupted.

"Les Deux Magots off Rue de Seine, upriver a ways in the Latin Quarter."

"The Two Maggots? Seriously? Jesus, how do you find these places?"

"You asking Jesus or me? I don't know if he drinks much these days. I do and I follow my nose. I can smell a good brew in the next Arrondissement."

"Who were these guys?"

"That's what I'm telling you. At first, I thought they were just guys, you know? It was a Frenchman and a Spaniard with a broken nose. Both are a dime a dozen in Paris. Then I moved closer. The Spaniard kept playing with his nose and I didn't recognize him at first on account of two black eyes and his face being swelled up. I figured the nose must have been your handiwork because they were talking about somebody that sounded a lot like you and your girlfriend. Man, he was crazy mad and the Frenchman asked him to lower his voice more than once."

"It was self-defense," I said.

Bobby glanced over at me.

"Well self-d or not, I'm telling you this guy wanted your dice dangling from his rearview mirror. The Frenchman swore on the blessed virgin that no one was going to touch you except him. The Spaniard wasn't having it. He wanted your hide right then and there and he was going to get it. The Frenchman looked like he was going to strangle the guy on the spot. Finally, he gave Ricky Ricardo a green light. Your buddy said everything was in place anyway so Ricky could do what he wanted. He said he didn't care anymore. That's what I wanted to tell you, man." Bobby paused.

"What did the Frenchman look like?"

"Oh, he was your boy all right. He was charming, cunning and callous all at the same time. Good looking, muscular. I guess I would do him if I were a girl."

"It sounds like him."

"I'm telling you, it was him. He turned and stared at me once when he thought I was paying too much attention to the conversation and my blood dropped into frostbite range in about two seconds. No expression, you know? Eyes like ice picks. I felt like I was dead right there, from that moment on. I think I'm only breathing today because he allows it."

"Bobby, did Chaban give any details about what he was doing?"

"Nothing I could understand." He thought about the question. "He did say there was one more test to run before the final bang."

"Is that what he called it?"

"Yeah, that was when the Spaniard turned around and we freaking recognized each other. It was Calderón. He's the guy I was trying to pump for 411 on your boy. Hell, I didn't know they were sleeping together. Chaban looked at me with those cold eyes and smiled my death sentence. I was out of that chair and gone faster than a brother who woke up at a Klan meeting. I didn't stop running for three hours. Man, I gotta go."

"What are you going to do?" I asked.

"You got to be crazier than your old man. I'm blowing town and I recommend you do the same, brother. These guys are as serious as a swan dive off Eiffel and twice as deadly. They don't live in the same world as us normal people." He paused. "Well, I can't speak for you."

"Watch your mouth. You haven't been normal since '67 when we dropped a quarter sheet of acid in the dorm. I remember you thinking you'd turned into a real black panther and wanted to roam the campus naked. Man, it took me an hour to find you and get a leash around your skinny neck." We smiled.

"I don't remember that," Bobby said.

"Are you heading to Italy?" I asked.

"I thought about it but the girls are too hairy and they don't bathe regularly, not that I do. But judging from your honey, I might like to visit England before I die, which may be sooner than I plan." He paused. "You know, tie in with what's left of the hippie movement before time moves on and we find ourselves living with the Cleavers again."

"I don't think the world is going back there any time soon." We sat in silence.

"Yeah, you're probably right," he said, finally.

I stood with him.

"When you bubble up to the surface again, give me a holler."

"Watch your ass, man," he said.

"Coming and going. You too."

Bobby walked away, resuming his quick pace by the time he reached Pont Saint-Louis at the end of the park. He pulled a cigarette from his pocket, stopping long enough to light it and toss the match into the Seine. His dark figure took long strides across the narrow footbridge. I concentrated on him as he vanished into the crowds on Rue du Pont Saint-Phillippe thinking I had seen him for the last time. When I turned away, Zita was standing in front of me.

"Let's go. It's not safe here," she said.

"Thanks for watching our backs."

I put an arm around her and we strolled quietly down the path into the black shadows of Notre Dame's east side.

CHAPTER 37

I was sitting on a cold marble floor with my back against an unforgiving wall. It was a challenge sitting upright because the hard white wood of inlaid wainscoting caught me behind the head. My legs were drawn up to my chest. I couldn't tell where I was. A thick haze swirled through the air.

A strange, distant buzzing rode a stale draft from somewhere, and the stink of death was all around me. A sudden chill gripped my shoulders, and I shivered. My teeth chattered and I squeezed my legs tighter, but the cold stayed with me.

The fog thinned into a shadowy mist and I saw I was in a great open room. The wallpaper above me was covered with a fleurs-de-lis design intricately arranged in golden fields of faded lilies. The ceiling was hand-frescoed, depicting a hunting scene with two dogs and a fox frozen in a mid-air struggle of life and death while four horsemen looked on.

To my right stood an enormous hearth made of stone. At three meters across and more than two meters high, the firebox was bigger than most French bathrooms. Heavy embroidered curtains hung closed on tall windows, diffusing traces of light as the afternoon sun tried to find a way through the dense fabric.

People were in the room now. Some were sitting like me. Others were sprawled oddly on the bare floor near the lone piece of furniture, an expansive dark oak desk. A woman was lying on her side with her head gently resting in peaceful repose on an outstretched arm. Her dead eyes were locked onto my soul. There

221

were more bodies too, but this one scared me. I stared at her a long time before I could let go.

Above it all stood a man at the desk speaking into a handset extended from a long, stretched cord. In clouded profile, his fierce lips were moving, but there was no sound. He had one shoe resting on an inert torso at his feet.

"You see, there is your man," a small voice said at my ear. The little girl was sitting beside me. I was surprised to see her pale blue eyes reflecting my face with delight, and she was no longer bleeding from a mortal bullet wound. She was simply a beautiful little girl, full of innocent life and childish anticipation. When I smiled at her, she giggled with pre-teen excitement and perhaps a little embarrassment. There was no sign of fear or fate in her expression.

"It's only a dream," I said. "Why did you bring me here?"

"So you can see for yourself and learn."

"Learn what?"

The man angrily threw the telephone receiver on the desk. It bounced twice and snapped away like a rubber band as the cord recoiled. The receiver rolled to the floor, taking the heavy base of the telephone with it. The man removed his foot from the corpse and straightened. He looked at me and, for the first time, I recognized Chaban's stark features as they resolved on the formless face. Pure evil oozed from his smile then I realized he wasn't looking at me. Chaban's indifferent eyes had focused on the little girl.

As though awakening from contented sleep, one by one, the dead bodies rose and floated listlessly through the locked front door. A sweeping trail of slick, wet blood marked their path on the marble as it moved past us. The bright red smear was the only shock of color in the otherwise pastel scene. The stain radiated a peculiar light that shimmered translucently in the haze of the room.

"Learn what?" I asked a second time.

Chaban was talking on the telephone again though there was still no sound.

"Chaban is not like you," she said, suddenly turning serious. "You are plain to see, but him? He doesn't know how to love yet he harbors no hate, no remorse, really no emotion at all. He does not believe we are people, only targets and opportunities. He sees miserable creatures, yearning to live, but deserving to die. The few who believe they are accomplices will end up dead too," she paused. "I've said I don't know how he thinks but this is what he thinks."

She turned to Chaban. Their eyes fastened uncomfortably on one another. With a vicious smile, he raised his automatic weapon and pulled the trigger. The little girl's head exploded with tremendous fury, battering her body against the wainscoting and back again.

I caught her before she slammed face first onto the floor and pulled her to me. Pressing a palm to her head, I tried to cover the wound so she might live this time. Blood was pouring through my fingers and I couldn't stop it. I pushed harder, but I couldn't stop it.

The little girl calmly took my forearm and brought it down to my lap.

"Don't worry," she said. "The pain is already gone and I have accepted my death. It cannot be changed."

I was having trouble focusing through the returning fog. I held her tight. Her eyes were now the dead eyes that haunted me, staring blindly somewhere above my own. I was talking to her but my voice was fading. I shouted but she was melting back into the mist.

"Wake up! Do you hear me? Wake up!" Zita was shaking

me. "You're screaming in your sleep. Are you all right?"

"A nightmare," I said, rubbing my face with both hands. I sat up in bed.

"Was I there?"

"No."

"Thank goodness," she smiled. "I never want to be in anyone's bad dream." Her eyes met mine. "Please don't go mental on me. I need you in more ways than one."

"I'll be okay."

"Well, dear, I'll continue to worry about you, if you don't mind."

"We need to recheck Eiffel and the others this morning. Something's not right," I said. "Chaban knows we're scrutinizing every tourist attraction in Paris yet he's going forward with his plan regardless. Why? The man's not the suicidal type so he has another play we aren't seeing."

"I told our team to be obvious so everyone who approaches knows he or she is being observed. One can't miss the watchers so you may be correct. But why another test before he hits Eiffel, and what is it?"

"I don't know."

CHAPTER 38

The Eiffel Tower was a magnificent piece of architecture, pointing proudly skyward like one of Kennedy's missiles ready for its launch sequence. It was a curious contradiction that transformed this oddity from an embarrassment to the nineteenth century French consciousness into the single most recognizable structure in Western Europe. Not another such design can claim to capture the essence of a city like the Eiffel Tower does with Paris. Nowadays, self-respecting tourists would never think of leaving France without their own personal likeness of Eiffel's iron lady.

We walked across Quai Branly and entered the park from the northwest. One of four massive feet was only thirty meters from the edge of the road, looming up on the unsuspecting visitor like some mythical giant from one of my dreams. Holding Zita's hand, I squeezed through the morning crowds huddled under the base. Her surveillance team was here somewhere.

I glanced up at the bottom of the second level, more than thirty-eight stories away, and remembered the first time Zita had taken me up to the landing. Because the elevator components were still the original operating mechanism from 1889, I had asked if we might walk the stairs. That had been my first mistake of the day. The outdoor iron staircase had stripped my bravado with each subsequent step. In a matter of three flights, my life had gone from George C. Scott in the movie "Patton" to "Coward's Run" starring Mr. Magoo.

"I'll be right back, darling. Enjoy the view," Zita said.

Winded and progressively more scared with each step, I had climbed the last flight of stairs on all fours, just trying to hang on. I couldn't breathe, not from the exertion of a difficult climb but from my easy ascent into cold fear. I had been glad Zita couldn't see the pitiful, sweating slug behind her.

Standing on the platform 115 meters above Mother Earth had not been much better. I couldn't raise my head and shoulders fully erect, ready to hit the floor and hold on in case this metal dart decided to show me the Left Bank up close and personal as it fell. The open sky had been calling me, drawing me to the edge of sanity, and eventually it had coaxed me to the rib-high railing before I understood what had happened. The pull of gravity had been relentless, and it had taken the rest of my strength not to throw myself over the barrier into free fall.

To clear my head of paralyzing thoughts, I had started reciting useless facts about the Tower I'd learned in school. It weighed 7,300 metric tons, which was about the same weight as the air surrounding it, making the structure extremely light. Before I could envision a tornado carrying the whole thing off to Kansas, I had gone on. It was essentially a large erector set with 15,000 iron pieces and 2.5 million rivets. And I had heard one could see London from where I stood. I found out it helps if your eyes are open, so I never verified that.

For some reason, this had not forced the death wish out of my brain fast enough. With my mouth continuing to mumble dysfunctional details, people must have thought I was praying, but that was far from the truth. In fact, I hadn't wanted to take the chance God might actually hear me for once and remember he had owed me one from the day before. I hadn't been in any mood for paybacks, so I had broken off my soft whispers and forced myself to focus on the insect colony below.

The overcrowded cement path had been covered with ant-sized pedestrians crawling aimlessly but calmly over one another. A herd of ladybugs had marched in twos along Quai Branly, and I remembered seeing part of a yellow leaf covered with dozens of ants leisurely puttering along a narrow stream. No one had been in a hurry and all had been as peaceful as Silent Night.

Zita was winding her way toward me through the throngs of tourists milling about the southeast pylon, and I dropped my thoughts about the second level. She wore her ever-present smile riding high on alluring lips and greeted me like she had been away for weeks.

"Do your people have any news?" I asked.

"No, they've seen nothing larger than a nappy bag on the back of a pram."

"And what was inside the pram?"

"A babe was in one and all. One of our gents is posing as a photographer to get close to visitors with prams and wheelies."

"So, there's nothing as large as a bomb? I suppose he could be bringing it in pieces intending to assemble it here."

"The locals sweep the park, here and up top after closing each day. Security stays all night, along with our chaps. Any articles left are removed from the premises and taken to lost and found which is a short distance from here."

"Then, let's widen the search area. Chaban might have gotten his hands on a surface-to-air missile. Have your men check the rooftops in the surrounding neighborhood for potential launch sights. What about the sewers?"

We checked with the other surveillance teams at the Arc de Triomphe, Sacre Coeur, Sorbonne, Notre Dame, the Louvre and a few other minor museums. The reports were all the same. There were no threats. Were we wrong? Bombing Eiffel was a guess but it was a damn good one. It wasn't making sense. Evidence of

Chaban should have turned up somewhere by now if tourists were the target. What had happened to the test Bobby mentioned?

I had to admit many of these sites weren't right. The Arc de Triomphe didn't attract enough tourists at any one time and security at the Louvre was always tight. It was the same for some of the others but Eiffel was perfect for him. What else could cause widespread terror other than destroying the single most identifiable and most visited tourist attraction in Europe?

An explosion here with a death toll of thousands would send a message to the world through its tourists and bring travel commerce to its knees. Fear would become the overriding factor in every decision from now on and it would cost Europe billions in lost tourist revenue. I would have bet my old '68 Camaro on blocks back home Chaban's goal was to bring down Eiffel. If not, what then?

We didn't have to wait long for the answer.

CHAPTER 39

We found a small café along the Seine and decided to sit outside, where we could talk over a late lunch. A mild wind out of the south blew softly across our table in the direction of the river current. Early March had given us a clear, beautiful afternoon. The sun was already coming back north with renewed energy. The unexpected warmth felt good as it loosened our winter-weary bones.

A glass boat passed, touring the city by water. Camera flashes spotted its windows. Down the way, Pont Neuf crossed over the river to our right and Pont au Change was a little closer on the left. My attention was drawn to a woman across the river on Île de la Cité riding an ancient bicycle with fat tires and fenders. A canvas grocery bag filled the small basket that hung off the handlebars.

She tried navigating around an approaching gang of five or six children when our waiter arrived. Zita ordered the smoked salmon salad and a glass of chardonnay. The little barbarians laughingly forced the bicycle into one of the sidewalk posts lining the street. I opted for ham and cheese on a buttered baguette. The woman had managed to keep the bicycle upright but lost her bread and fruit in the gutter. Discouraged by the behavior of kids in Paris, I ordered a glass of Guinness draft.

Before the waiter returned with our drinks, I glanced back across the river for the woman and her bicycle. There was no sign of either except for a lone Valencia orange still lying in the gutter where it rolled. The punks were gone too, no doubt searching for another victim.

In recent years, roving bands of pre-teen juveniles had bombarded European cities. When these gangs of miniature thieves were on the clock, they were surrounding families of tourists, pulling, poking and grabbing at their clothes while begging for candy. Sometime later, the surprised vacationers would discover that their wallets, purses, cameras and gold teeth were all missing. If tourists were not convenient, these little hoodlums resorted to terrorizing the locals for fun.

I dragged the Guinness closer. There was an outline of a shamrock drawn in the creamy head with the last of the drippings as the dispenser shut down. An Irishman was working the tap today. I took a long pull of the beer and let the heavy syrup slowly drain down my throat. With only the slightest bitter taste, the Guinness stout on draft was by far the smoothest beer I have ever tasted.

But I did learn in an off-hours Dublin pub not far from St. James' Gate Brewery the year before that one pint was definitely my limit. Matching a woman drink for drink and after losing count at five, I had awoken in a strange bed with nothing but a three-day headache to remember her by. She had taken my wallet and my shoes. At the time, I believed the shoes were part of an initiation into some clandestine Irish group, though I hadn't been taught the secret handshake. Or maybe I just couldn't remember that either.

Zita swirled the wine in her glass and wrinkled her nose as if the grapes had suddenly soured. Her thoughts were miles from here, but she was doing her best to appear in good humor. She finally turned to me with concern in her expression. There was something else there too, something far worse. Her beautiful eyes reflected the fear in my own and it broke my heart. The situation was totally hopeless and I never felt so powerless to affect it.

"I wish I could think like a bloody Frenchman!" Zita said.

"I wish I could think like a psycho."

"You do Sunshine. That's what I love about you."

"If that were true," I said, "we'd already be using Chaban's privates for croquet balls on the back lawns at Buckingham Palace."

She sighed.

We ate in silence when the food arrived. My sandwich went down quickly without much conviction. Afterward, it seemed dry and tasteless.

Did I really think like Chaban? Granted, I was paranoid and a bit of a freethinker in our world of stark realities but I really didn't know how to summon at will that insane place in my brain where there was no logic, no judgment, no balance, and no right or wrong. It simply called me whenever it needed a day out.

And that was more often than I liked. To be honest, they were rages I couldn't stop, once started. I had gone berserk hundreds of times over the smallest thing. Hell, over nothing at all. Sometimes it even started as a joke, but soon rose to a fever pitch so hot that everything around me was eventually burned. There was just no controlling the what, when or why.

I couldn't depend on drugs to help either. Grass would never find its way to madness, cocaine was afraid to go there and acid couldn't guarantee to bring me back once we entered. Frustration and self-doubt shut down any psychotic breaks I may have conjured.

"I think we should squeeze the girl some more," I said. Before Zita's smile widened into an off-color remark, I added, "For information on Calderón."

"Your girl?" she asked. "What was her name?"

"You know very well. Therese Bertrand."

"Oh, yes. Indeed."

"I have an idea. If we can't find Chaban, then maybe we can find Calderón. Bobby said he wants to get his hands on me. Let's find him before he finds me, then it's on our terms. I thought he would have turned up by now anyway. As you keep reminding me, I'm not all that hard to find. Christ, you can't depend on anything these days. Let's lean on her a little more. I'm certain she'll give him up with a bit of persuasion."

"Oh, that sounds exciting," Zita cooed. "Unfortunately, we released her from the safe house early yesterday and she is back home by now. She seemed harmless enough and we needed the space for a Russian lad defecting from the Moscow Ballet. I'll have our man pick her up again for another chat. She ought to love that. I know I will! However, I do so love your technique. Would you like to interrogate her this time? Face to face? Or…?"

"You're a funny woman," I said.

"I don't want you to miss any of the fun, darling."

Our conversation was interrupted when the volume on a television somewhere close was abruptly turned loud. The sound was coming from inside the restaurant; a special news report was beginning. Waiters and other restaurant personnel were gathering around the small set in the bar to watch and listen. We heard the words 'dernières nouvelles,' breaking news. We moved inside and joined the growing crowd. No one spoke, except once when the kitchen man joined the group asking what was happening. The news announcer's face was grim as she presented her report.

We have just learned that a jumbo jet departing Orly International Airport in Paris within the prior hour has crashed into the Ermenonville Forest northwest of the city. Initial unconfirmed reports from the scene are telling us that everyone on board has perished in a massive explosion. At the current time, it is unclear whether the explosion occurred in the air or as a result of an impact. Please stay with us. We have a news crew arriving at the scene momentarily.

The bartender set half-dozen snifters on the bar along with an open bottle of Calvados. He opened his hands and raised his eyebrows, inviting us to join him. Pouring himself two fingers of apple brandy, he passed the bottle along. When we all had a drink in front of us, Zita and I sat quietly on stools and focused again on the television reporter.

Authorities at Orly are now confirming to us that an aircraft has disappeared from radar. Communications with Turkish Airlines Flight 981 bound for London were interrupted just seconds before the craft vanished from tower control instruments. Flight 981 was loaded to near capacity because of canceled flights at British European Airways due to the baggage handlers' strike. Several airlines rerouted travelers from canceled flights to Turkish Airlines minutes prior to its departure. It is feared that as many as 350 people may have been on board. The fate of these passengers is currently unknown.

At this time, we have the spokesman for air traffic control on the telephone line. Sir, are you able to give us any details on what happened today? 'I can only confirm that Flight 981 departed Orly at approximately 12:30 p.m. this afternoon for its short trip to London Heathrow. The airplane took off in an easterly direction, and then turned north to avoid Parisian air space, which is required by law. Shortly thereafter, the DC-10 Series 10 aircraft was cleared to flight level 230 and turned west toward London. One of our controllers did overhear a garbled transmission from the flight deck shortly after that. The words were indecipherable but the aircraft's pressurization and over speed warnings were clearly heard in the background of the dispatch. We are presently investigating and have no further information at this time.' Thank you, sir.

Sources are telling us that among the flight's passenger list were almost 200 British nationals, including 17 rugby players returning home after a match here yesterday, four prominent fashion models, British trade union leader James Conway and Olympic double silver medalist John Cooper. In addition, 25 American travelers, 48 Japanese bank trainees en route to London for a seminar, 44 Turks on holiday, 16 French citizens and 11 crew members were all listed on the manifest.

We understand that the area surrounding the suspected downed aircraft is uneven, heavily wooded natural forest with dense undergrowth in places, which will make rescue efforts quite difficult. Kilometers from the nearest motorway, the terrain is impassable to all but well-equipped outdoorsmen and very small vehicular traffic. Our news team has set up an impromptu roadside staging point near the crossing of N330 and D126 south of Senlis where fire and rescue personnel have begun to assemble. We are working to establish a live uplink back here to our studios for direct voice communications with our news crew. We will go there as soon as our technicians allow it.

We are joined now by McDonnell Douglas flight engineer, Dr. Pierre Armont, specialist in the relatively new DC-10 super jetliner. Dr. Armont, can you please tell us a bit about this type of aircraft? 'Yes, I can. The DC-10 was designed for medium to long-range flights, capable of carrying a maximum load of 380 passengers. The craft has the characteristic feature of two turbofan General Electric CF6 engines mounted to underwing pylons and a third engine at the base of the vertical stabilizer, or tail fin. To date, the DC-10 has been a reliable airplane with relatively few maintenance issues.'

Can you speculate on what could have possibly gone wrong with Flight 981? 'Certainly any number of failures could have occurred but I believe all of these would involve human error.

The DC-10 is the most technologically advanced piece of precision equipment in the world, quite capable of flying itself and during any type of emergency, I would rely 100% on its capacities and decision-making faculties over all types of human intervention. Now, if indeed the DC-10 did fail its purpose and mission, I would not rule out a devious plot perpetrated by those with murderous intent.'

Do you mean to say foul play? 'Well, yes. For example, a relatively small explosive device placed in the cargo hold, let us say in a piece of luggage, may cause a crack along the fuselage as it detonates. This principle is true of any aircraft. Because a confined explosion tends to force its containment casing outward, a normal consequence of such an explosion causes structural damage to the integrity of the frame. When this occurs, the basic laws of physics must inevitably triumph, allowing the strength of the wind to tear metal from the exposed fuselage. In turn, this action causes depressurization of the cargo and possibly the passenger compartment. Of course, the DC-10 is designed to fly quite well without pressurization, however, with any further level of tampering…well, I cannot say.'

Thank you, doctor. Let me interrupt you there for a moment. I believe we have confirmed communications via satellite telephone with our team in Ermenonville Forest. Yes, hello? 'Hello, I am reporting from the Flight 981 staging site for the search and rescue teams. Directly behind our position, we are able to see a thin plume of black smoke floating skyward. Early responders returning from the scene are confirming that there was indeed an air crash not two kilometers in from the motorway where I stand. The fire captain reports it is impossible to describe the untold horror he witnessed there. The entire airplane appears to have exploded on impact, but there was little to no fire on the ground. This fact negates what we know about other crashes when the fuel tanks are teeming with petrol, leaving this reporter to speculate on a probable mid-air explosion.

'We have heard from other sources that a farmer near the town of Saint-Pathus, approximately 15 kilometers south of here, is claiming to have several large airplane pieces and a number of bodies in his turnip fields. Because the aircraft has been reduced to mere fragments in the forest behind me, it will take some time to determine if any pieces are missing. If the farmer's claims are proven true, then the sky over his fields, again some 15 kilometers from here, may have witnessed the initial incident that caused the failure of Flight 981. In the meantime, a rescue team has been dispatched to Saint-Pathus. I can tell you, with these facts coming together, that rumors are epidemic here regarding an on-board bomb that may have played a major role in 981's demise.

'I am reluctant to tell you that early responders are reporting there are no survivors at the crash site and only a few dozen bodies, perhaps as many as 40, may be all that are visually identifiable. All else is unknown at the moment. Beyond that, we are getting conflicting reports from the impact site of rampant confusion everywhere. It is chaotic with no clear direction on where or how to start. Rescue teams are currently meeting there to determine how to approach the situation. I will keep the line open as more details are announced here at Ermenonville Forest. Until then, this is Jean Bleu, reporting for Channel 3 News.'

We will have much more information as the situation unfolds. Please stay with us. Now, we have two additional aeronautical experts who will discuss various scenarios that may have caused the failure of 981 and the ramifications for immediate air travel, as well as a doctor of psychiatry from the Sorbonne, to help us cope with this tragedy. Let me start by asking…

I finished the Calvados with a huge gulp and glanced at Zita, who still held her eyes fixed on the television screen. Here it was. Chaban's final test and we were caught flat-footed.

CHAPTER 40

Before 6:00 a.m. the next morning, Zita and I were crouched behind a yellow Peugeot in a tiny parking lot across from a long, continuous block of three-story apartments. We were on a well-hidden side street, about a kilometer southeast of Jardin du Luxembourg in the heart of the university district. The heavy wooden door bearing the weathered numerals 329 was the fourth from the left along the blanched-white building front. Interior lamps illuminated several flats, but the middle window remained dark. The Rue Amyot neighborhood offered comfortable housing for Sorbonne's post-graduate students and, as it turned out, also afforded a great safe house for our friend Marcus Calderón.

The early mist swirled upward in the grainy darkness, the dew steadily evaporating as night reluctantly gave way to day. Within the hour, the sun would be rolling over Paris, leaving a warming breeze in its wake, but for the moment, the predawn chill still clung to the bones with numbing sincerity.

I rose from behind the car and stood at the edge of the building at one end of the parking lot. My legs were stiff from the cold, so I tapped my heels against the brickwork. I peered in both directions, not expecting to see anything moving, and massaged the back of my neck with a cold hand.

It had been a very long time since I was forced to rise at such an ungodly hour and I felt sick. My stomach was off. I glanced at the time, wondering how far away lunch might be, but it was difficult to focus on something as close to my face as a wristwatch.

To make matters worse, I was getting a headache that began with a pulsing shot over the right temple and hammered against my skull like a rhythmic beating with a policeman's sap. I faced the sidewalk and squeezed my lids roughly over a pair of dry, burning eyes. The next time I need to get up at 4:00 a.m., I thought, I'd just stay up all night from the evening before. The feeling couldn't possibly be any worse than this.

Reflexively, my eyes rose to the dark windows of Calderón's apartment. We knew he wasn't there. I already picked the lock in the dead of dark and we searched the studio as silently as a couple of mice. The room was empty. Junk mail lay inside the door, there were dirty dishes on the counter, and the bed was still unmade from the day before. We thought we knew where he had been last evening when an MI6 surveillance team had followed Bertrand to the Hotel St. Michel. When she had come out alone at 9:30 p.m., a promising lead had evaporated in the wind.

Zita's man had picked up the lady after midnight when she reported for her shift at Chaud. He had been patiently waiting, nodding his head to the revving music and taking a curious interest in one of the female patrons. The agent had been saved from making a huge mistake with a transvestite he had been chatting up when Therese Bertrand strolled through the door still a little flushed from the evening's workout.

The lady had been cooperative. She understood now that we were not interested in taking her money. Allowing her to maintain possession of her purse while we had questioned her, she said Calderón had unexpectedly stopped by her flat at 7 p.m. wanting desperately to see her. She had been on her way out but took a few minutes to alter her plans. The man had deep pockets and he treated her very well. Besides, Calderón was handsome, and he was better than most where it counted.

"Why didn't you call us?" Zita asked.

"I was a little busy," she said.

"How long did he stay at your flat?"

"No time at all. He has this thing for hotels so we always go out. I told you, we were at the Hotel St. Michel."

"Yes, well, he's no longer there, is he?"

"Do you blame him? After the last reception you gave him, he is a little paranoid about doors bursting open. We arrived separately. Markie waited outside and came up the back stairs when he was certain I hadn't been followed inside. He was agitated, not at his best this time and he was gone before I woke up."

"What time was that?"

"I don't know. I dozed off. Perhaps it was 9:30 or later."

"Did he say anything about what he's doing in Paris? With whom he's meeting?"

"No, but he was laughing quietly to himself when we were finished and I thought it was because of me. You know, like I was good for him. He said no, it's not that at all. The man he works for had a very successful day today so he too was happy."

"Did Calderón mention what this success entailed?" Zita asked.

"No, but he did say the joke was on the American who had broken his nose." Then speaking directly to me, "he said you are stupid, no offense, and you won't find Chaban because you search in the wrong places. Markie said he'll deal with you soon in his own way."

"Do you know how to contact him again?"

"I don't know his telephone," she hesitated. "Markie had a package with him tonight he said he needed to deliver later. It was addressed to him and I remember because the flat's so close to mine. It is 329 Rue Amyot, number 6."

"You do know, if you're lying, we can and will put a hold on your bank accounts?" Zita mentioned.

"Both of them, how will I live?" she fretted.

"Nice try. We have found four so far in addition to your Swiss account." Therese Bertrand's body visibly shrank in her chair.

"It's the truth," she whispered.

Bertrand was on the verge of tears, focused on her folded hands. I pulled her small black purse from my pocket and laid it on the table. With three fingers, I pushed it across the space between us until it nudged her knuckle. Slowly she pulled the bag to her lap and, hiding her face, said thank you almost inaudibly.

I rejoined Zita behind the ugly, round-backed Peugeot. She was sitting on the ground with her legs stretched out flat resting her eyes. Her knees bounced slightly to keep a small spark burning in her ankles. I squatted next to her.

"Is he coming?" she asked, without opening her eyes.

"He'll come."

"My fingers are so cold I may not be able to shoot him."

"I don't want you to shoot him. I want to talk to him." Zita gaped at me like my eyeballs had just rolled down my face.

"Since when do you take the logical path?" she asked.

"I have a plan."

The plan involved using myself as bait when Calderón turned up. I needed to know how much he wanted to get his hands on me. I hoped it was bad enough to risk his freedom, bad enough to sacrifice Chaban's work. It all depended on how he reacted when we surprised him. What could possibly go wrong with that plan? I guess that's why no one lives forever. Shallow plans always lead to shallow graves.

The sun climbed above the horizon but had yet to break over the tops of the buildings. Light was crawling across us like ground fog and the asphalt was beginning to warm. The dampness was comfortably receding.

I pulled Zita to her feet. She straightened unsteadily and stiffened both legs before she could walk. We stood at the edge of the building, staring down the empty road. Dammit. Where's Calderón? 'He's coming,' I heard the little voice say. 'He's coming.'

Apartment lights across the way were switching off and people were hitting the street to take on the first day of the week. Students carried knapsacks and messenger bags. Some had books tucked under an arm. Others held school folders and papers pressed to their breasts to ward off the morning chill but all walked with an urgency that only comes with youth. I silently urged them to keep moving and clear the area before Calderón appeared.

When he eventually turned onto Rue Amyot from Rue Lhomond, I smiled. He ambled along the avenue with his eyes to the ground, either to feign privacy or to hide his drunkenness. But, it was my experience focusing on one's feet only helped with uneven pavement and finding pennies. Calderón should have had his attention directed on what was ahead.

I waited for two young docents to pass our position. One was waving his arms telling a story the other looked like he'd already heard a hundred times. The second man was nodding impatiently as they walked past. The narrow lane that lay between a row of parked cars and the building was now clear.

I stepped out onto the sidewalk as Calderón staggered closer. Thirty meters, twenty meters, ten meters. He sensed something blocking his path and straightened slowly. He squinted, trying to focus.

"Puta madre pendejo!" he said when he finally recognized me. "I owe you something."

"Do you want to wait in line or take your shot now?" I asked, as I dropped my coat to the concrete.

Rage flashed. Hot fire consumed Calderón. Laying all reason aside, he charged. I stood my ground, legs apart in a slight crouch, muscles fixed against the impact. At the last second, I stepped into a roundhouse kick that landed below the stomach. Uncontrolled momentum carried him forward and down as he lost his balance. His hands hit the pavers hard and slid forward. Layers of skin were sandpapered to smooth muscle. The rough surface was splashed with the blood smear of a very angry man.

Adrenaline coursed through Calderón's veins like lightning along a 12-gauge wire. There was no way a scrape was going to slow him down. He righted himself and sidestepped to my left, anticipating another kick. The man was huge, over 180 centimeters and built like a brick house. I tried to stay away from him until his energy surge dissipated. He swung wildly in my direction with a right hook that missed by a kilometer.

Calderón surprised me with a quick lunge, dropping me to my back. Hungry for the kill, he punched me high on the cheekbone. A second blow caught me on the temple. We wrestled, trying to find the best grip. Calderón wrapped huge hands around my throat, but seeping blood made his fingers slick.

Finally, lifting my head by the ears, he slammed it to the pavement. The impact caused both of us to lose our hold. We grabbed again. I heard the hollow sound of metal as it tapped on cranial bone. Zita slid the gun barrel past Calderón's cheek so he could see the tip out of the corner of his eye.

"Enough," she whispered. Calderón reluctantly let go of my face and hair and staggered to his feet, breathing heavily.

"I had this under control," I complained.

"Yes, I thought so but we don't have time for you boys to swap machismo. Runaway evolution stops here," she said. Zita turned to Calderón. "If you fight again, I will shoot your arm. If you attempt to run, I'll shoot your leg so please don't experiment with thinking."

Calderón understood. He was visibly calming, mostly because he wasn't looking at me any longer. The gun held at the back of his head took priority for the moment. He grimaced and gingerly pressed raw palms to his pants.

He clenched and unclenched his fists. I could tell from his expression the pain level was sharply rising. The fasciae were gone from the palms and most of the fingers. Probably some muscle as well. Blood wasn't dripping from the palms any longer, but they were both candy-apple red and slick from the oozing of exposed capillaries and veins.

"Let's go upstairs and take care of those hands. We need to talk," I said.

CHAPTER 41

Calderón was tied to the arms of a breakfast chair, palms up. Zita poured alcohol on the open scrapes and it burned like soul blistering torture. His body shook as antiseptic ran through his raw fingers. Calderón didn't utter a sound, but his wrists strained against the bindings and his back arched as pain shot through him. I thought he was going to pass out but somehow he held it together.

There were no bandages in the tiny flat so we laid linen hand towels over each palm to temporarily keep contaminants from settling on the exposed flesh. Proper medical care would have to wait. Calderón's breathing was returning to normal when the air abruptly caught in his exhale and he was forced to refill his lungs to capacity. Life's energy slowly escaped again with the next breath and he squeezed his eyes, resigned and defeated.

"We need to talk," I said.

Calderón made no sign he heard me until he slowly turned in my direction.

"I have nothing to say to you," he said.

The stubborn man was not going to give up Chaban so I thought I would try something a bit unusual.

"You are in big trouble here, Mr. Calderón."

"From you? I don't think so."

"No, there's no trouble from me. In fact, I actually admire your cleverness. It was quite brilliant but, you see, I don't make the laws. With yesterday's criminal act having international ramifications, I would say you'll be charged with the death penalty in a half dozen countries. So unless you have whiskers and like to lick yourself, it seems you're going to come up short on lives to give for your cause."

I paused until he looked at me.

"On the other hand, there's no capital punishment to speak of here in Europe. If you cooperate, we can possibly make sure you remain here to live comfortably in the French penal system. You know, smokes when you want them, a girl friend or two, released on weekends."

"You're not serious."

"Of course not. You're going to wish you had died with your victims. Here's what's going to happen. The Japanese will soften you up with a good full-body caning and, buddy, that's going to sting worse than those hands there. Then, the Americans will cramp your sphincter with a date in the electric chair. It's an inhuman way to die so you'll get a chance to appeal the verdict. Honestly though, we'll still fry you, then send your body to England where the Brits will dangle the toasted remains over Trafalgar Square until the crows pick the meat from your carcass and your bones are covered with pigeon shit."

Zita's eyes widened slightly.

"Don't think that your immortal soul will fare any better. You do have one, don't you, Marcus? Pope Paul tells me he's preparing your excommunication as we speak. It appears you won't be making that ascent into the light any time soon. Do you know what a nice Catholic boy like you is going to be doing for the next millennium as penance? Any guess? Come on, take a guess."

I waited.

"You, my friend, are going to be picking up dog shit in St. Roch's pastures. It's right in the papal decree, man. If you were paying attention in school, you know Roch is the patron saint of dogs and he collects every soul from every dog that ever lived. They all do their business on the meadow grass and someone has to clean it up. That guy is you. Otherwise, his nightly strolls would be through ankle-deep dog doo and that wouldn't be very saintly, would it? On the upside, there's no need to worry about the stink because you won't exactly be breathing anymore.

"After a thousand years of that, you'll get to know Roch pretty well. He's also the patron saint of bachelors, surgeons, tile makers, invalids, diseased cattle and the falsely accused. I don't know how he was granted guardianship over so many of these soulless creatures but you can ask him. Hell, over tea and biscuits sometime you can tell him the sad story of how you were framed."

Calderón smirked.

"And don't get too excited that Christ will end up with what's left of you. Remember, it was his old man who invented the holy practice of an eye for an eye. You probably know He's not keen on someone blowing up His children. When people explode, it's difficult to sort the souls from the bodies with anything except a nut picker. It really is a mess. But He's going to put them back together and, if you ever get there, they're all going to be waiting for you."

"Don't ask how he knows such things," Zita offered, softly.

"You're both loco," Calderón sneered.

"You have no idea, mi amigo," I said. "But right now, you should be thinking about what you need to do to pry yourself out of your current situation here with me, and get to the safety of the nearest police station. Life's funny that way, you know. Yesterday, you were taunting their ignorance. Today, you need the authorities to pull your fat from the fire because I'm about to show you just how loco I really am." I tugged the Laguiole knife from my pocket and opened the blade. "Pull his pants down."

Zita unbuttoned his fly and pulled the loose trousers down at the knees. Calderón struggled, making it easier to strip the pants. The material fell around his ankles.

"What do you think you're doing? I'll have your balls for this!" Calderón screamed.

"Well, that is the point, isn't it?" I threatened. "Don't worry. I only need the sack for a tobacco pouch but I think Chaban may want your marbles so they won't go to waste. Right about now, he should be opening the message I sent saying you're confessing faster than a drunken sailor to his shipmates so..."

"Lies! I'm loyal. He knows that. In fact, if I don't report in soon, he knows he can find me here."

"Mr. Calderón," I sighed. "We need to get down to business. You've put us on a very tight schedule. I'll give you ten minutes to talk to me or I will leave you tied to that chair without your bag. I'll put your balls on the counter over there and you can discuss your loyalty with your boss when he gets here."

"I don't know anything!" he said.

"Well, you know Chaban better than I do and it's apparent to me you've outlived your usefulness to him. Help me out and I'll help you out."

Calderón dropped his head and shook it.

"I don't know what you want from me."

"Tell me about your little trick at Orly."

"There's nothing to tell," he insisted.

"Nine minutes."

"You can't stop him anyway. I'll tell you." There was a twinge of defiance, and maybe a little pride, in Calderón's voice. "It was easy. Airport security is a joke. For a week's pay, the gate guards would sell their mothers' teeth. The plans were no problem to obtain either, a little money, a few threats." He tipped his head. "You understand."

"What plans?" I asked. "Do you mean the airport or the airplane?"

"Well both, you fool. I arranged for the exchange and brought the Douglas drawings down to Paris. Le Roux delivered the airport schematic. Sadly, later on he became greedy and demanded more money for his part."

"So you killed him."

"Look, we knew you were in Marseilles at the same time as us. Yeah, we had eyes on you all the time. I told Le Roux if he took you down I'd give him a bonus, but he failed. After that, I had to convince him to do the right thing. Without more money, he said I'd have to pry the plans from his dead fingers." Calderón shrugged. "I thought it was a choice."

"What happened to Flight 981?"

"We were going to use a big charge like Blanco's because we were unsure of just how much it would take to get the job done. But, the arrogant engineer told me all we needed was a small bomb in the right place to do the same damage."

"Go on." I cleaned a fingernail with the knife point.

"The idiot told me a few grams of your military-grade C4 on the cargo door would give the desired result. It would be barely noticeable, a small explosion to loosen the lock and jar the seal. When the wind took the door away, the reduced pressure would stress the system and down comes the airplane."

Stress the system was the understatement of the year. Passenger exits on a DC-10 were designed to roll inward, preventing them from opening while the cabin was pressurized. The cargo hatch, however, had a contrary design. Due to its size, the designers didn't want the door to swing inside the bay because of the large amount of valuable cargo space it would consume. Instead, it was built to swing outward, allowing freight to be stored directly behind the opening. But, in the event of any failure in the locking mechanism, the hatch would be forced open by the high pressure inside and the thin atmosphere outside.

As the cargo hold depressurized, the difference in pressure between compartments might cause the deck separating them to buckle, sucking out rows of seating down through the ruptured cargo hatch. The aircraft's guidance cables, buried in the flooring, would also rip loose. The pilots would be unable to control the airliner and it would fall like a skydiver without a parachute. All things considered, it was a deadly compilation of designs.

"And this was a test?" I asked.

"What do you think?"

"What were you testing? What more can you do?"

"He said you were stupid."

"Stupid and crazy," I agreed. "It's a very unpredictable mixture, amigo. That combination is known to explode and permanently disfigure someone's face or at least take the skin off his hands if handled improperly. Oh, wait. We've already done that." Calderón growled like a wild animal.

"I'm not your friend. Stop calling me that!"

"I'm the only friend you've got left, as sad as that might be for both of us. You better be nice to me," I said. "But don't worry, we won't be swapping any spit today."

"You disgust me," he muttered.

"Okay, Marcus. Let's see how well I was listening. Squeal when the story goes off track. You get lucky and find out how any 16-year old can bring down an airplane. Your buddy has a thirst for death and somebody has your backs with a crap house full of money. Maybe it's the Palestinians, maybe the Syrians or some other pack of lunatics. It really doesn't matter though, does it? The two of you walk away with the cash while these misplaced martyrs are filling their Islamic brothers with whitewash about heaven's virgins just waiting for them to die.

"So, you run your test and it works perfectly while we're all sightseeing at Eiffel with fingers up our noses. I was just thinking too small, mesmerized by one tree while you were gearing up to napalm the whole damned forest. I was thinking maybe Paris but you were thinking Europe."

Calderón was staring at the wall again. The muscles in his jaw were working like he was slowly chewing gum. He was thinking, even though all expression had flushed from his face.

"What could possibly live up to the marketing hype created by Flight 981?" I continued. "Let's see, blow up another airplane? No, Orly is too hot. Were you ticked because we camped out at your primary target? Did you hit the airport to pull us away from Eiffel?"

Calderón laughed.

"We considered the Tower but it was too much trouble. The airplane was easy."

"So, we're jacking a couple hundred tourists on an airplane? Wait a minute. Now I see the forest and the cities around it. Paris, Brussels, London, Frankfort. One plane crash is bad luck. Two downed planes put a pebble in Europe's panties. Three planes start looking like the Angel of Darkness riding across the continent. Four planes, well you get the idea."

"Fuck you!" Calderón struggled against the leather wrapping his wrists.

"Is that all you've got? After the terrific conversation we've had, that's all you've got?" I asked.

A pall filled the air.

"Well, you cooperated and gave us all of this great information," I finally said. "As a reward Zita, what do you think about leaving him here for his friend to pick up? No harm, no foul. We'll call it even."

"Okay," she answered tentatively.

"Let's go." Then to Calderón, I said, "You can keep your bag and balls for now, and good luck explaining your cooperation to Chaban."

"I told you nothing. Nothing!" Calderón yelled through the door as it closed behind me.

"So, what do you say? Does he believe I'm crazy?" I asked Zita.

"I do. Do you know how many laws you just broke? Do you even know the law?"

"Which one?"

"Any of them, Doc!"

"Not really."

"Please tell me you were joking about leaving him for Chaban."

We started down the stairs.

"Of course, Angel. Let Calderón think about it for an hour or so then have your men pick him up. I want that clown to spend the next 100 years in prison married to the guy with the most cigarettes."

"What exactly did he tell us, then?"

"Honestly, not all that much but he gave me time to work it out. His reaction at the end confirmed it. I hit a nerve."

"And...?" she asked.

"And, I believe he told us the goal, for Chaban and his backers, is economic failure in Europe. Imagine the impact of five planes crashing on the same day. Chaos would rip the world apart. You can forget about ever getting on another airplane. That one act would define the meaning of terror forevermore and nothing would ever be the same.

"On the plus side, I'm not convinced that Chaban has the wherewithal to accomplish this feat in more than one city. Two or three cities could mean total collapse of the world's economic structure. God help us if he has that capability. To be safe, have MI6 alert the surrounding countries and we'll take care of Paris."

"However, like you told Calderón, Orly is cranked down tighter than my old granny's knickers. How do we know where he'll hit?"

"I believe Calderón also told us where. Chaban will stay where he's most comfortable, the place he knows the best, right here in Paris. Why you might ask? Remember the code I found in his room at Montparnasse Hotel? T1 S5 G17 9151. Terminal 1, Satellite 5, Gate 17...?"

Zita smiled as she understood.

"Terminal 1 at the new Charles de Gaulle Airport opens in four days."

CHAPTER 42

The planning and construction of Aéroport de Paris Nord began in 1966 on 32 square kilometers of land not far north of Paris. Renamed Charles de Gaulle International Airport after the president's death in 1970, France's architectural masterpiece was finally set to begin service on March 8, 1974. As the first to open, Terminal 1 boasted the avant-garde design of architect Paul Andreu. It was a massive, 10-story circular structure surrounded by eight satellite pods. From the sky, the image reminded most people of a giant octopus.

The main floor of the central complex would serve as a home for waiting travelers while seven of the satellite pods would house four departure gates each with boarding rooms where passengers embarked on their journeys. The eighth satellite was primarily employed as access for cargo vehicles, temporary storage, preflight preparations and final customs inspections.

A white painter's van unhurriedly rolled into the parking garage and down the incline under the base of the passenger complex. The name on the side panel of the small transport read La Chapelle Familia, Peintres Professionnels above an address in the 18th Arrondissement. The vehicle followed the temporary signs to the second level below ground before the driver parked opposite a contractor's battered equipment truck.

The high-pitched drumming of the pistons sounded like the effortless chattering of a motorcycle in the enclosed canyon of the underground garage. The engine suddenly raced and coughed before abruptly shutting down. The van sat patiently while the exhaust system cooled with a constant tick, tick, tick.

The driver stepped out. He stretched his arms above his head and walked to the rear of the van, listening for movement on the incline. He was tall and slender, dressed in a personalized white jumpsuit. A cap was pulled down low over his eyes. Adjusting his sunglasses, he smiled. The area was empty, quiet.

The painter walked across the ramp to the back doors of the contractor's van. He pulled up a pant leg slightly and bent to tie a shoe. While crouching, he slipped a length of pipe from a sleeve, set the timer and rolled it a little more than an arm's length under the contractor's truck. He opened the back of the painter's van.

"We have an hour," he said to the figure inside.

A second man stepped out of the darkness in the rear cage and jumped to the ground. Also dressed in a white jumpsuit, he was a few centimeters shorter than the first and not nearly as thin. He sported a bushy, light-brown mustache that hung down over his upper lip. It must have been itching because he kept fidgeting with it.

His gaze shifted up the ramp at a sudden noise.

The sound of scraping metal on concrete preceded an old gardener as he came around a blind corner. He was carrying more tools than a sane man needed to manicure the airport's entire green space. A shovel had slipped from his grip and it partially dragged beside him, tapping out the rhythm of his tired feet. Instead of stopping to rearrange the load, the old man persevered until he reached the tailgate of a motorized three-wheeled wagon. He dropped the tools on the concrete, causing a loud clatter that punctuated the scraping of the shovel.

"Bonjour," said the short painter.

The old greenskeeper nodded without meeting his eyes. He tossed his tools in the bed of the wagon one at a time before finally working his way into the tight driver's seat. He fired up the two-cylinder engine, and the motor jumped to life. The vehicle bucked backward, moving in a quick reverse arc down the incline.

The wagon rolled forward with the gardener hunched over the wheel, paying no attention to anything except guiding the vehicle to the surface without incident. Riding the brakes all the way to the top, it took a long time for the tiny truck to disappear.

The painters retrieved their brushes, rollers, pans and a five-liter bucket of paint. The tall man loaded a canvas bag with the small items and pulled the straps over his shoulder while the other lifted the heavy bucket. The two trudged down the ramp to where the service doors stood open.

They stopped, surprised at the size of the expansive room. The open warehouse beneath the passenger terminal was a circular 75,000 square meters. Around the outside wall were eight identical openings at set intervals, exposing underground passages leading to the satellites. There, passenger luggage, airline equipment, raw materials, retail products, mail, medicine and every other type of cargo one might imagine would be loaded into waiting airplane bellies and shipped to worldwide destinations.

Although currently strewn with electrical and plumbing supplies, construction materials and assorted other finishing products, the main hall was scheduled to be emptied sometime today and initial inventories would find their way into brand new bins and chain link storage areas. Air transportation was swiftly becoming critical to many logistics networks, essential to managing an increasing demand and ever-expanding flow of goods and resources such as people, products, services and information. Without the airlines, it was virtually impossible today to execute a national or international trade strategy, moving commodities from manufacturing sources to points of sale in a timely manner.

The painters weaved a crooked path through the warehouse and entered Numéro Cinq du Tunnel. The entrance widened into a well-lit, two-lane highway running a half kilometer to the satellite's 10,000 square meter loading and unloading facility. It was a long walk. Neither spoke, afraid the echo would carry.

The man with the mustache pressed the button, raising the large metal access door to the jet bridges. The sun's rays bounced off the tarmac like a black mirror and flooded across the floor as the barrier rose. The bright light was blinding.

So far, so good. I shaded my eyes with both hands and looked out across the asphalt. The airport felt oddly abandoned, like all the people and machines had inexplicably vanished. A swirling wind danced a sad dance with the dust under the passenger walkway, circling like two lost souls searching for the doorway to heaven. I turned to Zita.

"Clear," she said, looking back down the passage.

I ran for the staircase to the movable jet bridge at Gate 17. Taking the steps two at a time, I landed on the steel platform in under twelve seconds. Faced with a single-core, aluminum alloy door, I glanced through the small window.

Embedded in the door was a pushbutton combination lock. I pulled Calderón code from my pocket to check the number sequence and punched in 9151. The door popped open. I smiled. A billion dollars was stuffed into a cookie jar and for safekeeping, the key was handed to a thief with a sweet tooth. Entry couldn't have been easier.

The air inside was fetid and cold despite a heavy tarp hanging across the open end. I blew into my left fist and steamy breath flowed between the curled fingers like cigarette smoke. It felt like a damp coffin. The hallway was a gray, unforgiving tube that would soon funnel passengers down a descending ramp to destinations unknown. A thin but durable carpet covered the center of the bleak runway. The three vacation posters framed in thin silver and screwed to sheet metal walls were as good as the decorations were going to get.

Friday begins here in this dismal place, I thought. Chaban would have set his plan in motion long ago; each detail calculated and verified a thousand times over. Problems had been defined and solutions had already been documented. Every component was in place long before the fun would begin. I imagined waiting for opening day was the hardest part for him.

Because the combination to the door was included in the code, I knew the best chance of finding explosives was right here, specifically in the guidance mechanism that coupled the bridge hood to the waiting aircraft. It was the only safe place with easy access. The juice had to be here if it was anywhere.

I pulled a Phillips head screwdriver from my back pocket and kneeled in front of the ramp steering device. Carefully removing the screws along the top and sides of the plate beneath the control panel, I set them aside and loosened the three screws at the bottom. The heavy steel plate wanted to fall away, but I held it in place until I tucked the screwdriver between my knees.

Cautiously, I lowered the top a few centimeters and peered inside. A lone wire taped to the plate was connected to a mercury tilt switch wedged safely for the moment in a bundle of steering wires. If I dropped the plate to the floor, its weight would pull the switch free and detonate the booby trap. That would have seriously damaged my complexion, right through to the back of my head.

There was still a little play in the wire so I lowered the plate another five centimeters. Tucked painstakingly among the wires in the cavity were one, two, three, four, five, six, seven, eight apple-sized balls of putty individually sealed in Saran Wrap. I carefully lifted one out and hefted it. It weighed about the same as a baseball.

The combination lock clicked and the outside door swung open. I dropped the explosive in front of me. Despite the cold, sweat ran down my back. I delicately closed the plate and fumbled for the screwdriver.

"Que faites-vous?" A man's voice asked.

"Vérification mécanique en finale," I said, without turning around.

"Tout va bien?"

"Fil lâche dans cette unité. Tout est bon maintenant." Bad wiring caused a short in the steering system but I was able to change it out. It looks like it's working now.

The man hesitated like he was waiting for something. I felt him watching as each screw was reinserted. He started to walk then stopped when I dropped the last screw. The air was heavy. It pushed on my shoulders and squeezed my chest. I waited for the man to make his way up the ramp before I removed the screws again.

From a space beneath the C4, I pulled a paper lunch bag free, careful not to disturb the mercury switch. Inside were eight detonators. Each was approximately six centimeters long, connected with thin wiring to tiny twist timers.

It was worse than imagined; eight balls of C4 found, eight airplanes lost, and Europe was doomed; all within a few hours. How could so little destroy so much? Terrorism was about to go mainstream and once done, consequences could not be undone.

The putty suddenly gave me an idea. Replacing the cover plate, I bounded down the stairs and rejoined Zita.

"What happened? I almost came after you when that guy went through the door behind you," Zita said.

"Found it," I said.

"Where is it?"

"I left it in place."

"Are you daft? You left it?" she asked.

"Yes, my lady. I have a plan. I need to get to a toy store—one that sells American toys."

"Toys? Now you remember a birthday back home?"

"Hardly, I'll explain on the way."

We jogged back through the tunnel to the staging area beneath the main building and walked from there. The area was now crowded with uniformed CDG laborers piling construction equipment and leftover materials on pallets while forklifts transferred loads to the ramp entrance. Private trucks were backed up as close as they dared and journeymen sorted through the gear for personal tools. We slipped through workers and around pallets.

Zita retrieved the length of pipe she had rolled under the contractor's truck. It was our backup plan when everything went south at Gate 17. If we were not able to return within the hour, Zita had designed a device to create a thick stream of smoke without an actual explosion. It would be enough to divert attention from us to a possible car fire in the underground garage.

"Seventeen minutes remaining. This is a new record for you," she said.

"No, wait. Remember the time in Rome when I was back earlier?"

"Doc, we were at the wrong address."

"Oh, right," I smiled. "Let's go shopping."

CHAPTER 43

Celebration activities around Europe's premier air traffic center at Charles De Gaulle International Airport were relatively low key during the week leading up to its long awaited opening. In atypical French fashion, there was little pomp and circumstance surrounding the launch of this high-tech, ultramodern facility. Several newspapers proclaimed France as the new economic leader of Europe while one independent radio station chastised the government for mismanaging such a disaster prone project, but in general the media was also uncharacteristically quiet.

It was true this day was postponed a number of times in recent months. With any multi-year development project, unforeseen delays setback construction progress; most notably once to repair a huge crack in the dome of the main hall and again when a crane tipped, damaging a section of the tarmac required for runway access. As a result of such debacles, it was inevitable that even the usually exuberant French public had been forced to accept a stance of wait and see. The airport would open when the airport opened and not before.

In spite of it all, CDG officials were preparing for lengthy inauguration ceremonies complete with live orchestral music, champagne, hors d'oeuvres and high-ranking political guests. An afternoon start to the first day's flight schedule was designed to accommodate planned festivities, expected to start promptly at 8:00 a.m. and properly consume the full morning.

President Georges Pompidou was booked as keynote speaker during the program but he had suddenly taken ill. Two consummate politicians had already stepped up to fill the void. Secretary General Édouard Balladur and Jacques Chirac, the newly appointed Minister of the Interior, would now address the audience instead. It was Chirac who would dedicate the new airport to honor the war hero and former president, General Charles De Gaulle.

There would be no further delays to the commencement of initial operations at CDG. Inaugural flights would begin on Friday, March 8, 1974 without incident and this would be a historical day to remember. Additional staff had been hired to ensure dignitary and traveler experience from day one would be nothing short of astonishing. Airport personnel were busy with finishing work inside the main terminal, along the concourse and inside boarding salons. The machinery behind the curtains would have to catch up when it was able.

Because no protests or other disruptions were expected to delay opening activities, full security forces were not yet in place but were due to begin phasing in on Thursday, the day before planned ceremonies. Already thin police details were on notice they would be working with skeleton crews until the airport was fully up and functional. As a result, with inadequate numbers during the first weeks of operation, protection teams were likely to be overwhelmed if what Chaban wanted to happen actually did happen.

While keeping a close eye on Gate 17 in particular, Zita and I spent Wednesday and Thursday in maintenance uniforms hosing down tarmacs and sweeping up leftover construction debris surrounding the base of the satellites. Sanitation trucks came through on the first morning and left more of a mess than they had cleaned. Instead of sucking up the rubble, the water and hard bristles of the giant brushes saturated the smaller chunks and ground them into a light brown, pasty mud that oozed into the cracks and uneven surfaces of the new asphalt. That was not coming off with a push broom, though I might have tried harder if I had known when the mud hit the fan on Friday that no one would ever be clean again.

By the end of the second day, we had checked the other gate ramps a dozen times without finding any further criminal intent. Using a magic marker, I ran a thin line across one screw on each of the steering system cover plates to make it easier to identify tampering. But there had been none since I initially removed each guidance system cover, searching for more explosives. Gate 17 was the only storage location and even that went untouched.

We took a huge risk by not alerting the locals to the coming danger, but increased activity around the airport would have warned Chaban and his team. He would have seen too many policemen for too little circumstance and immediately known the situation was all wrong. He needed to feel his plan had been undetected and authorities were simply clueless, despite the disappearance of Calderón.

I wanted him to appear at the airport right in front of me. I wanted this to be done here and now. If tomorrow didn't end in Paris, I'd be chasing this man all over Europe, always a step behind.

I fell asleep early Thursday evening, waking briefly when Zita folded her arms around me and rested her head on my shoulder. I slept the sleep of sweet nonexistence, without dreaming, without moving, without breathing. Time passed or maybe it didn't. I had no idea but when I opened my eyes, I was standing in the gritty haze of early evening at the foot of a freshly covered grave.

The small white marble marker had a simple phrase chiseled

in the stone, 'Un Ange Vit Ici,' an angel lives here. Nearby a large bouquet of flowers had tipped over and lay withering on the ground. This was all that remained of the little girl, I thought, nearly a year after her death. I reached down and re-centered the flowers at the headstone.

She was sitting on a small incline beyond the grave with her head dipped low over crisscrossed legs. Completely motionless except for the slight rising and falling of her tiny shoulders, her figure shown as soft light against the black that engulfed her. Occasionally, she would straighten to casually throw a clot of dirt into nothingness. She turned her whole body toward the sound of my footsteps and smiled. The little girl wiped at the blood on her face.

"I hoped you would come," she said.

"How've you been?" I asked, immediately realizing it was no doubt the dumbest question I had ever asked.

"I'm dead," she said. Her face reflected a peculiar mix of expressions; anguish, amazement, amusement, and awareness.

"I'll get Chaban. This will end tomorrow."

"At what cost?"

"No cost," I said, confused. "I have a plan that'll save many lives. I catch him or I don't. Either way, it'll work. I'm changing what he thinks will happen tomorrow. My plan..."

"Yes, yes, your plan," she knowingly snapped. Then, more gently, "If only life and death were as simple as the plans we make."

"What do you mean?"

"A plan merely defines an outcome we wish to happen. Surely, you know that. We think in terms of plans but we are driven by the choices we must make." She threw another clod of dirt and continued. "They're nothing more than compromises that create more choices which lead to even more compromises. All of us are unintentionally pulled along random paths. Somewhere wishes and wants are lost and reality arrives. Have you ever wondered how and why you end up where you are?"

"Every day," I admitted.

"Be careful that vengeance does not become confused with righteousness." Her opaque blind eyes revealed no emotion.

"Are you worried about me dying?" I smiled.

"No," she whispered. "I'm worried you don't change tomorrow but tomorrow changes you."

I sat next to the little girl and threw a dirt clod of my own as the twilight descended into near total darkness. The half-moon looked like a loose button on the cloak of night and did little to light the shadows. I could barely make out the black tree line in front of me. Details of the surrounding forest and graveyard were disappearing quickly.

"Do you know what this place is?" she asked absently.

"Is it your home?" I asked tentatively. I didn't know what else to call the place where her body had been laid to rest.

"These are the woods that shuddered when Flight 981 surrendered to its misfortune," she corrected.

"But," I stammered, pointing toward the grave that I thought was hers.

"It belongs to another," she said. "And yet we are all one now."

I don't know if it was her suggestion that slipped through my defenses or if it was a nightmare of my own creation but there was a sudden movement in the field. I saw people. A man foraged for his head and left arm. He bent once to pick up something. Examining it closely, he eventually dropped it and moved on. A mother walked aimlessly. She held her arms as if she was carrying an infant even though there was only emptiness at her breast. Stopping in front of me, she unfolded her arms and held them out to me. The pain in her eyes was crushing. I was helpless to do anything.

I slammed my eyes shut. I didn't want any more of this. I wanted them to be monsters. I didn't want them to be human beings, though I knew they were. People were so much scarier than monsters.

When I opened my eyes, near total darkness had closed in on me. I half-heartedly focused on the field through the eclipsed light, very afraid there might be another movement. I was happy it was too dark to detect anything beyond a few meters in the soundless obsidian.

I closed my eyes again and was content to quietly sit beside the little girl. I didn't want to know about the horror in the forest. I didn't want to think about the lost lives and unsettled souls wandering Ermenonville. I was frozen with fear, afraid I now had a whole generation of people who would haunt my sleep. I wanted to look at the little girl, but I couldn't. God, please, there is no room in my head for more than her.

I felt fire beneath my eyelids. A fever flashed through my head. Demons flooded the emptiness in my chest and rhythmically poked at my insides. I shut down and concentrated on quieting the taunts. Nothing helped. I quit breathing until the storm around me quieted. My body rose up on soft cloud.

Then I dropped through the darkness; picking up speed, falling faster and faster. I tried to raise my hand to steady the universe but I couldn't move. I was strapped down in an airplane seat. I squirmed, trying to free myself. People were on both sides. They appraised me curiously but no one said a word. An icy wind burned my face, forcing my breathing to a minimum.

"Hey," the little girl shook me. My body moved clumsily like the bones had melted away. I swallowed hard on a dry throat. "Hey, it's time to go. Are you going to sleep all morning? It's half past six."

I opened my eyes, expecting to see the little girl or something far worse. Instead, I was greeted by Zita's smile. "It's time, love."

CHAPTER 44

Yesterday's gusting winds had finally died down by the time we walked across to the truck. The new day was already warming and I could smell the sweet fragrance of fresh flowers above the fading scent of the night mist. New blooms overflowed the gardens surrounding the single-story safe house that lay on a quiet avenue off Rue de Charonne, not far from Cimetière du Père Lachaise. The early morning was promising another beautiful spring day in Paris' 11th Arrondissement and I counted on this fortune stretching north to the airport.

We arrived at employee parking on the ring road sometime before 7:30 a.m. A crowded bus shuttled workers to the lower level of the main terminal where the employees filtered past two dozen time clocks. People were courteous, an unusual gesture for Parisians. They were looking forward to inauguration activities and the promise of new jobs. Today was a day they wanted to remember and I could almost guarantee that would happen.

I started to thank Zita for believing in me, but I already saw the answer in her eyes. Until the end of forever. She smiled.

"Ready?" I asked.

"Please don't get yourself killed or maimed," she answered.

"I'll do my best."

"Right, lash that to your brain and I might feel a little better."

"Always," I grinned.

"I do hope your plan works."

"Have I ever let you down?"

"Amaze me, yes. Bewilder me, certainly. Infuriate me, absolutely, but let me down, never." She smiled.

I lifted Zita's right hand and kissed her palm. We parted without another word. I had misgivings as she walked away but realized Zita was already far better at this job than I would ever be. She would be fine, I thought. It was me I should be worried about. A hand instinctively went to my throat to ensure St. Jude was still hanging safely in place. But honestly, if I was going to have half a chance of surviving today, I would need a living, breathing saint beside me wielding a two-meter staff like a Kung Fu master.

Zita worked the passenger lounge inside Gate 17, watching people around the ramp door. Nervous Nellies were prime suspects and loiterers were not far behind. She stopped to chat with fidgety folks and carefully followed dawdlers. If the C4 was removed via the boarding area, she would follow to determine where it was going.

With her vacuum set to low, Zita worked her way close to the boarding door to examine the lock. How was it secured? Was a key required on both sides? Was it double bolted? She twisted the knob hard, but it didn't move.

"Il est verrouillé, mademoiselle," said a man in an Air France uniform. Of course, the door was locked, she thought. It would remain so until the first passengers flooded into the waiting area later this afternoon.

"Oui, monsieur." Zita returned to her vacuuming.

Workmen were finishing water pipe maintenance in the ceiling. A soundproofing panel had been moved aside and an employee was buried to the waist making final adjustments to a leaking sprinkler seal. Judging from the conversation he was having with himself, the man had lost all patience with the project. Though muffled, his running narrative was punctuated by many of the colors in the rainbow. It took two co-workers to steady the ladder as he danced on the top step.

Boarding personnel were performing last-minute inquiries on a state-of-the-art data processing system that used a new text terminal. This innovative interface brought information inquiry into the space age, reducing response times to just fifteen seconds. In recent years, advances in technology went from zero to sixty, pushing computer capabilities far beyond our dreams. As a result, human imagination and expectation were going along for the ride. Most large information-intensive corporations like banks, insurance companies and airlines had already jumped on the bandwagon, integrating electronic genius into common information handling procedures.

I milled around outside the terminal where sixteen aircraft were poised for an invasion of passengers marking the start of flight services out of Charles de Gaulle International Airport. Eight new DC-10s, fleet mates to the airliner lost during the crash of Flight 981 less than a week ago, stood ready to be the first to hit Runway 8R/26L and fly into history. Bound for New York, Dallas, London, Rome, Ankara, Delhi, Rio de Janeiro and Mexico City, these super liners could carry a full load of almost 400 passengers with a maximum takeoff weight of more than 263,000 kilograms. With a wingspan of fifty meters and a length of almost fifty-six meters, the DC-10 was the latest entry into the marketplace for McDonnell Douglas and already the pride of the Pan Am, BOAC, Air France and Air India fleets despite its dubious early record.

Twin DC-8s flanked one of their bigger DC-10 cousins at Gate 12. A workhorse in its own right, the DC-8 represented a distinguished chapter in commercial air travel. It was one of the earliest jet-powered passenger carriers and in the years following its maiden flight, the DC-8 established commercial transport world records for speed, altitude, distance and payload. Its good safety record made it a reliable passenger choice for the past fifteen years. Even though the DC-10 was gaining in public approval as the preferred way to travel, the DC-8 still commanded much of the sky over Europe.

Three DC-9s kept the other McDonnell Douglas planes company. Designed to operate on smaller runways, the DC-9 delivered jet service to short- and middle-range routes at regional cities previously able to only offer access to prop planes for its customers. The tail-mounted engines allowed for a cleaner design with full wing flaps to increase lift and shorter ground clearance to accommodate smaller airports. Destined for French cities, these Air France aircraft were set to deliver Charles de Gaulle's first consignments to local markets in Lyon, Marseilles and Nice.

Boeing was represented as well, with three Lufthansa 727s rounding out the sixteen passenger transports occupying gates on the Terminal 1 satellites. Still the best-selling aircraft in the world, the narrow-body 727 was arguably also the most versatile, though without a doubt the noisiest airplane ever built. It remained a crew favorite, however, because of its unprecedented low-speed landing and takeoff capabilities. At the same time, the 727 provided its passengers with exceptional jet luxury and travel comfort. A few years ago, a 727 was the stage for D.B. Cooper's very creative leap into history over the American Northwest with $200,000 in extorted money. But we were in for more than ransom this time.

The cargo doors were all standing open, waiting to be loaded with who knows how many metric tons of cargo, and a quarter kilo of C4. With close to 5,000 travelers taking their assigned seats prior to lift-off, Charles de Gaulle International Airport, Paris and the rest of Europe were in real trouble. It was already past 10:00 a.m. and I hadn't seen a soul near Gate 17. I second-guessed my plan and desperately wanted to double-check the steering mechanism to make sure the C4 was still in place.

"Qu'est-ce que tu fais ici?" Startled, I spun around. A strange little man was staring at me from the seat of an airport tractor. His head was tilted to allow cigarette smoke to curl up past a closed eye.

"What…" stumbled out of me.

"English, shit!" The man pulled the cigarette from his teeth. "What do you think you're doing here?"

"I'm your temporary baggage loader."

The man shook his head.

"Says who?"

"They told me inside that I have to report to Gate 17 and work here if I expect to get paid."

"I don't need you at this gate. Business here has been concluded. Everything except the luggage was packed in last night. "

I shrugged.

"Dammit! The luggage comes out in the next hour," he sighed. "If I must have you here, you'll stand outside and throw bags on the conveyor belt. I'll be in the belly. Otherwise, it'll be a disaster." Pausing, he glowered at me and shook his head adding, "Do your job. Mind your business and you'll stay out of trouble. Can I trust you to do that? There'll be something in it for you."

I nodded. He took one last drag on the cigarette and flicked the butt at my feet. I stepped on the burning ember as he drove away.

Prep crews began flooding the tarmac. A trio of aircraft fuelers worked diligently around a BP petrol truck on the next satellite down. Two were busy uncoiling a hose and the third man was already up a ladder uncapping an under-wing fuel connector on one of the DC-10s. He precariously balanced on the second step from the top in order to lock the nozzle in place.

An electrician attached lines from the nose section of another DC-10 to a waiting power cart. One mechanic inspected the brake hydraulics in the wheel well of a 727 while another furiously took notes on crucial diagnostic information. A man walked with a radio pressed to his face. As he passed me, it sounded like he was reporting to the control tower.

And suddenly there he was. An uncomfortable young fellow approached the ramp stairs. He was a child, really, appearing too young to hold an airport job and behaving like he didn't belong on the tarmac, anyway. With one hand on the bottom rail he swung his head from side to side to see if anyone was paying attention. Our eyes locked, and he awkwardly nodded before starting up the steps.

"Hey, Englishman," the little man shouted from the tractor. "It's time to earn your pay."

He pulled tandem baggage carts to a stop close enough to catch a foot. I stepped back. Another cigarette burned between the stained fingers of his steering wheel hand. I stared at the kid on the jet bridge platform.

"Now!" the little man commanded.

He cranked the tow truck and swung the small train in a large circle toward the far side of the DC-10 where the loader was already in place at the cargo door. I made a mental note to throw this guy under his tractor before the end of the day.

I was counting on the kid to get it right. He needed to do one thing; deliver the explosives to the DC-10s. After that, it would only take a few seconds to press each baseball in place, insert a detonator, set the timer, secure the cargo door, and seal Europe's fate. Chaban had to believe his plan was working.

The little man switched on the rolling conveyor. Getting my attention, he pointed to the baggage cart and made a pitching motion at the rubber runner slowing making its way to the top. So much for my training, I thought. I nodded my understanding as he hopped aboard, rode the belt to the open bay and disappeared inside.

After throwing the first bags on the belt, the kid exited the ramp door and bounced down the stairs carrying a thin canvas pouch. Step one was complete; he didn't blow himself up. I expected him to come to the DC-10 but instead he turned under the jet bridge in the direction of Gate 20.

I glanced up from the conveyor to the aircraft windows. Passengers were in the cabin, placing carry-on items in the overhead and settling into assigned seats. A few strained to identify their bags and ensure each was properly loaded. One teenager continued to watch from an aft window until I was finished unloading one cart and halfway through the other.

"Où est François?" It was the kid. The canvas bag was gone and he was holding the last blob of C4 close to his body like a baseball pitcher eyeing a signal.

"Do you have something for him? I'll pass it along," I said, reaching for the putty ball.

"No, sir, this is my last delivery and he has my money," the boy switched to English.

I pointed. The kid jumped on the conveyor and rode it up to the cargo hold. Watching the pair closely in the opening, I continued to pitch luggage onto the belt until François called for me to stop. The two spoke for a few more seconds. As I lifted the last suitcase from the baggage cart, the boy pocketed his money and turned to leave. Three steps down the ramp, François raised a suppressed semi-automatic pistol and shot the kid in the back of the head.

The bullet hit the nasal cavity and splattered brains and eyeballs as the boy fell. The inert body gently returned to the cargo door and dropped inside. François glared sharply down the ramp and purposefully waved the weapon for me to load the last suitcase. He pocketed the pistol and laid the C4 at his feet before dragging the kid farther into the interior of the aircraft.

I raced up the conveyor belt and was surprised to see François already returning. Without breaking stride, I slammed against the killer, knocking him sideways. He landed on a bed of suitcases and I was on top of him before he could recover. I hit him under the right eye with the heel of my hand and delivered a savage punch to his Adam's apple.

Desperately gasping for breath, he swung his arms wildly and caught me with a forearm across the face that stung as his uniformed arm scraped flesh. I blocked his next attempt. Rising up I punched him in the heart, stunning him.

"You stupid son of a bitch!" I screamed. "Did you have to kill the kid?" I pulled François by the feet off the luggage pile, bouncing his head on the floor. He twisted out of my grip and staggered to his feet with the revolver in his hand. He coughed and wiped tears from his face. François backed away from me. He stopped in the open door to pick up the C4.

"Who is stupid now huh, Englishman?" He coughed again and spat blood on the floor. "You are dead and I am rich. So, who is stupid now?"

"That would still be you. You're the one holding a fist full of silly putty."

"Silly putty?" he asked, grinning. "Do you mean my little explosive here?" he sneered.

"Smell it. Not C4. It's silly putty; just a child's toy."

"You're lying. All Englishmen lie!"

"Not English either. I'm an American so you're stupid yet again."

He lifted the gun quickly with a stiff arm. When François

cocked the hammer, I swear I saw the bullet fall into place at the back of the chamber. His lips formed a crooked smirk as his neck exploded in a fountain of red.

Dropping the gun, the killer clutched awkwardly at the wound but lost his balance and fell. His body went into spasms. I watched his legs jerk as blood pulsed onto the cargo floor. Unlike what the movies teach us, this was not an instant death. Bleeding out through an artery could take 45 to 60 seconds. Final death may even be a little later if adrenaline had constricted the vessels.

Zita stood in the doorway. She guided her shooting arm around the area expecting additional danger.

"Are you all right?" she asked.

"He was alone. There's no one else," I said.

She relaxed her stance and slid the weapon back inside her jumpsuit.

"How many times have I told you to carry a gun?" she reprimanded me. "I cannot continue saving your sorry rear."

"Let's close this thing up and get out of here."

CHAPTER 45

I had replaced the C4 baseballs with a popular child's toy called Silly Putty. Mixing the putty with a little soil to dull down its light pinkish hue made it a passable replica for military-grade explosives, especially when wrapped in cellophane. Experts could easily differentiate between the two when held in the hand but if most of us were not paying great attention or didn't know any better, color and consistency were generally uniform, the weight of equal amounts was roughly within grams and both burned slowly when set on fire.

That's where the similarities ended. Silly Putty bounced almost as well as a rubber ball and could lift print from a newspaper, but it was usually not coveted for its explosive capabilities. The detonation velocity of C4, on the other hand, was more than 8,000 meters per second. It was extremely good at focusing a blast and punching holes in anything from sheet metal to steel plate and everything in between, including airplane cargo doors.

Zita shut down the conveyor belt as I swung the heavy cargo door closed and secured the latching mechanism. It was tricky getting the seal to seat properly but it finally engaged and I shoved the handle home. My foot slipped and I nearly fell seven meters to the ground. Zita was laughing at me when I pulled the loader clear and joined her at the terminal wall.

The powerful GE engines began to spin and gas fumes sucked oxygen from the air. It was impossible to breathe deeply and swirling grit chipped at our faces as we jogged the perimeter of the main building. The jet exhaust followed us through the tunnel formed by the curve of the satellites.

A DC-10 began its slow roll across the tarmac with the honor of first to depart from Charles De Gaulle International Airport. The departure crew at Gate 13 was backing out a DC-8. Other planes waited for these two to clear the lane. The noise was deafening this close to the revving engines. Zita covered her ears and was trying desperately not to succumb to the hurricane-force exhaust.

I was positive Chaban was close. He needed to see the aircraft lifting off with his precious cargo and all were en route to disaster. He would then find a quiet place to celebrate the murders of countless innocent people and revel in single-handedly driving Europe back to the Dark Ages. If the detonation timers were set full on, we had possibly another hour to an hour and a half before Chaban became suspicious, he hadn't heard about an explosion or two.

The observation deck was the obvious choice to watch the activities. It was right below the restricted control center on the top level of the Traffic Management Tower and had a clear view of the tarmac. The area was crowded today, filled with dignitaries, politicians and other attention seekers, but Chaban would be there all the same. He would be enjoying the ground hustle, the fueling, the loading and the last-minute maintenance checks.

I imagined him pressed to the window, paying close attention to the baggage handling operations, especially around the cargo doors. I could see him nudging onlookers aside for a better view. He would watch while each jumbo jet was prepared and secured. He would see no police, no dogs, no precautions of any kind. Chaban would wait patiently for the bomb-laden aircraft to receive final ground clearance and he would smile as each flight lifted off to the east before turning toward its destination.

A blood-bath would result if we tried to take him on the observation deck so we decided to wait for his descent to ground level and pray everyone didn't decide to leave at the same time. We had no way of knowing how many bodyguards protected him but we thought perhaps one or two at most.

There were only two ways down from the tower, a single elevator to the left and an enclosed staircase to the right. The small lobby was tight to say the least. It was either the very worst or the very best place to engage your enemy, depending on whether or not you liked to hug and kiss the guy you were going to kill.

I did and Zita didn't. She liked to shoot and she said one needed space to shoot properly. I liked to fight, partly because guns scared me and partly because I believed I had the advantage if I could disarm someone before the guns started blazing. Zita reminded me a weapon can also be drawn in close quarters and when that happened, one couldn't run fast enough or far enough to get away. We decided to take them outside the lobby entrance.

"Do you have a gun for me?" I asked.

"Do I have a gun for you? Oh, now you want a gun?" she responded, in disbelief. "No, I do not have a bloody gun for you. Why didn't you retrieve the one the cargo chap was pointing at you?"

"I didn't think of it at the time. Fine, I'll stay with my knife," I said. "I'm betting Chaban will be the first to leave the party but I don't reckon it matters. He has to come out this way. Is it all right to stand here by the door or would you prefer to move further back so you can shoot properly?"

"How about I shoot you right now?" She asked, humorlessly

I intended my comment to be sarcastic but the more I thought about it, I realized standing off ten meters and shooting Chaban in the back was a brilliant idea.

The entry to the lobby swung inward like many in Europe. This was usually not a good thing if you were trapped inside a crowded building during an unchecked gas fire. But, since glass doors had a tendency to reflect images in the arc of the swing, these doors were proving beneficial for two people pressed against the exterior walls who needed to remain hidden. We waited.

The ding of the elevator broke the silence as it descended to the main level. I thumbed open my knife with an audible click and held it in a reverse grip with the blade toward my wrist. Zita's weapon hung on the far side of her profile. A woman's sultry laugh vaguely seeped into the foyer as the elevator doors rattled apart. The sound grew stronger when half of the double door swung in. We turned, ready to advance on whoever appeared.

An older man and a woman barely out of her teens came through the doors. The man, sporting a rich suntan and trying to look twenty years younger, glanced in my direction and I nodded. He stared through me as if he didn't see a human being standing there and nonchalantly turned back to his companion, saying something rude I didn't quite catch.

I thought I should have cut his throat on the spot to teach them a lesson about why we should be courteous, even to menial cockroaches. Even insects have feelings and who knows what might set off a murderous rampage, like saying something rude.

I watched the pair as they turned toward the car park, uncertain they would make it to a hotel before need and nature crossed paths. The girl's hand slipped from her partner's waist to his backside as she playfully grabbed a handful of derrière. The man pulled the young woman closer and leaned his cheek down onto the top of her head. It was difficult to walk so entangled, but both were making the best of it. Swaying along like a couple of drunken friends, they eventually made it through the VIP entrance to the underground garage.

A glint of sunlight off the vertical stabilizer of a Boeing 727 caught my attention. It was the last to leave the gate area, slowly rolling across the tarmac toward Runway 8R/26L. I cringed as the revving thrusters peaked at 140-decibels.

The initial aircraft departure window would close with this lift-off and the arrival window would open. Departures were intentionally choreographed with no overlap today to enhance the excitement of inauguration day. If scheduled arrivals appeared early over the skies of the new airport, they would be held at the inner marker until all the aircraft had taken off.

Chaban would leave soon. The eight aircraft under his control were en route to an odd sense of history affecting Europe for many years to come. He would now be very excited, perhaps a little arrogant and without a doubt expecting great things in his psychotic future. But expectations were a bitch when they turned out to be the opposite of what was expected.

I felt the electronic thump of the elevator mechanism engage, followed by the vibration of the 1000-kilogram motor coming from the machine room behind me. I counted to myself, four seconds per floor, level three, level two, level one, ground floor. The doors parted. Multiple, fast-moving footsteps echoed in the lobby. Both double doors swung in.

A gun came through the door nearest me, followed by a beefy arm. The weapon was a Spanish single-action, blowback-style pistol manufactured by Astra, which I thought went out of service in the 1950s. The Astra 400 had been the sidearm of choice during the Spanish Civil War because of its accuracy and stopping power, even though it was bulky and difficult to operate.

Weighing more than a kilo, it took a strong person to carry such a cumbersome weapon.

Before the man completely cleared the door, I grabbed the gun hand by the wrist, pulled him off balance, and ripped across his forearm with the knife. The blade sliced through his light jacket, down into skin and muscle, before hitting something hard. He screamed but didn't release the gun. I drew him in closer and sliced the waist flab along his right side before I heard the sound of metal hitting concrete. The stunned man staggered backward. I kicked his knee, and he went down in a heap.

I learned to knock a man down when he was injured, otherwise adrenaline would keep him coming. He needed time to realize he was hurt, which always happened when he tried to get up. It was a simple distraction, and it worked every time.

The man rolled over and tried to sit. His right arm wouldn't support the weight. Falling to his face, he wailed and grabbed the gushing wound on his forearm.

Zita was rolling around on the concrete with another gunman. I wasn't sure how it happened, but she appeared to be doing fine. They were wrestling over the man's gun when it went off. The bullet hit the ground above their heads and skittered across the tarmac.

Zita's weapon was near the wall. I started for it when I heard the unmistakable click of a revolver's hammer not far from the side of my face. It was the only sound that could make you review your life and regret every decision you ever made. And right now, I regretted not expecting another gunman.

"Very good," Chaban said. "I'm truly impressed. I almost hate to kill you now." The weapon was within a finger's length of my chin. "I assume I have Calderón to thank for this? You'll want to put a bullet in his brain before I find him."

"Police have him."

"I really thought you were stupid."

"So I heard."

I folded my knife and slipped it into a pocket. I was done for the day and raised my hands.

"Put your arms down." He grinned. "Please, this isn't an American movie. I don't plan a long conversation. I intend to kill you directly, though I do need to tell you, as usual, you are late. The game's over and I win again."

"What exactly did you win?" I asked, trying to buy time.

"Everything, obviously," he said. "Don't you see? The world is about to fall apart."

"And when the dust settles, you'll walk in and sort it all out for us?"

"Hardly," his voice came out in a chopped laugh. "I couldn't care less about these pathetic beings. I was paid to present Europe with a creative situation. Why that was and what they do with it is of no interest to me. Please don't think I'm some sort of grandiose psychopath with world domination cravings. That, my young friend, is just too much work."

There was a long silence, like he was considering something.

"You and I are two sides of a coin, aren't we?" He asked, finally. "I love to watch people die, and you love to try to save them. What a perfect pair. Nothing else will ever be as much fun, will it? It's a shame I won't have you to play with in the future. I was really starting to like you."

Chaban's extended arm tightened. The revolver steadied against my chin. He was going to shoot me and go about his day. I peered into his steel-gray eyes and saw something I hadn't expected.

I wanted to see a total lack of empathy. I wanted to see the black bottom of fourth-world paranoia. I wanted to see swamp alligator crazy. Instead, the crystal-clear sanity of reason and right was staring back at me. I saw the calm intelligence he used to calculate and recalculate every brush stroke in his masterpiece. I saw the untroubled conscience allowing him to pull the trigger without another thought.

A gunshot exploded under the overhang, shattering the door glass. I flinched. Chaban glanced at the two struggling on the ground. I ducked below his outstretched arm and slammed him viciously to the ground. He landed flat on his back, cracking his head on the concrete. The pistol flew onto the service road.

On top of him, I smashed his head on the sidewalk twice more before he punched my elbow and I collapsed. Chaban staggered to his feet and lashed out blindly with a furious kick catching me on the right shoulder. A second kick missed as I rolled away. Off balance, he fell to his hands and knees.

Chaban stood too fast and reeled from the pounding his head had taken. He took a step and tried stomping on my face but I diverted the thrust into the curb and twisted his body away from me. I steamrolled into the back of his legs and he fell across me. He elbowed my stomach, and I dropped to my back.

Chaban was on his feet again. I couldn't prevent the next assault from catching me below the breastbone. A heavy shoe crushed my stomach. The air coughed out of me. He followed with another kick to the chest. I folded in, trying to breathe, expecting another jolt to the gut. The next blow glanced off my temple and nearly finished me.

Chaban stood unsteadily over me. He vomited. Blinking hard, he tried to clear his vision, but it wasn't working. He swayed. Where was the gun? I couldn't move. Chaban vaulted over me and trotted unsteadily for the car park. Where was the damned pistol?

Chaban burst through the glass doors at the pedestrian entrance, barely able to catch the handle to stop himself from collapsing. I deliberately wheeled up to one knee to check my own vitals. My body was a pincushion of pain but otherwise everything felt about right. Nothing seemed broken.

Zita had lost the advantage and her assailant was straddling her. With a hand still on the weapon, she struggled to keep the barrel out of her face. The man pushed her head away. He pried at her fingers. He choked her and still she fought back.

Opening my knife on the run, I landed with my knee in the small of the man's back and my right hand under his chin. He lurched forward, then snapped back like a rubber band. The momentum almost threw me off. I pulled his face up and away from Zita, but the determined gunman would not release the weapon.

"Relax or die," I said. "Comprendre?"

The man didn't move, so I inserted the blade under the lowest rib two or three centimeters deep and held it there. I had his attention now but still he didn't move.

"It's loyal of you but your boss has left you here to die with us. Living might be a better choice under the circumstances. Which will it be?" He remained silent. I sighed. "I'm about to sneeze and there's no telling how far the blade might slip so please hurry with your decision."

Matter-of-factly, the man relaxed and surrendered the weapon to Zita. Extracting the knife from his ribs, I pulled him backward to the ground and pressed a knee on his chest. He moved calmly under me, not offering resistance but rather testing the severity of his wound. His breathing quickened at one point, returning to normal when he moved again. Expressionlessly, he stared into my eyes.

"Nothing vital," I said. "It's in the fat above the kidney and below the lung."

Zita grabbed the man's wrist forcefully and handcuffed him

to the handle on the shattered door. Without a word, she handed me his weapon and picked up her own. Examining it closely, she found a scratch on the automatic slide caused when it hit the rough concrete. She concentrated for too long trying to buff the nick with a thumb, then ejected the chambered round and pushed the gun into a pocket.

I bent over the other man. He was still clutching a bleeding forearm. His breathing was heavy and irregular. I raised an eyelid. The pupil was constricted, and he was at the point of passing out. I pulled his shirttail from his pants and cut a strip from the bottom. Wrapping the material around the man's upper arm, I tied off a makeshift tourniquet at the elbow.

"Sir, can you hear me?" There was no response, but I continued even though I drew a blank on any French I'd ever learned. If the man heard, I'm not certain he understood. "Help is on the way. You'll be fine. Slow your breathing down and try to relax." I looked at Zita. "Let's get that bastard."

CHAPTER 46

The overhead illumination in the car park was sporadic. Workers had installed every other fluorescent tube in order to meet opening day deadlines. It took a few seconds for our eyes to adjust from the spiking sunlight. Tires screeched around the curve of the up-ramp and an engine gunned for its top speed. The driver swerved in our direction, crushing the passenger door on a concrete support as the car flew by.

Zita stepped from behind the pillar and fired three times into the back of the blue Renault sports car before it disappeared through the exit gate. Two bullets shattered the back glass, and the third lodged in the rear mounted-engine compartment. Chaban was on the move, and Zita was right behind him.

Within half a minute, I had an old panel truck hot-wired and caught up with her outside the car park on the airport road toward Lille. Pulling alongside, she jumped in before I came to a full stop.

"Which way?" I shouted.

"To the right onto A1. North," she pointed, breathlessly.

I took the ramp to the motorway and sped up to 140 km/h, hoping it would be enough because I doubted this old dog could do much more. The highway was empty except for an 18-wheel tractor trailer plodding along at slow speed. Our van came up behind it too fast and I barely avoided a collision by breaking out of the semi's draft at the last second. The van jerked into the left lane and almost tipped on its side before stabilizing.

In the rearview mirror, the flashing headlights of a fast-approaching vehicle grabbed my attention. I awkwardly guided the van in front of the large truck as a motorcycle blew by us at over 250 km/h. Without a helmet, the rider was laid out flat behind the tiniest windscreen I ever saw. Dammit! I didn't think we'd ever catch Chaban's sports car in this old crate. I wished I'd found something faster to steal.

We hadn't seen Chaban since leaving the airport; more than twenty kilometers without a sign. The sports car was capable of 300 km/h. If he had floored the high-performance machine, he was in Munich by now wearing an alpine hat and drinking a liter of Roggenbier. I shook the steering wheel, so frustrated I could have cracked his skull and eaten his brain with a pair of chop sticks.

I rammed the gas pedal to the floor, practically standing on it, but the old van wouldn't move any faster. There was nothing left. She was already giving me all she had. The small Volvo engine was struggling under the pounding the four pistons were applying to the cylinder head. Come on, baby, hold it together a bit longer! The truck sailed around a long curve in the highway and I slammed on the brakes.

I stomped the pedal five or six times as the backend fishtailed. Steering back and forth like a crazed bumper car driver, I managed to get the truck stopped within a meter of a 15-year-old brown Citroën. Brake lights glared red across the roadway all the way to the horizon.

While daydreaming about finding the sports car with a blown engine on the side of the road, we had almost run into the back of a massive traffic jam. I threw open the door and jumped to the ground.

"What are you doing?"

"He's here somewhere," I called.

I ran down the center of the road with a line of cars on either side. Several people had grown restless of the jam and rolled down side windows, craning long necks into my path. One curious man stepped out of his vehicle right in front of me. As I bumped by him, I told him to remain in the car. It was police business.

I ran 100 meters as the highway inclined to a small summit. There it was. The metallic-blue Renault Alpine A110 sat five or six cars in front of me in the outside lane. Its wheels were cranked hard to the right and Chaban fisted the horn intermittently, but the accident blocking the highway wasn't about to move any time soon. A multi-car crash beyond the crest of the hill had ripped apart two cars, and another was on fire. The police and fire brigade were busily attending to victims and vehicles.

Chaban saw movement in the rearview mirror. He engaged the transmission and forced the Renault to the narrow berm on the outside, clipping the tail of a Ford Cortina as I ran up on his bumper. Swerving half off the pavement, a spray of deadly shrapnel was launched as the Renault's right tires dug into the golf ball-sized rocks on the soft shoulder. Hesitating only slightly, I ran after the car as it vanished in a dust cloud.

I heard horns blaring above the crushing of stones under my feet and someone was shouting off to the left, but I kept running. A low red compact turned out into my path. I slammed across the hood. Barely stopping long enough to glimpse the shocked woman behind the steering wheel, I kept going. There were flashes of movement all along the line now. Drivers were gunning engines, inching out of their lanes.

A sudden burst of gunfire caught me by surprise. People were shooting; I guess the French really didn't like traffic jams much. Shotgun pellets tore into a Volkswagen bus next to me and a sliver of glass bounced off my cheek as I ran through the explosion. Someone was coming up fast, and I heard the sickening thud of a body against solid metal. Another barrage split the thick air around me. Chaban had backup.

A policeman jogged toward me, waving his hands. As he dodged in front of a small black truck, his chest exploded from a third shotgun blast. I jumped headfirst into the ditch. The speeding car swerved toward me, hit a boulder and veered back on the shoulder. Up and running again, I counted three men in the vehicle before an arm reached around and fired at me. Hitting the gravel again, I watched as they vanished into the cloud behind the blue Renault. I threw a handful of rocks after nothing and swore in three languages.

The old truck braked behind me.

"Get in!" Zita yelled. I ripped the passenger door open and Zita floored it as I stepped onto the running board. The momentum of her acceleration threw me headfirst into the seat. The door hit my leg and bounced open again. When I righted myself, I reeled in the handle as the heavy metal recoiled back toward me a second time. I was choking and my eyes were stinging from the churning dust, but I managed to point in the direction of the exit off-ramp. "I saw them, I saw them!" Zita shouted.

"Where did those guys come from?"

"Two cars behind Chaban!"

The van sped through the dust cloud as it slowly rained over the restless blob of stalled traffic. Punching out the other side, we came to an abrupt halt in the middle of the intersection past the stop sign at the bottom of the overpass. The truck idled noiselessly, exposed on the open road.

"Which way?" Zita yelled.

We were in the outskirts of Villenueve-sur-Verberie

scanning up and down the D100 for some indication of Chaban. Turning left took us to the center of the medieval working-class village famous for its premium beef cattle. The right led us through the less-populated rolling forests southeast of here. It was a 50-50 chance.

"Right," I said. "The forest."

Zita cranked the steering wheel toward the tree line and gunned the engine roughly over the ditch on the far side of the road. Slowly, we picked up speed over the first hill. By the time we reached the next summit, the van was traveling fast enough to launch over the top. I braced my hand on the cab roof, waiting for the impact as the vehicle finally smacked down. The bounce bottomed out the chassis with a scrape that sent sparks flying out the back end.

"You've got a steering wheel to hold. I'd like to catch Chaban before I visit space!" I said.

"That's not going to do either of us any good if you keep distracting me, love," she said, without taking her focus from the unpredictable pavement.

I held on by wedging my straight arms between the ceiling and the dash. At the top of the next incline, I concentrated on scanning as far down the way as I could before the hollow in the highway swallowed us again. There was no sign of either car and I was wondering why I thought going through the forests was a good idea.

The old truck sailed through the only intersection in the tiny village of Mont L'Eveque before I had a chance to yell. Zita slammed on the brakes and we skidded to a shaky stop.

"What?!"

"Back up! Back up! Back up!" Throwing the manual transmission in reverse, Zita backed the van until we were on the other side of the cross street. Confusion filled her eyes.

"There!" I pointed. "Do you see the tire mark?"

"Where?! That could have been there for days," she protested.

"No, see how wide the arc is. It comes from the left lane here and curves off to the right toward the river. The marks end over there. Whoever made this turn was traveling at full speed." Zita was thinking.

"Do you have anything better?" I asked.

The Alpine had veered right onto a twisting country road that circumvented lakes and bisected the many streams marbling the woodland landscape. We crossed one bridge and within seconds, crossed back to the original side of the river. The road narrowed considerably. Trees came up to the edge of the truck on both sides.

Zita slowed the van to 60 km/h from necessity. It was still too fast, but we had no choice. The trees and the undergrowth were as thick as I'd ever seen. Vegetation blocked three-quarters of the daylight except for an occasional golden meadow that broke the solid green-black with a brilliant beam of stark white.

Zita stopped the van at one of the meadows after we crossed the same tributary three times. Her attention was focused on a pair of men standing in the driveway of a hilltop chateau. The pair was dressed casually, wearing baggy pants and short-sleeved knit pullovers. Both were muscular with short-cropped hair.

Pointing, Zita asked, "What do you see?"

"I see a couple of clowns chatting in their front yard."

"And…," she urged.

I glanced again before she engaged the transmission and moved out of sight behind the tree line, obscuring the large house on the hill.

"And they finished their conversation so they walked to opposite ends of the building."

"No wonder you are so easy to follow. You noticed nothing else?" Bewildered, I shook my head. "Your man is there," she said.

"What makes you say that?"

"How many farmers do you know who wear shoulder holsters?" She answered a question with a question.

"Farmers, none," I grumbled. "Moonshiners, 27 in central Alabama alone."

Zita drove another 100 meters. We found a packed clay driveway that wound its way through the trees toward the chateau and thirty meters beyond that, she pulled off into the trees. She ejected the magazine from her Beretta to ensure the clip was full. I checked my weapon, too. It felt like the thing to do. My clip was missing four of eight cartridges. Who leaves home with a half loaded gun, I thought?

CHAPTER 47

The approach to the chateau was heavily wooded only so far up from the road. The final fifty meters on the front and sides were open, green space with shrubs barely large enough to hide a medium-sized goat. We walked cautiously through the cover of the trees until most of the long driveway and the front of the chateau were visible. The blue Alpine was nowhere in sight, and I raised an eyebrow questioningly. Zita gave me her beautiful 'patience, my dear' smile that always irritated me because she was asking for something I had in short supply.

Making slow progress in a wide half-moon to the left, we moved toward the back of the house, hoping there might be a better chance of reaching it unseen. The footing was uneven and treacherous as we picked our way through the woods. I stumbled once and slid partway down the incline, but we finally made our way through the undergrowth to the rear of the chateau.

One of the men from the second car stepped through the back entrance. He carried a pump shotgun cradled lightly in one arm as he hiked toward a large storage barn further up on the left. He switched arms with his baby, hefting it a little to a more comfortable position. Zita removed a suppressor from her pocket and attached it to the Beretta.

At a tiny window in the door, the man peered in, shielding his eyes against the sun's reflection. He debated something with himself. Hesitantly setting the shotgun against the wall, he pulled a ring of keys from his pocket, found the right one and opened the heavy door. The rusted hinges creaked loudly and a flock of birds took flight.

We came out of the tree line at the side of the building and peeked inside. Two vehicles occupied four bays in the garage. Farthest away sat an old McCormick International four-wheel drive in bad need of repair. The hood was removed, and the engine lay open. The guard's attention, however, was on the other vehicle. He was unfolding a canvas tarp over a metallic-blue Renault Alpine A110 sports car.

I followed Zita through the door, weapons raised. The man was startled by the sudden movement. In panic, he swung his head trying to remember where he had kept the shotgun.

"Non, non! Attention ici, s'il vous plait," Zita said. Their eyes locked. I sidestepped further into the garage, searching for a better angle as the man dropped out of sight behind the car.

"Guard the door!" She shouted.

While watching for the others from the far side of the McCormick International, I heard feet shuffling on the dirt floor. A short quiet was snapped by the sharp scrape of metal on metal. In quick succession, two bodies hit the garage wall, the sounds of close-in fighting, a high-pitched grunt from Zita, someone's head banged twice off the car's fender, a heap hit the ground, and quiet again. I swallowed hard, ready to spring from my crouch if I heard the familiar ching-ching of a shotgun chambering a shell.

"Clear!" I heard Zita's breathless voice and the tension poured out of me as if I lost all bowel control. I stood up weakly. Zita was bent over two straight arms propped on the sports car.

"Are you all right?"

"No, I am bloody well not all right," she smiled, wearily. "Let's go."

She tossed the shotgun over the car and I caught it one handed.

"Where is he?" I asked.

"Well, if you must know, darling, he's tied to the axle. Chaban's not leaving with the Renault unless he intends to drag this bloke with him."

Squatting at the open door, we heard leaves rustling high in the trees, but everything at ground level was calm, quiet. At one time, the courtyard had been beautifully maintained with multi-colored flowers and a fruit garden. Now, all that lingered on the barren ground were two sickly apple trees and some kind of thorny bush.

The back of the chateau was a two-story façade of stucco and brick that must have been 200 years old. A weathered, reddish-brown tile roof overhung whitewashed sides. A heavy, windowless door stood in the middle of the building flanked by half windows. Above that, a balcony with dark floor-to-ceiling windows ran the length of the top floor. Thick wooden latticework supported the remains of last year's flowers growing four meters high at both corners. That looked like an invitation to me.

We ran the fifteen meters across the open yard and lay flat against the wall next to the trellis. We waited for men to rush around the corner with weapons blazing, but no one came. I climbed the wooden structure, placed the shotgun over the rail and hopped onto the balcony.

As soon as Zita had also pivoted over the railing, I fished the lock tools out of my coveralls and went to work on the closest door. The key slots were so large and worn from age that I could have used ballpoint pens.

We stood in a large bedroom that was sour from sickness and old sweat. The bed was unmade. The sheet and duvet were in a pile on the floor. I listened at the door, opened it a crack, listened, opened it another few centimeters and listened again. There was a television, or maybe a radio, blasting somewhere below. I finally recognized the broadcast. It was France 3, a local television station offering news and political insights throughout the day. Channel 3 was the station that first reported the downing of Flight 981.

We checked the other rooms on the top level. An old couple was in the bathroom. Both were dead, lying face down in a claw-foot tub. Running water washed over the bodies, mixing with blood as it circled the drain. I turned the faucet off.

Sick, I stood at the top of the stairs watching the darkened ground floor. Light from the television flickered up ancient stone steps lined with plaster walls and it reminded me of a tunnel descending into the fires of hell. By now I was wielding the confiscated shotgun like it was made for me, but Zita took the lead anyway.

She crept down the gritty steps one at a time, with her Beretta pointing the way. I was three steps behind. At the bottom, she took a quick peek around the corner. I pointed to my chest. Chaban was mine.

Passing over the doorway like a translucent angel, Zita positioned herself at the front door. I listened to the reporter's voice. The man was finishing a report on the morning's opening ceremonies at Charles de Gaulle International Airport. And there you have the complete story. What a beautiful centerpiece of French culture this airport is going to be. Now we move on to other news. Before I could spin into the doorway, Chaban screamed above the newscaster's voice.

"Fils de pute! Ça fait deja deux heures que les avions ont décollé. J'ai du entendre quelque chose," he shrieked, hysterically. He was leaning over the television with a hand on each side of the console, staring down at the screen. He screamed at the reporter's image, "Where is it? Where's the story? I know you're keeping it quiet on purpose to piss me off! Come on, where is it! It's been two hours. I know there are bodies all over the countryside! I want to see them."

He shook the huge television.

"Tell them. Tell them everything! Come on, you can't keep it quiet forever! Do you want to make it personal? I'll do twice as many planes next time!" His face was flushed red with fury. Dried blood was still evident where I had cracked his head earlier. "And I'll make sure you're on one of those airplanes because I'm going to personally shove a wad of C4 up your ass to start everything off right!"

The reporter paid no attention to Chaban's rant, going on about an Assemblée Nationale debate regarding the creation of an inquiry committee to investigate new immigration policies to be implemented later this year.

"You're going to make me wait, is that it?" Rage fully consumed him now.

He rattled the console again. Taking a step back, he lashed out with two severe kicks that landed across the reporter's face. The blows careened off the thick picture tube while the reporter continued undeterred.

"God damn it! Why are you bastards waiting? Tell the story. I want to see your silly faces! Eight! Eight bombs, count them! Tell the world! You have to know about it by now! Show me the bodies!"

I interrupted Chaban's harangue by chambering a round in the shotgun. He spun. Hatred flooded his eyes.

"What?!" he screamed. "You can't be here?"

"It isn't going to happen," I said. "There won't be any explosions today."

"You have no idea," Chaban spat, bitterly.

"Actually I do." I prayed he didn't see the gun shaking in my hands. "I exchanged your C4 for child's clay."

"I saw it going into the airplanes myself. There wasn't time to switch it before the doors were sealed."

"Yesterday," I grinned above the twin barrels.

"You're lying!" He screamed.

"Yeah, that's what François said."

"Impossible! You're too stupid! Everything was planned."

"Well, I guess your plan wasn't stupid proof."

Chaban charged, leaping a love seat that separated us. I fired and the big gun jerked on a 45o angle toward the ceiling. Some of the buckshot struck him in the side of the abdomen and the left shoulder before the rest went wide above his head.

He kept coming, possibly not aware that he was wounded. Before I could pump another shell into the chamber and point the shotgun again, he smashed into me, knocking over a small table. My elbow hit the floor hard and the weapon flew out of my grasp.

At the first sound of the shotgun blast, Zita swung the front door wide and stopped both of the pistol-wielding guards as they bounded up two steps to the porch. The first went down with a single shot to the chest before he could draw his weapon and the second caught a round in the thigh and another in the shoulder. She stepped out to attend to them.

Chaban was trying to choke me but had trouble finding a strong hold because of his injured arm. I brought two fists in hard against his stomach then smashed my open hands against his straight elbows, forcing the hands away from my neck. As I rolled over on all fours, he was on me again, fumbling for a good grip on my back. I threw my legs out in front as far as I could to break his grip and twisted my body to face him. On hands and knees, we stared at each other.

Chaban tried to stand. I leaped for his legs and forced him to his back. He held my torso to his chest and pounded the side of my head with his fist. I applied as much pressure as I could to his stomach wounds. I probed the holes with my fingers to rip the incisions wider.

He screamed and released me, but he was not weakening. He was on me again and we fell across an armchair. Seeing the shotgun, I scrambled over his body, but he caught my leg and jerked me back.

His saliva was dripping onto my shirt, mixing with blood. Seizing a brass vase that had tumbled to the floor, Chaban raised the weapon ready to strike. He swung the heavy object at my face. A single bullet struck him in the forehead, spraying blood and brains across the back of the loveseat. Chaban hesitated then dropped. His head hit my chin, splitting my lip. I rolled him off me and sat up, breathing hard.

"You will never make a proper agent, will you?" Zita asked, with a smile.

EPILOGUE

"I'm here to say good-bye."

"You can come any time you like," I said.

"No, it's time to go." She shook her head. "I cannot stay longer." The little girl stood in front of the open window with light from the half-moon filtering through her lucent body. The lace curtains shifted around her.

Her eyes were cast down and her arms were folded across a delicate body. The blood was gone from her face and her eyes were a clear blue when she looked up at me. She smiled, with some embarrassment.

"Thank you for watching over me." I said.

"It was nothing...nothing at all."

"I'm glad it's over."

"It's not over," she said. "You do know there's more to come before you can rest, don't you? There are many lessons to learn before you know who you are. It's your beginning and my ending."

I already knew I was destined to be an unintentional voyager, running from my mistakes, failings, frustrations and disillusionments that always hounded me, living with uncertainty, indecision, addiction and endless conversations with myself, swinging at darkness and demons, enemies, friends and lovers, and choosing as my personal penance to right Shakespeare's slings and arrows of outrageous fortune that visit us all from time to time. I really didn't want to know more.

301

"What will you do now?" I knew it was another silly question, even as I asked it.

"The same as you. Go on." She was amused.

We did go on. Andrew Chaban became nothing more than a deleted footnote in history when 1974 hit the earth with the impact of a red hot meteor. It became the deadliest year on record for terrorism. Insurgent activities continued to evolve in more varied, more widespread and more unpredictable ways. Airplanes remained a prime focus on the Continent, but the message was sent to subversives around the world. Everything was now fair game. Embassies and government buildings were targeted. Open season was declared on pubs and restaurants, theaters, trains, subways, automobiles, city streets and even tourist attractions.

"I want to go back to when it was safe," I said.

"Life goes that way." She lifted a thin finger toward the apartment door. "You must go through that door, wherever it leads. And when it closes behind you, fortunately or unfortunately, you will carry this new world on your shoulders."

She was right, though it was difficult to admit at the time. While the sixties changed us in thought, the early seventies changed us in circumstance. We were forced to act and react to our own human situation. The world was becoming more about *we* than me. Even though the population crept over four billion for the first time, the planet had somehow grown smaller during the past few months. Whatever affected one of us now affected all of us.

When I turned back from the doorway, she was gone. A soft breeze filtered in from the raised window, warming the suddenly cold room. It had rained sometime overnight and I could smell the musty scent of Paris as it awakened for a new day.

I wandered to the window and stood looking down on Quai des Grands Augustins and Notre Dame Cathedral lying across the

Seine. The river had an inky sheen in the hazy light, but then some things would never change. The last of the city lights were twinkling out as the sun crept up over Île de la Cité.

It was a long time before I realized the shower had stopped running. Zita was standing behind me wrapped in one towel while drying her hair with another.

"Come on, Doc. Get a move on," she said. "It's time to catch the plane to London. I'm going to show you the best time you've ever had."

"I believe you already have," I smiled.